WARNING!

Adult Fiction
Sexually Exquisite

*If you are not eighteen or older,
do not, seriously, do not read this book.*

MARRIED ON MONDAYS

GC
GRAND CENTRAL
PUBLISHING

NEW YORK   BOSTON

This book is a work of fiction. Names, characters, places, and incidents are the product of the author's imagination or are used fictitiously. Any resemblance to actual events, locales, or persons, living or dead, is coincidental.

Grand Central Publishing
Hachette Book Group
237 Park Avenue
New York, NY 10017
www.HachetteBookGroup.com

Printed in the United States of America

First Edition: March 2010
10 9 8 7 6 5 4 3

Grand Central Publishing is a division of Hachette Book Group, Inc.
The Grand Central Publishing name and logo is a trademark of Hachette Book Group, Inc.

Library of Congress Cataloging-in-Publication Data
HoneyB
    Married on Mondays / HoneyB. —1st ed.
       p. cm.
    ISBN 978-0-446-58232-2
    1. African Americans—Fiction. I. Title.
    PS3563.O87477M27 2010
    813'.54—dc22
                        2009027118

Book design by Charles Sutherland

Why I Cherish Our Love

Date:

Given To:

Given By:

Personal Message:

To Stella Morrison

MARRIED ON MONDAYS

Pussy is a terrible thing to waste.

G-spot Genocide

Is Your Pussy on the *Hit List*?

Sexually liberated women are in high demand but there is a low supply.

I've moved the section I originally placed here—"Would You Marry for Love?"—to the end of the book, because since I've started hosting HONEYB Adult Slumber Parties, I'm not surprised, I'm shocked at the number of women who are unconsciously sabotaging their G-spot with sheer neglect. It's like walking by a plant every day and not noticing the plant until it starts to wither. "Oh, you poor thing." And instead of watering the plant, what do you do? "Let me take you out of your misery." Some of you actually throw the plant in the trash. Just like you've done with your G-spot, you're letting your pussy slowly deteriorate.

The G-spot is named after the German gynecologist Ernst Gräfenberg. Ladies, Ernst is our hero and we will not let his research be in vain. Some women don't know their G-spot exists. They haven't lost it, but don't know where to find it, or they're having sex with men who are clueless about the G-spot and other female erogenous zones.

The HoneyB wants you to stop. Stop right now, raise your right hand, and tell the truth. Is your pussy on the G-spot genocide hit list? If it is, I want you to take yours off today, especially if you've never experienced an orgasm. With pussy, all things are possible. Let me rephrase that. With good pussy, all things are possible. A good pussy is an untamed, well-trained pussy.

Here is my twelve-step program to G-spot vitalization:

1. Make sure your fingernails are smooth to avoid painful kitty cuts. And I have to slip this in for good measure, never let a man with jagged or dirty fingernails touch your good pussy.
2. Take a shower or a bath to get your pussy ready for you. Never serve what you wouldn't eat. Taste yourself, girl.
3. After cleansing your body, wash your hands (yes, again) and be sure to get all the soap off. Some pussies are more sensitive than others and you don't want to irritate her before you get started.
4. Now insert your middle finger as far as you can into your vagina. (There's a reason why the middle finger is about two inches long, and when inserted, your middle finger naturally faces the right direction. God didn't make any mistakes.)
5. You're not searching for orgasmic stimulation at this point. Right now you're discovering the sensation and location of your G-spot.

6. Your finger may veer to the left or right as if running off the road and falling into a ditch, or as I call it, *the trenches*. While you're in the trenches, clean them out. Scoop, ladies, scoop. You'll taste better. Okay, let's get back on the road to finding your G-spot.

7. Feel the fleshy part of your vagina, aka the hump, or as I call it, the speed bump. A speed bump serves a purpose. It signals a man to do what? Yes, slow down. Right there. That's your spot. Slide your finger along your bumpy hump. That's how the G-spot feels, bumpy. To give you a comparison, press the tip of your tongue against the inside of your bottom teeth. Now slide your tongue back and forth in the bottom of your mouth. That's very similar to the feel of your G-spot. Now let's get back to the G-spot. Close your eyes, get in the zone, and pay close attention to the sensation. When you awaken your most sensitive spot, hey, girl… you're on track. Keep on stroking. When you know how to pleasure yourself, you have no problem telling your lover what turns you on.

8. If the finger test did not work for you (or even if it did and you want more stimulation), dry yourself off and head to the adult toy store. This is not the time to be shy. Don't forget the mission. You are taking your pussy off what? That's right, the *hit list*. No G-spot genocide for your pretty kitty.

9. Tell the assistant you want to see *all* of their G-spot stimulators (these are different from clit stimulators). Ask all the questions you need to ask, and make an educated decision on which G-spot stimulator is best for you.

10. Go home, get naked, get in your bed, sit on a stool or the edge of a seat, or, if you bought a waterproof stimulator, get in the tub. As long as it's a safe place, the HoneyB doesn't care where you sit or lay—it's your house, not mine.

11. Don't turn on the vibration just yet. I want *you* to find your G-spot first. Repeat step 7 above.

12. Once you are in tune with your G-spot you will have more powerful orgasms. Congratulations! You've successfully completed HoneyB's twelve-step program and you have officially taken your pussy off the *hit list*. Don't forget to awaken (water) your G-spot regularly.

I'm no G-spot genius but I do consider myself a sexpert. I can't speak in more technical terms as a gynecologist would, but I have helped women become sexually liberated. I'm like the orgasmic midwife who helps to deliver orgasms instead of babies, except I don't make house calls or booty calls. I do consultations. If there is anything I don't know about sex, I want to learn, therefore I'm more educated on the female anatomy, sex, and sexuality, and have more hands-on experience than the average person.

The right person or persons, a clean environment (I am a Virgo, okay), and a healthy frame of mind free from judgment of self and others can lead you to the most incredible orgasmic moments you'll ever experience. Most people worry too much about what others think and not enough about how they feel. When your life transitions, the only person you have to answer for is you. Do not deny yourself sexual healing or pleasure. But first you must learn what pleases you.

Want to see actual pictures of a woman's G-spot? Want to learn more about your G-spot, orgasms, and vaginal exercises? Here are a few of my favorite websites:

1. www.MaryMorrison.com
2. www.doctorg.com
3. www.speculum.com

You cannot overeducate yourself on sex or sexuality. Now that you're equipped with the tools to stimulate your G-spot, if you desire you can learn how to fill your urethra with ejaculate and learn how to… squirt, baby, squirt! Men love it when women squirt, so the HoneyB has incorporated female ejaculation into the story line of *Married on Mondays*.

If you want me to host a HONEYB Adult Slumber Party for your book club or your event, email me at honeyb@marymorrison.com.

CRÈME CITY

The Pulse of the USA
Population: 6.9 million

PROLOGUE

Foxy

Four years of marriage.
Three years of adultery.
Two men.
One woman.

Mondays were her hardest days to stay focused. Being one man's woman and another man's wife was physically manageable but emotionally draining, especially on Mondays when she had to spend "quality time" with her husband.

Four years ago she stood at the altar. Vowing to forsake all others, she longed to fold back her veil and kiss her ex-fiancé, who sat center aisle, fifth row. She glanced over her shoulder, blinked him a kiss with her eyes, then faced her husband. The tall, dark, and handsome man who stood in front the pastor wasn't the only man she was in love with. Her ex-fiancé could have easily been the better man. No matter how hard she tried, she couldn't stop loving him.

"If anyone has cause why this man and woman should not be joined in holy matrimony, speak now," the pastor said.

Whew! There were valid reasons why she couldn't honor or obey her ex-fiancé, but she cherished him the same as her husband before and after she'd said, "I do."

Foxy leaned across her desk, handed her sister DéJà the deposit envelope for the money earned from servicing their customers and clients. She stood, hugged her sister Victoria. "I'll see you guys in the morning."

"Everything will be all right," Victoria said, hugging Foxy. "Open up to your husband tonight. Tell him the truth. If you don't want to tell him, pray. God will show you the way."

Foxy pushed Victoria away. Her half smile represented her love for her sisters. The other half that should've shown her happiness to see her husband remained suppressed. A wise wife never confessed her affairs.

"Be on time tomorrow," DéJà scolded. "We're not going to keep baking your pastries for you."

"Why can't you empathize with Foxy? You know she's emotionally distraught," Victoria said. "Take your time tomorrow. I don't mind covering for you."

"Well, I do," DéJà retorted.

Hugging DéJà, Foxy said, "I love you too, sis. Bye Victoria and thanks. Y'all have fun for me this evening." Carrying assorted pastries to her car, Foxy exhaled, placing the white box on the passenger seat.

Opening her legs led to opening her heart. Or was it the other way around? Loving two men had emotionally torn her apart. Three years into her affair, she didn't know how to end her marriage or her relationship with her ex.

As she exited the driveway of Crème her cell phone buzzed. Seeing his name on her caller ID, she smiled from the inside out, then answered, "Hey, you."

"What's wrong?" he asked without saying hello.

"Same ole, you know. Got that Monday morning blues straight through Monday afternoon."

He moaned in her ear, "How's my pussy?"

Her pussy contracted with excitement. Her body tingled.

"Touch her for me," he whispered.

This time when he spoke, she came. Her vaginal muscles pulsated repeatedly. She hadn't touched herself. The sound of his alluring voice made her cum. "Stop it. I'm driving."

"Then pull over and take off your thong for me. Stick your finger in your pussy for me. I bet she's hot just the way I like her."

"Good-bye," Foxy said.

His voice softened with sincerity. "I love you, Foxy. I will always love you."

Why did he have to constantly remind her how much he loved her? Flowers, gifts, massages, dancing, movies, art galleries, museums, comedy shows, Broadway plays—all the things her husband used to do her ex had never stopped doing.

She reflected on the day he'd taken her to see *The Color Purple* the night before the Tony Awards. Fifth row. Aisle seats. Oprah and Gayle sat five rows behind them in the middle of that row. When Celie and Nettie cried, she cried too. Her tears played patty-cake with her ex-man's soul. He was her best friend. Everybody needed somebody to hug, to love. Her ex was always there for her. That was more than she could attest to for her workaholic husband.

"I love you too," she said ending the call.

Foxy made a U-turn to take the long route home. She drove slower than usual. Headed north instead of south on Shoreline Drive to avoid passing her ex-fiancé's house. Three-thirty traffic was light. Her pussy was moist. When would her husband realize she was no longer a happily married woman? Did he care?

She pressed the engine button, turned off her car, then watched shoppers load grocery bags in their trunks. Women with kids, unaccompanied by men, got in and out of vehicles. She wondered if the women had husbands that used to grocery shop with them the way her husband used to shop with her.

Walking into the store, Foxy called her dad.

He answered, "Hey, how's my number one princess?"

Hearing his voice made her smile. No man had treated her better than her father. When she was a little girl that was a good thing. Now that she was a woman, when her father gave her away, she thought her husband would treat her better. She was wrong. "I'm good, Daddy, how are you?" she asked, inspecting the filet mignon.

"Doing great. You sound perturbed. What's . . . ah, the Monday blues," he said. "I told you to think like me. If you decide to do something, don't worry about it. If you're going to worry about it, don't do it, princess."

"I'm not you, Daddy."

"I know, princess. And I know you're not happy, but whatever you do, don't have an affair. We men aren't as forgiving as you women. Hey, I'm trying to downsize without layoffs. I have to go into a meeting. I'll call you later. Love you," he said.

"Love you too, Daddy," Foxy said, dropping her phone in her purse. She tossed red potatoes, fresh spinach, and a bottle of her husband's favorite merlot into the shopping cart. Thinking about her husband somberly, she scanned her debit card, waited for the bagger to place her items in the cart.

Foxy missed her man. She visualized his dick inside her, his hands caressing her breasts. She smiled placing the bags in the trunk. Her body jerked. Another orgasm surprised her. Hadn't seen him since Saturday night. Yesterday she was at church with her sisters. She refused to go to the altar when Victoria had asked. Her sister was not her savior and going to the altar would've only satisfied Victoria. Foxy knew she was no saint but neither were her married sisters.

On her drive home from the store, Foxy called her man. "Hey, baby. I just called back to say I miss you."

"Stop by for a minute so I can hug my sweet baby," he said.

"You know I have to have dinner with him. I'll see you in the morning. I love you."

"Love you too," he said.

Foxy carried the food to the kitchen where she seasoned the meat and chopped the potatoes. She showered, brushed her teeth. Gathered her hair in a ponytail, put on a canary yellow gown and red three-inch slip-on heels.

She'd finished cooking by six. Heard her husband's car in the garage.

"Hey, gorgeous. Smells good in here," he said, bypassing her. No more kisses when he walked in. No hugs. No slaps on her juicy booty.

She set the table, prepared their plates, put extra servings of potatoes and dessert closest to his seat at the table. Her husband entered the dining room. He'd traded his suit and tie for the clothes he'd sleep in, a pair of gray baggy sweats and a wife beater.

His behind was barely in the seat before he beamed. "Got a new client today, gorgeous. You'll never guess who?" His grin was wide.

All he ever talked about was work, work, work. But this smile was different.

"Yeah, who?"

"Nova," he said like he was on a first-name basis with whoever she was.

"Nova, who?"

He nodded. "Scotia, baby. Nova Scotia." His lips curved upward like a kid who'd just gotten his first cell phone.

"That's nice." His enthusiasm for another woman had ruined more than her appetite.

Was there anything about her that excited him that way? The remainder of dinner was quiet. Squirming in his seat, her husband hardly kept still. She excused herself from the table, brushed her teeth. She went to bed early. He crawled in beside her at midnight. No touches, no kisses, no hugs.

Her husband turned his back, hugged his pillow, and squirmed himself to sleep.

CHAPTER 1

Foxy

Sandwiched in a love triangle—her husband on one side, her ex-fiancé on the other—Foxy was able to sustain her marriage. Her husband should thank her ex-fiancé for sexing her senseless. Her ex-fiancé would soon be indebted to her husband. Neither man satisfied all her needs, but together, her two men were the perfect blend.

She didn't marry for money. Had a separate bank account. She didn't marry for love. Nowadays, love didn't last long enough. Had her heart broken twice by the same man. Wasn't going to be his fool again. She didn't marry for mind-blowing sex. She knew how to pleasure herself before she surrendered her virginity at the tender age of sixteen. She didn't marry to gain social recognition. Her self-esteem was so high no man could scorn her. She didn't marry to validate her womanhood. She was a woman solely in charge of her life.

Tuesday morning she opened her eyes, glanced at her husband's side of the bed. As usual, he wasn't there. His getting out of bed before her shouldn't bother her but it did. No more making love, morning quickies, or light kisses on her lips before he got out the bed. The burgundy sheet on his side was neatly tucked underneath the mattress.

She placed her feet on the ginger-colored carpet, sat on the side of the bed, unlocked her G1, then texted her lover, "Hi baby. Be there after 6." She locked, then placed her G1 on the nightstand, and sat on the floor. Her morning ritual—crunches, hip thrusts, squats, and pushups—proceeded, stretching her legs, arms, and torso. Bypassing the sixty-five-inch flat screen television she used to watch pornography on with her husband, she entered her bathroom.

After she married him, moved into his house, she learned her husband's habits. He didn't like sharing his things or his space. His bathroom was on the opposite side of their master bedroom. His study was his. The kitchen, family and living room were hers. The dining room was shared one day a week. Neither of them would return to the table until Monday. To her, marriage meant the property under their roof—including her husband—was legally hers and she had the right to dispose of whatever she chose.

Her "I can have it all" attitude was ingrained by her father the four years she lived with him. Moving from her mother's two-bedroom condo in Boise into the largest mansion in Crème City to live with her dad and attend high school with her two sisters changed her life forever.

Thanks to her dad, she had the opportunity to live with her sister from Baton Rouge and her sister from Boston. Three girls, the same age, with three different moms, from three different environments, experiencing puberty under one roof while being raised by their dad were the hardest yet most rewarding years of her life. Their father taught them to stick together and to never marry anyone who had little to give or nothing to lose.

Disgusted with her husband's selfish, egotistical behavior, she stared in the mirror. She lathered cold cream on her forehead. Her piercing hazel eyes narrowed. Divorcing her husband wasn't an option she wanted to exercise, but one she'd considered numerous times.

Give my fine-ass rich husband to some other woman? I don't think so.

She bit her bottom lip, cursed, "Damn you! Why do you act like I'm your servant? Selfish-ass bastard! I hate you!" Love made her hate him. Hate made her love him. A live-in maid could easily fulfill her wifely duties. A better question was "Why had he asked to marry her?"

Her random outbursts were occurring more frequently. She prayed she wasn't on the verge of a nervous breakdown. She wasn't crazy. Just terribly frustrated. Headed for self-destruction if she didn't make a change in her life.

She kept staring at her reflection. The high arches of her thin brows were waxed to perfection, not a single hair was out of place. Thick layers of chestnut hair caressed her honey golden shoulders with more affection than her husband's hands. Her nose—not wide enough open as her mother would say—complimented her round, firm cheeks.

She smeared cream above and below her soft lips, wondering what her life would be like if she hadn't married him, if she'd remained single. Would she be happy? Content? Lonely? Would she have risked having her heart broken a third time by her ex-fiancé?

She brushed her teeth, rinsed her face with cold water, then went to the study where she knew she'd find her husband sitting in his favorite, worn bourbon-tinted leather chair surrounded by his wall-to-wall law library.

"Morning, baby," she said, softly kissing his lips. Calling him baby was a habit not worth breaking. There were no sentiments in her greeting.

Looking up at her, he smiled, then whispered, "Hey, gorgeous. What was all that noise? Were you yelling at someone on the phone?"

Did it matter? He hadn't bothered to check on her. "Oh, nothing, just dropped something on my foot," she lied. She removed his black-framed glasses, folded, then placed them on the end table beside his chair. Exhaling, she looked down at her husband, then asked, "Baby, do you still love me?"

He frowned. His eyes narrowed. He patted his thigh. "Sit. Talk to me. Why would you ask me something like that out of the blue?"

Exhaling, this time through her mouth, she wanted to remove his hand from her ass. His touch irritated her. He no longer excited her. "Guess I'm tired of . . ." Her eyes scrolled toward the crystal chandelier that hung high above their heads. She thought about the fatal ending in *The War of the Roses* and understood how couples could kill one another physically or emotionally. Agitated by his nonchalant attitude, she paused thinking, *Tired of spending more time with my ex-man than with my husband.*

He touched her chin, tilted her face, then stared into her eyes. "Tired of what, baby?"

She cringed, gripped his wrist, moved his hand to her lap atop the hem of her yellow gown. "Haaa . . . barely seeing you, that's what. You work hard on everything except our marriage."

CHAPTER 2

Foxy

Shaking her left leg as she'd done whenever she was nervous, she asked her husband, "How did we get here? Don't you remember the way we were? For a whole year after we got married, every day was our honeymoon."

He used to bring her roses, buy her jewelry, take her dancing, hold her hand in public. There was a time he wouldn't keep his hands off her. She closed her eyes and could hear the way he used to proudly introduce her. He'd say, "This is *my* wife."

Opening her eyes, she continued, "Something changed you. You started spending more time at the office, less time at home, less time with me. Then you took up golfing on weekends, and now . . . I barely see you. It's like you'd rather be anyplace where I'm not."

She swallowed the remaining words not worth mentioning.

If she were so gorgeous, as he'd often say, why couldn't she have all her needs met by him? *Girl, don't cry. Please, don't let him see you cry again.* Her emotions ejected a waterfall of tears over her eyelids and down her face, soaking her gown. Maybe if her husband were home more, she'd be home more.

Kissing her tears, her husband answered, "You are my everything. Don't you know how much I love you?" He tucked her hair behind her ear, cupped her face again, as he stared into her eyes.

He knew all the right words to say to avoid arguing. She looked away from his empty words. Her eyes rested in the corners. Love without action didn't mean much. She yearned to grab his hands, fling them against his chest, pound on his broad shoulders, scream in his face . . . but she didn't. Like a good wife, she held it in, placed his needs ahead of hers.

"I keep telling you I feel like I'm married to myself. All I want is my husband back. A few days a week is all I'm asking. Hell, one more day a week would be a good start. You're the only partner at the firm who works after midnight five days a week."

He kissed her lips. "That's why I'm better than them. That's why they come to me for my opinion. Clearly, they need me more than I need them."

She interpreted his words with her thoughts. *Yeah, I bet you feel the same way about me.*

"And don't compare me to them," he said. "You have no idea what goes on at the office. Just because they go home every night doesn't mean they're faithful. Hey, listen. If it'll make you happy, I'll do better. I promise."

She hadn't mentioned anything about being faithful. Why had he? Was he cheating too? "Better or your best?"

"Fair question," he said. "Both. But I told you I have this new client," he lamented as though she shouldn't be pressuring him for more time than the one night a week he dined with her.

Excuses already. "Yeah, I know. International supermodel Nova fucking Scotia. If the deranged bitch hadn't ran over her boyfriend with her brand-new sports car she wouldn't need you to represent her ass. And you make sure you stay away from those triple XL collagen-injected lips that she's always plastering all over every man's damn face."

She wasn't the type of wife who felt her husband wanted to fuck every woman with a big ass, shapely legs, nice breasts, and juicy lips, but Nova had to have starred in every man's wet dream, including her husband's.

As if he were a raging bull preparing for attack, a puff of air shot from his nostrils. He leaned back. His lips tightened, then curved to one side. "Calm down, sweetie, calm down. I only have eyes for you, baby," he said, patting her thigh.

Wow. It wasn't his eyes she was concerned about. If he could've looked in a mirror, he would've seen what she saw. His body language was the opposite of what he'd said. He petted her like she had four legs. Maybe she should run over her husband with her car. Bad idea. Then he'd be a bigger burden, and she'd have to take care of him. She wasn't stupid. *What man wouldn't want Nova's juicy lips performing fellatio on him?*

"Take care of this for me, baby," he said, massaging his erection.

Oh. Now he wanted her to suck his dick. Probably while he'd fantasize about Nova giving him head. Whatever. She'd learned the mechanics of giving a great blow job had nothing to do with love.

She knelt before her husband to begin her next morning ritual. Gazing up at his irresistible dark brown-sugar masculine body, her heart ached. Was his love and affection that important to her? Or was his covert rejection driving her mad? How could she despise and desperately need him at the same time?

Her husband held one end of the thick, knotted rope; she held firm to the other. She was losing this round of tug-of-war with him. Later her heart would tug for another man.

Her husband's sultry, almond-shaped eyes slowly closed. His slanted cheeks narrowed toward full kissable lips, large perfect teeth, and a well-trimmed mustache. His face was as mesmerizing as his wide, strong shoulders and bulging biceps. No matter how hectic his day was, her husband dedicated one hour to exercise, and his herculean physique proudly showcased the results. She refused to give him up and risk having him date Nova. Surely Nova's boyfriend wasn't stupid enough to take her back.

Foxy massaged the curly hairs on her husband's chest mounds, then teased the few strands surrounding his hard nipples. The lightest touch of her husband's hairy chest, abs, thighs, legs, or arms layered chill bumps over her body and made her pussy pucker with pleasure, craving to have her breasts scrub against his hairs. She enjoyed touching him. If his affection weren't contrived, she'd welcome her husband's touch.

His affection had changed. He used to embrace her with his eyes, massage her with his breath, love her with his heart. Not anymore. His touch had become cold, robotic. His words flat as though ordering off a fast-food menu. Love, like life, was what she'd made it. Over time, her reality of being a happily married woman had become an unfulfilled fantasy.

She kissed his chest, his abs, his navel; buried her face in the richness of his pubic hairs; then inhaled. Lowering the elastic waistband over his dick, she wrapped her hand around his incredibly long shaft. His shaft was too thick for one hand to circle. She rotated both palms to cover all sides. Sliding her hands to the base of his shaft, slowly, ever so slowly, she suctioned his head into her wet mouth until her jaws caved in. She refused to release his shaft until his dick was too stiff to bend.

Although they spent less than six hours a day together—including the four hours she slept beside him—she never wanted her husband to justify soliciting sexual gratification from another woman, especially not that Nova *Scot-ti-a* woman. For years he'd revealed his crush on her.

"Baby, you are so damn good," he moaned as though it were her first time giving him head. He pulled her neck toward him, thrusting his dick down her throat, then grunted, "That's my girl. Take all of this dick."

Months after their marriage, twelve to be exact, *your* dick had become *this* dick. Maybe if she'd addressed his subtle changes early in the marriage, their relationship wouldn't have failed. To her, going through the motions was the same as failing.

Four years of marriage and she'd never missed a morning sucking her husband's dick unless he was out of town, which was most weekends. She believed her newfound wifely duties were to keep her husband not happy, but satisfied. Keep as much peace as possible in their home by doing the thing that mattered most to him. His morning blow job was his way of starting each day stress free.

Since he was the one neglecting her, it was okay for her to have an affair. But his biggest mistake would be letting her catch another woman riding or sucking his dick. He'd asked her to marry him. That meant he was ready to commit to her. She tried convincing herself that marrying him would make her faithful. Help her to change her promiscuous ways. Make her forget about her ex who sexed her senseless. She wondered what would happen if he ever caught her sucking another man's dick the way she devoured his. How well did she know her husband? Getting caught might be her biggest mistake.

Taking her father's advice, just in case her marriage ended, she'd kept her maiden name on all her legal documents except her marriage license. Foxy Montgomery married Winton Brown for the same reasons her sisters Victoria and DéJà Montgomery married their spouses—for the two things money couldn't buy, prestige and respect.

"I'm cumming, baby," he said, grabbing a fistful of her hair.

Cum squirted against her tonsils, dripped down her throat. She'd rather swallow his sperm than to have her husband ejaculate inside her. She kissed his head, then asked, "You good?"

Thanks to her dad's advice, she'd have a baby when she was ready to become a full-time mother, not to keep or please a man, even if that man was her husband. She didn't want to be a married woman who'd end up a single mom like her mom was.

Winton smiled, then nodded. He knew she'd get him off again if he wanted. "I'm good. Real good. Thank you, gorgeous," he said, meticulously tucking his dick inside his boxers.

Her clients had more gratitude than her husband. The only thing missing from Winton's *thank you* was the two thousand dollars she charged her clients for the same type of blow job.

CHAPTER 3

Foxy

Her husband was priceless in many ways, but not when it came to sexually pleasing her. He'd never dug into the buried treasures of her G-spot. The place that made her squirt like a fountain remained a mystery to her husband. Best not to teach her husband the plethora of tricks she shared with her ex-man and her clients, or she'd arm him with tools he could use to please other women. Other women could wreak havoc in her marriage if they became hopelessly devoted to her husband the way she was. As long as her husband was partner in the number one law firm in the nation, Foxy was no fool—she'd settle for getting her pussy licked elsewhere.

She'd continue to maintain her husband's trust if she kept him away from her real occupation. It would serve neither of them well if he discovered she was more than a waitress at her family's pastry shop. Sexing clients after hours was a career, not a job. Along with her sisters, Foxy was an owner of Crème, a neighborhood bakery that prepared pastries and fulfilled adult sexual desires by asking one question: *What is your fantasy?*

Hurrying into the bedroom, she showered, then dressed for work. The uniform—a tapered, short-sleeved red button-up blouse, a matching A-line skirt, and Crème's signature cream slip-on stilettos with 14-karat gold heels—would soon be in a closet next to another man's clothes. A man she'd known before she'd vowed to remain faithful. A man she'd promised to marry but couldn't. Couldn't let him break her heart a third time. No sense in her entering a marriage with preexisting trust concerns. She knew him too well, and although she catered to him five days a week, he strove to occupy the one day a week she shared with her husband and the Sundays she spent with her sisters.

Sundays consisted of going to sunrise church service with her sisters, then to the spa with her sisters, shopping with her sisters in the afternoon, then having a late lunch with her sisters. Monday evenings Foxy had a standing appointment to share quality time with Winton, if that was what one could call having dinner. She hadn't been vaginally penetrated by her husband in three years.

"Have a good day, honey," Foxy told her husband, kissing his lips. "Think you'll be home by midnight?" she asked, hoping to encourage him.

Shaking his head, Winton answered, "Not tonight, sweetheart. The new client, remember? You know her case is going to be all over the news today, so I have to get on top of this one early. Don't wait up." He gestured for another kiss. "Oh, and I need to call your cousin Dallas about his DUI. Figured out a way to get the charges dropped."

"I appreciate you so much, baby," she said, giving him a lingering kiss.

Why couldn't she be honest with her husband? In a man's world, a man having sex with multiple women wasn't perceived the same as a woman sexing multiple men. Winton's coming home after midnight meant she'd cook, have dinner, fuck her ex-fiancé Dallas, make it home before midnight, bathe, then fall asleep before Winton eased into bed beside her.

Winton put on his eyeglasses, snapped open his *Crème City Times* newspaper, lowered it to his lap, then said, "I love you, woman," staring at her ass.

Foxy swayed her booty. The attitude in her butt should've conveyed to him that she was getting dicked-down really good by some man. Her husband was either too blind to notice, didn't want to see the truth, or like most foolish husbands, he assumed she'd never cheat on him. She turned her head, gave her husband a wink, and smiled before strutting out the door of their lake view home on South Shoreline Drive for a morning quickie with the man she could've married.

Chapter 4

Winton

His wife wasn't out the door two seconds before he'd started getting prepared for Nova. Winton was excited and nervous to meet face-to-face for the first time the woman men all around the world fantasized about fucking. Nova had graced the cover of sports magazines with swimsuits the width of shoelaces. He was anxious to find out if her perky breasts were real. One lingering, tight embrace and he'd know.

He retrieved the warming gel from his medicine cabinet, turned on the shower, saturated his left hand, then stroked his dick. He was proud to have a dick the size of a ten-inch-long salami. He had no idea how Foxy swallowed his entire billy-stick, but she was the only woman that had.

The heated sensation of his dick got hotter with each stroke. "I bet Nova's pussy is hot like this," he said, stroking faster. "Open your mouth." He visualized his dick waxing her lips.

"Ah, yes. Suck the head, baby. Harder. Harder." He grunted. "You ready for this hot cum. Hold your titties together. I'm getting ready to . . . ah, yes." He imagined cumming on her nipples, then watching her lick his creamy cum, as his seeds washed down the drain. "Damn, that bitch was good, and she doesn't even know it."

He shaved extra close. In case she initiated a hug, he didn't want his mustache to scratch her multimillion-dollar face. His Sexualé cologne was usually reserved for after work but not today. He brushed his teeth twice, rinsed three times, and shoved a handful of peppermints in the inside jacket pocket of his five-thousand-dollar suit before getting in his luxury sedan.

The second he started his engine, the Bluetooth connected. He dialed the office from his cell.

"Brown, Cooper, and Dawson, how may we represent you?"

"Hey, this is Winton. I'm on my way. I should make it there before my client, but if I don't, call me immediately when Ms. Nova Scotia arrives," he told his assistant.

"Sure thing, Mr. Brown. Anything else?"

"That'll be all," he said, pressing the end button on his steering wheel. His standard commute time was thirty minutes.

Six-thirty Tuesday morning there was moderate traffic on the freeway into the city. Another hour and cars would be bumper-to-bumper the way he wanted his dick on Nova's ass.

The golden pyramid landmark, owned by his firm, occupied one square block and marked the center of Crème City. Winton parked in the garage, rode the express elevator to the fiftieth floor. The top floor was exclusively his. Its peak marked the highest point of all the downtown structures. His partners shared the floor below. The forty-eighth floor was their court-room, the place where they conducted mock trials prior to going to court.

Winton fully extended his office windows six inches, then inhaled the fresh air. He had the most amazing 360-degree panoramic view and was the only man that could look down on every business and residence in the city whenever he wanted. He gloated at being the envy of all his counterparts. Winton refused modesty. He'd worked exceptionally hard to become the best lawyer in the country, taking on cases others believed impossible to win. His ethics and consistency earned him first right of refusal on the majority of big cases like Nova's.

His intercom buzzed, then he heard, "Ms. Scotia has arrived."

Spraying air freshener, he pressed the button, then replied, "Great, send her in."

The strong air-conditioned breeze blowing through his office floor vent blew Nova's sheer white skirt above her hips as she entered. He struggled to keep his focus on her and off her hot body. The exposure hadn't fazed her, but her super-protruding nipples made him feel like a deer caught in her headlights.

"Have a seat," he said, gesturing toward the two chairs across from him.

Nova slid her chair from the opposite side of his desk. She sat diagonal, facing him. If she extended her leg, she'd touch his. Normally he'd tell his clients not to move either of his chairs, but he was glad she'd taken the initiative to come closer.

His eyes scanned from her lap, up to her lips, and back to her nipples. If he were ordering from an à la carte menu as he'd done countless times, he wouldn't know what delicacy to choose first. He felt the gleam in his eyes shining from her light.

Lord, why me? Yield not to temptation again, man, he thought, then said, "Excuse me." He inhaled long and slow, lowered his eyes, stared at the V that had gathered between her thighs, scratched his brow, tapped his pen on the desk, then pushed back his chair. Her headlights commanded his attention. The wheels glided along the plastic mat giving him, giving them, three feet of space. His eyes lost contact with her nipples, but the image was etched in his mind.

The morning sunrays beamed through the windows, over his shoulders, and onto his computer screen making it difficult for him to enter data into her file. Bypassing the thermostat that registered sixty-seven degrees, he closed his office door, considered locking it, but didn't. That wasn't a good idea. He twirled the rod until the interior blinds closed. Didn't want his staff or counterparts walking up observing his interaction with Nova. He pressed a button. The wooden horizontal blinds covering the exterior windows tilted upward, redirecting the sunshine toward the ceiling, away from his computer.

Winton glanced at Nova's silky legs. Her French pedicure, long thin legs, and slender feet exemplified . . . *sexxxy.* If he were fortunate, he'd have them wrapped around his waist soon. He didn't believe in luck.

Her crushed diamond slip-on stiletto dangled across toes he'd dreamed about kissing, sucking, stuffing in his mouth while fucking the shit out of her missionary style, so he could admire her beauty and observe her distorted facial expressions as she came for him. The lace straps of her glittery candy-apple red thong stretched over the elastic waistband of her skirt, shaping her butt cheeks into an incredible heart. He'd love to bury his face in her butt and lick her asshole.

Damn. Winton wasn't sure if he should thank Nova's man or curse him. His timing sitting back in his chair was impeccable as she uncrossed her thighs, fanned her skirt above her knees, then crossed her ankles. He got a whiff of her sweetness and almost got a view of her crotch. Was her pussy fat, flat, cameltoed? Did she have a landing strip? Was her pussy bald?

Smoothing his hand over his mustache to shield his parting lips and hard tongue, Winton exhaled into his palm, then said, "Start from the beginning, end with telling me how you became so mad with your boyfriend that you ran into him with your car."

CHAPTER 5

Winton

What attracted a married man to a woman other than his wife?

During his twelve years of practicing law, he'd represented many gorgeous women. Short. Tall. Plus size. Bald. Long hair. Average looking. Thin. He'd sex a woman less attractive than his wife without reservation, knowing he had a better-looking wife at home. If he ever divorced or separated from his wife, if only to make his wife jealous, he had to have a woman more gorgeous and more successful than his wife.

A few times he'd slipped into the arms of his clients for comfort, three women to be exact. An attractive woman could do many things for a married man—make him feel good about himself, remind him he was worthy of praise and pussy for his hard work, or let him know the grass wasn't always greener (on her side), giving him good cause to redirect the generosity he exhibited toward her toward his wife.

Nova's succulent lips, the lips his wife obviously envied, parted just enough for him to see her sparkling Lumineers. Did she taste minty, fruity, or like sugar in the raw? The red rouge on her upper lip blended into a vibrant pink tease on her lower lip. Her mouth was surrounded by a hint of chocolate liner. He imagined her inner and outer pussy lips and her shaft were the same, a blend of red, pink, and chocolate.

"My boyfriend is hot. The tabloids just announced he was voted the sexiest man in America. You know that? Of course, you do. Everybody knows he's the hottest man alive. But I can't control these groupies. He has women in heat all over him, all the time. I mean, I have my share of men flirting with me, but the difference between how fans respond to a male celebrity versus a female celebrity is women are bitches. And desperate bitches in heat will do anything to get a man. Those bitches make me *soooo* mad," she said, making fists. "I want to"—right, left, right she punched the air—"beat their asses to the ground."

She inhaled, then continued, "But I refuse to be their financial ticket out of poverty because most of them don't have anything to offer my man except their broke-ass pussy. Those bitches have no respect for my man. They have no respect for themselves. And they damn sure nuff don't have respect for me."

Nova stood, stepped to him, then said, "Let me show you what I mean. One woman tried breast-feeding him in front of my face. Can you believe this?"

She raised her skirt, straddled his chair, shoved her irresistible 100 percent authentic titties in his face, grabbed her blouse, lowered her top, then rubbed her super nipples across his mouth.

Fuck! It took every ounce of fortitude to keep his hands off her. He recalled squirting cum on her nipples while he masturbated in the shower earlier. He nibbled before leaning back. Squeezing her biceps, his dick hardened against her thong. He felt her engorged shaft grinding against his billystick.

"Ou, you've got a nice big one," she said, retreating to her seat. "But you see what I mean. Men don't disrespect me that way in front of him, so why do these bitches keep testing me?"

Precum oozed from Winton's dick. He'd done nothing wrong this time. How was he to know she'd show him her tits and tell him things that made him want to fuck the shit out of her sexy ass right now? He loved her edginess. Her fire was what he desired.

The growl of Nova's voice when she said, "One way or another this will come to an end," turned him on.

He visualized her ripping off his shirt, pushing him on his desk, yanking his dick out of his pants, and wildly slopping those hot juicy lips over his head, slobbering his precum in her mouth, then smearing it on like lipstick.

Bitch, you are so fucking fantastic you can have any man you want including me, and you are sitting here tripping over this one guy who obviously doesn't deserve you. Why?

Lifting her skirt, she'd push her thong aside, then mount him, this time squatting on the big-ass dick his wife loved to suck but hadn't fucked in years. Nova would sit there and let her pussy muscles work his dick out until he exploded inside her.

"Hello! Are you paying attention? I said . . . why do these bitches keep testing me?"

CHAPTER 6

Winton

Oh-damn. Massaging his erection underneath his desk, Winton regained focus, then asked, "Is this really about the other women, your strained relationship with your man, or do you have anger management and control issues?"

"Pick one. Hell, pick 'em all!" Nova yelled, leaping from her seat.

Her titties bounced. He picked up his pen, tapped it on the desk. Her nipples were still hard as his dick. She probably never needed nipple suction cups like his mistress. Isis had worn the cups so much she'd trained her small introverted nipples to protrude. Inputting insignificant data, he tapped on his keyboard. He'd get the facts during her deposition.

Nova was taking client confidentiality to a new level. What if one of his partners Acer or Naomi had walked in his office while Nova was straddling him? She knew what she was doing to him. Or did she? Did he? Was his assumption that she wanted to fuck him conclusive? Struggling to maintain professionalism, Winton eased his hand from his computer midway down his thigh and choked his dick, forcing his erection to subside.

"Now what really pisses me off is when he flirts back at women in front of my face. That's blatant disrespect. And why is his fucking ex-girlfriend always showing up at every one of his concerts? I hate that trifling bitch. She sits in the front row and she makes her way backstage, and he fucking talks to her like I'm not there. I hate her ass! If she was so fucking hot, why did he leave her for me?" Nova shouted, flopping in her seat.

The answer was standard. Men were dumb, nah, make that stupid, when it came to dealing with women. And men acted a damn fool when they dealt with supermodels.

Men who mistreated fine women made it easy for other men to slide their dick into home plate. Winton hadn't been attracted to a woman other than Foxy during the first year of their marriage. Shortly after their first anniversary, he started spending less time at home. Why bother exerting energy to make love to a woman who refused to have his baby until she was ready?

Cumming in his wife's mouth allowed him to stop praying for the son he desperately wanted to carry on his name and inherit his empire. Until Foxy was ready to have their baby, he'd deny her the pleasure of having his dick make her cum. And he'd keep wrapping his dick up while fucking his mistress.

His first affair lasted longer than he'd anticipated, an entire year. His subsequent affairs were back-to-back and each also lasted a year. And while he hated ending each relationship, he had to. Soon he'd have to end his affair with Isis. Perhaps he could replace Isis with Nova. New pussy excited him.

None of the women he bedded was worth leaving his wife for. He'd told them that. Not the "not worth" part. He'd told them he wasn't leaving his wife no matter what. No way would Foxy walk away with half his assets. Being with a woman that he'd never leave his wife for evoked emotional pain for those women, but not for him. The more he sexed them, the more attached they'd become. The better he had sexed them, learned their bodies, discovered their erogenous zones, made them cum hard, the more possessive they'd become.

Better for him to let them go before any of his women showed up at his front door, or worse, in the courtroom during one of his trials. He'd stopped answering their calls. Stopped responding to their messages, knowing if he'd let go, eventually they'd let go too. The advantage to living in the largest populated city in America was that he could easily avoid the places he used to take his ex-mistresses and start over. Find a new mistress and take her to new places.

Isis claimed, like his previous, she understood he was married. He tried to train Isis to keep her mouth shut by telling her, "You have to keep this between us. I'm a private man. Everyone knows me, so you can't go around telling my business. What happens between us is our thing. It's special. If you tell your friends, they'll mess it up for us and I'll have to let you go."

Lately Isis had told her family and friends that he was close to popping the question. That was a lie. She'd asked, "Baby, do you think we'll ever get married?" And he'd replied, "The way my wife is acting, we should." How she interpreted that to be a semiproposal was beyond him. A few more hits on Isis's pussy and she'd be history.

Winton wondered if Nova's concern was losing her man to another woman or that, if his ex won him back, she'd single-handedly make Nova a paparazzi disaster. Would he become a public failure if Foxy left him for another man? Nonsense. His wife would never cheat on him. Foxy was faithful to him, and she deserved a little of the extra time she'd pleaded for this morning.

Why did he have to take Nova on as a client? Acer had passed. Naomi too. Maybe he should try to convince Acer to reconsider representing Nova. Acer was the only serial monogamous man Winton knew that hadn't cheated on his wife.

"You hate your ex so you hit him with your car? Did he hit you first? Assault you? Has he ever hit you? Were you in fear of your life so you were trying to get away from him and *accidentally* hit him? Maybe you didn't see him standing on the sidewalk, thought you were hitting your brakes but *accidentally* pressed your foot on the gas?"

Nova frowned. Her mouth pouted into a sexy O as her lips exposed her teeth. Winton imagined pressing his dick head into her mouth, parting her lips and teeth wide enough to slide his dick inside. Fair exchange was amicable. If he covered her ass, she should polish his trophy with those humongous lips.

For a moment, he thought about his wife. Winton wasn't bored with Foxy. He hadn't sexed her in so long the desire to penetrate his wife was gone but his reason wasn't. Foxy was stunning. Any man would be proud to have such a great-looking wife. Part of the reason for his divided attention was sitting across from him; the other part, his latest mistress, was waiting for him to get off from work and come to her place. Maybe he was prewired like most men who enjoyed fresh pussy.

"Accidentally?" she said, first smiling, then frowning at him.

Winton wanted to grab Nova's breasts, bury his face in her cleavage. His tongue stiffened longing for a lick of her clit, her shaft. Did she taste like vanilla rock candy, sticky honey, or coconut milk? Were her vaginal juices thick like homogenized milk, whipped cream, slick like olive oil, slushy like applesauce, or watery? Was she hot like *fi-ya* or lukewarm? Was she tight or loose? Praying he was smarter than his dick and glad his erection had subsided, Winton said, "Let's continue this conversation over breakfast at a restaurant."

Without trying, beautiful women had a way of making men do foolish things. Winton Brown was many things, but he was no woman's fool.

CHAPTER 7

Foxy

The second she slipped the key into his lock, opened his front door, she was at home away from her home. Foxy locked the door behind her. The first time she hadn't secured the lock, Dallas complained, "Always lock my door, woman. I shoot first and ask questions later. Never know what ignoramus is bold enough to invade my house."

Breaking and entering on Shoreline Drive was less than 2 percent, but Dallas believed the low rate placed all of them at a higher risk. She understood his point. People who were comfortable or oblivious to their surroundings made easier targets.

That day when she hadn't locked his door, she'd had a lot on her mind. That day was the first time she'd used his key since she'd given back his engagement ring. She had no intention of using the key after she'd gotten married until Winton had pissed her off. She'd found another woman's red lace thong deep inside the inner pocket of her husband's suit jacket.

Foxy decided to leave the thong there and not confront Winton. That morning, three years ago, marked her reunion with Dallas. Dallas wasn't better or worse than Winton; they were different.

Dallas insisted she keep the key to his home. He gave her the attention and time she deserved to get from her husband. She was welcomed anytime and never had to call first. Dallas made her feel like a woman in and out of bed. The problem was, Dallas was a lot like her father, Mason Montgomery. With each of her engagements to Dallas came a baby by some woman she had no idea he was fucking. Foxy had accepted his ring. She refused to accept his children.

She tried convincing herself that Dallas's children and their moms wouldn't put a strain on her relationship with him. To some extent that was true. Dallas never asked her to do anything for or with his children. Told her, "You have an open invitation to join me when I have my girls." But Foxy couldn't imagine sharing her husband with four females who at some point would take priority over her. Maybe that was the real reason she didn't want a child. Having a child meant Foxy would have to put the child's needs before her own.

That day when Foxy showed up at Dallas's place, he consoled her. Comforted her. Reminded her, "I should've been your husband in your wedding photos. Not the man you introduced as your cousin. You should've married me." He told her she was where she belonged. With him. That he didn't understand why she kept running away from him when she was the only woman he wanted to marry. Nothing Dallas had said that day made her want to divorce Winton. Her cheating husband made her cheat too.

Foxy had to be equally yoked and equally stroked. Her position was non-negotiable. There was no reason for a debate or confrontation with Winton. She'd serviced enough married and single men to know that men knew the truth, but they'd never admit: pussy overruled dick. He'd made his decision to fuck around and so had she. But fucking around was getting old; thirty-one was knocking on her door, and she was finally ready to have a baby. She didn't want to be sixty years old sitting at a high school graduation.

"In here!" Dallas yelled from the kitchen. "Breakfast will be ready in a minute."

Entering the kitchen, Foxy bit her bottom lip, then smiled at Dallas. She removed her red skirt, handed it to him. "Morning, baby. I'll finish this," she said, taking the eggbeater from him. She stood at the counter scrambling eggs in her purple thong and cream stilettos.

Dallas's green eyes glistened. He tucked his tongue behind his upper lip, slapped her ass with her skirt, then shook his head. "Beyoncé, Maxwell, or you want me to surprise you? Think about it. I'll be in the bedroom."

Definitely no surprises again this Saturday. She watched him. His sunken spine separated his back. Firm shoulders narrowed to his slender waist. His hard ass with dimples on each side sat high as he swaggered. He glanced over his shoulder, winked. His lips curved to one side. She jerked. He smiled, nodded upward, blew her pussy a kiss. She raked the eggs on a platter. Tossed a few sausages and croissants on top.

As she entered the bedroom, he was stretched atop the

comforter naked with his dick resting on his stomach. Six foot five inches of muscle lay before her. His brown curly pubic hairs trailed from his navel to his nuts. The hairs on his chest spread shoulder to shoulder. After all the years she'd known him, Dallas still excited her each time she saw him. Should her marital obligations rank above her womanly needs?

Foxy sat the platter on the nightstand, crawled in bed, then lay next to Dallas.

He caressed her left breast. Kissed her hand. "Tell me how much you love me."

"I love you so much that my husband has found a way to have my so-called cousin's DUI charges dropped."

Dallas rolled on top of her. Smothered her with kisses. In a hearty voice he said, "Ha, ha! That's my girl. And that's why you should be my wife. There's nothing you haven't done for me when I've asked. Nothing."

That was true and the same was true for her. Dallas and her dad were the two men that would do anything for her, no questions asked. She wasn't sure about Winton. Although she still wanted it, she realized she no longer needed her husband's support. With the stroke of a pen, she could take half of Winton's possessions. If her husband continued ignoring her, she might have to file for divorce to get his attention. She could spend his money to get his money.

Her husband, like many men, defined himself by his net worth, capital gains, material possessions, and trophy wife. Not by the love of his mother or his wife.

Foxy shimmied out of her thong, spread her thighs to let Dallas's dick fall against her shaft and clit, then closed her legs. Soft or hard his dick made her pussy wet. "I love you so much it hurts." She squeezed her thighs, tilted her pussy toward his nuts.

Dallas shoved his tongue into her mouth. His hands roamed over her shoulders, biceps, then down to her waist. "If I ever find that genie in a bottle, my only wish would be to make you my wife. One day you'll be all mine." He sat up, unbuttoned her blouse. With a snap of his thumb and middle finger, he unfastened, then removed her bra while kicking off her shoes with his toes.

Foxy removed the clip from her ponytail, fluffed her hair wild the way he liked her to, lay her head against the mattress. Looking in his eyes, she demanded, "Stick your dick inside me right now." She didn't have to ask twice.

Dallas held his dick, slid the head down her shaft, over her clit, and into her wet pussy. Bracing himself on his knees, he sat on top of her and began thrusting his dick in and out her pussy, each time stroking deeper, repeatedly hitting the bottom.

Foxy pressed her thighs together and moaned, "Dallas, why do you fuck me so good, baby?"

"Because I always want you to cum, but I never want you to leave. Guess I have to work harder," he said, pulling out.

Her eyes rolled upward. Her body trembled. "Shit!" she screamed, releasing her marital frustrations. "This feels too good. Put him back in."

He slid his dick all the way back in. Dallas paused with his dick deep inside her until her pussy stopped quivering. He pulled out, stroked his dick. His cum shot in spurts, clung to her breasts, neck, and lips. He massaged his sperm into her mouth, then kissed her.

Quietly, Foxy made her way to the shower. DéJà would be upset with her again today for being late for work.

He followed her to the bathroom. Stepped in the shower with her.

"This makes no sense. We're perfect for one another. Why won't you divorce him?" Dallas asked. "I've got money too."

"Not again today," she replied. "It's not about the money. Maybe we're perfect because we're not married. Marriage is temporary. Infidelity lasts forever."

Foxy couldn't tell Dallas the truth. The only attorney more prestigious than Winton was the attorney general. Dallas was stable, successful, and handsome. If he didn't have those two oops kids, maybe she would've married him; who knew. If she had married Dallas, she may have cheated on Dallas with Winton. Dallas was well-known in his field as one of the top headhunters for CEOs. But his profession was subpar in comparison to her husband's.

She told him, "What we have is better than being married. We're inseparable. You love me. I love you. But you drive me bananas."

"Don't say that word. You know what happens to me when you say bananas."

His dick stood at attention. Maybe it was the way Dallas loved and made love to her that was causing her outburst and not Winton's rejection. She wanted her husband to be like Dallas but she didn't want Dallas to be her husband.

"You make it seem as though I'm the only one that has your heart, then a baby pops out of some woman's pussy and it has your DNA. Let's just keep things the way they are. It works, you know."

How many other kids did he have that neither one of them knew about?

"Works for whom? Not me. I want to wake up with you. Not have you stop by in the morning on your way to work and drop in to cook us dinner, then leave before midnight."

Foxy countered, "I do more for you than I do for my own husband," then stepped out of the shower.

"If you love him so much, then why fuck me every day? Do you fuck him every day too?"

"Told you. That's not your business," she said, making her way into the bedroom. She put on her clothes, kissed him. "Beyoncé. I'll be here when you get home. Bye."

No man was going to have her answer questions he wasn't willing to answer, then use her confessions against her. Dallas never told her whom or how many women he'd fucked, but the babies made it obvious he was fucking other women without protection even when he was engaged to her. That meant he'd cheat on her just like her husband was cheating on her.

Now that she was married, Dallas had a right to be nonexclusive. Foxy didn't ask probing questions nor was she going to answer any. Some things were better left untold.

Foxy drove ten miles along South Shoreline Drive to the most prominent side, the west side, where the sunset was breathtaking every day. Shoreline Drive was one huge horseshoe—west, south, and east—that stretched forty miles along Crème City's waterfront. The north side was the only side with a three-hundred-foot pier that stretched out over Lovers' Lake. At night, Winton's office building was lit like a Christmas tree. Wherever she was with Dallas, she could look toward the sky and see the tip of her husband's pyramid.

Seventy-five percent of the residents lived in the overpopu-lated metropolitan heart of the city. Blocks of luxury high-rise condominiums had views of the adjacent condos. The scenic view, serene water and beautiful landscaped front lawns on one side of the street, tall trees and mansions on the other, gave her time to rethink her life as she drove by both of her sisters' homes.

Foxy parked her car at 6969 West Shoreline Drive. As she prepared for another day of work at Crème, Foxy accepted her reality . . . men and women were created equal, but women were responsible for balancing their end of the seesaw.

CHAPTER 8

Foxy

The day went by fast. Servicing customers helped Foxy escape the woes of her bittersweet love triangle. While some women were trying to find a husband, if the law allowed, she could have two.

This Tuesday was busier than normal. The day after Memorial Day, kids should've been back to school and working folks back to their jobs. From opening until closing it seemed like the entire 6.9 million residents of Crème City had patronized their shop. Bustling for cinnamon buns, cream puffs, and chocolate-dipped macaroons, Foxy had to hand out numbers to establish order. Customers and kids socialized in the parking lot like they were at a tailgate party, waiting to hear their number. The daily three fantasies had become more popular than the state lottery, and DéJà had sold all three before Foxy had made it to work by eight.

"Foxy, come here," DéJà said, ushering the last group of patrons out the door.

"I already know what you're going to say. I've got to get in earlier."

Operating a family-owned business meant Foxy was her own boss, but not according to her tyrant sister DéJà, who had deemed herself in charge of Foxy, Victoria, and the day-to-day operations of Crème.

Locking the door, DéJà said, "That too, but that's not what I have to say. I heard Winton got Dallas's DUI charges dropped today. You'd better be glad Winton doesn't know you were in the car on a date with Dallas when he got the citation."

That night the cops ruined what could've been a perfect evening. They were headed to Lovers' Lake for a stroll along the pier when Dallas's cell phone rang. He reached for his phone, swerved into the adjacent lane. Before he answered the call, a siren blared, lights swirled, and the high beams from the patrol car blinded them. Fortunately she hadn't consumed any alcohol at the jazz club. On the way to his house, Dallas had asked, "Can you ask Winton to take care of this for me, cuz?"

The downside to DéJà and Victoria's spouses being partners in the Brown, Cooper, and Dawson law firm with Winton was that sometimes her sisters knew about her situations before she did. Foxy presumed her husband was too busy with Nova to call and let her or Dallas know the good news, but she had no doubt Winton would prevail. Winton's getting a DUI dismissed was a matter of having his legal assistant complete the paperwork for his review, having lunch with a judge friend, then filing the necessary documents. Her husband had never lost a case and a DUI surely wouldn't be his first.

"You've been hanging on to that all day?" Foxy asked. "Why didn't you mention it to me when I got in this morning?"

"Your idea of morning is our afternoon. Victoria and I get here at five a.m. The morning pastries are done by the time you arrive." DéJà stumped by Foxy, removed the cash drawer from the register. "I assumed you knew but y'all were probably too busy fucking to hear your phones. Acer texted me this afternoon, and you know I don't talk business in front of our customers." DéJà stared in her face, then said, "But it's time, sis. You know what I mean." Then changed the conversation, "Girl, it was a madhouse up in here. We must've sold over a thousand pastries to customers. Plus the three fantasy specials to our clients."

Customers were those who bought pastries. And for tax and legal purposes, clients were those who paid for catering services. Every day after closing Foxy and her sisters each serviced one client from four o'clock to five, occasionally until six.

Comparing the six thousand dollars they earned on the client-based side of the business with the five dollars per pastry they earned on the customer-based side, servicing clients always yielded more revenue for Crème in a shorter period of time. But the pastries made all of their revenue appear legit.

Not responding to DéJà's comment, Foxy answered, "Of course, my husband got Dallas's charges dropped, Winton is the best," then walked behind the counter, around DéJà, through the kitchen, into their office, and sat at her desk.

Their business wasn't a brothel or whorehouse. They didn't have esteem issues from fucking numerous clients. Their fulfillment of adult fantasies ranged from talking dirty, to spanking, to flogging, to teaching clients how to reach higher orgasmic states or how to prolong their ejaculations. If more people had healthy sex more often, the world would be a better place. There were a few occasions where they had intercourse or oral copulation with their clients. As with any business, they reserved the right to refuse service, and the use of dental dams and condoms was mandatory.

DéJà and her sister Victoria entered the office, sat at their desks.

DéJà hissed, "Acer and I, we are the best. You know this."

"What?" Foxy shook her head. "Don't get me started."

DéJà hated when anyone perceived they were better than she or her husband. There was no need to challenge her. DéJà definitely had the final word of every conversation.

The ivory circular revolving desk was sectioned into three triangles that merged into one large circle, allowing them to face one another while conducting business or trade stations without changing seats. In this case, the seating arrangement forced Foxy to face her accusers.

Victoria chimed in, "What you do with Dallas and your husband is up to you—"

Foxy interrupted her "I'm so neutral and the voice of reason about everything" sister and said, "But."

"No buts. Not this time," Victoria retorted. "Let's just pray Winton never finds out the truth about his pro bono services for *cousin* Dallas, who, remind you, is in some of your wedding photos. You're playing with fire. Don't be surprised if your husband beats you when he finds out you've made a fool of him."

That was the shit Foxy hated. What gave Victoria the right to predict Winton would lay hands on her? Foxy's husband had never hit her. Winton wasn't the type of man that would resort to barbarically resolving problems. He was a lawyer because he was smart, and intelligent men didn't beat women.

Victoria said, "I vote we tell Dad about your affair before it's too late."

Foxy's mouth gaped open. "The hell you will! If you tell Dad, I'm telling your wife."

"See," Victoria said. "You are miserable, and I will not be your company. If you don't want our help, fine. Go get counseling."

Psychiatrists were for crazy people; she wasn't crazy.

"Foxy, nobody's telling Dad," DéJà commanded. "Look at me. You are an eighteen-wheeler treading on melting ice in the middle of Alaska. Make a decision. Divorce Winton or divorce Dallas."

"Cute. Real cute." Foxy rolled her eyes at DéJà. She and her sisters were the same as when they were in high school, opinionated, stubborn, and different. Neither of them could tell the other what to do without opposition. "I'm not married to Dallas."

"You may not think you're married to him, but three years of fucking the same dick constitutes common-law pussy," DéJà said.

Victoria burst into laughter.

"This is serious, Victoria," DéJà scolded. "Foxy, what are you going to do? Don't force me to side with Victoria and vote we tell Dad."

"Why can't I have both of them until I make up my mind? Men do this shit all the time. Mistresses, second families, kids out of wedlock, making babies during engagements, creeping, cheating, baby mama drama, and what are women supposed to do? Keep our mouths shut and our legs closed and pretend we're sugar and spice and everything nice when we're really fed the fuck up? Fuck that shit. When Winton comes to his senses, maybe I will stop seeing Dallas, but I refuse to lay at home in my bed alone while my husband is sleeping with some other woman."

"You don't know that for sure," Victoria said.

"Oh, what am I supposed to do? Confront him about the nasty-ass cum-stained thong I found in his jacket pocket?"

Victoria shook her head, then said, "That was three years ago. You chose not to confront him. Foxy, you've got to learn to forgive your husband. This Sunday, I don't care what you say, we're taking you to the altar for prayer."

"That's very noble of you sister but no thanks. You first," Foxy told Victoria. "With the exception of Mondays, my dear sister, three years ago was the last time my husband made it home before midnight. I bet you wouldn't be so practical if your wife was fucking around on you or if she found out you were still fucking your ex-man, Mr. officer of the got-damn law, chief of police."

"My situation is different. Rain is my client now," Victoria explained.

"Client my ass. Yeah, right. You're servicing him for free? I don't see his two thousand dollars in the register when you schedule him."

Victoria replied, "If it'll shut you up, I'll put up the two thousand dollars. Damn."

"How about your shutting up. Keep your money. This isn't about money. My point is you're just as confused as I am. Does Naomi know Rain is your client now?" Foxy lamented.

DéJà interrupted, "Enough! It's three fifteen. Foxy, count the register; Victoria, you double-check the deposit; and I'll make the deposit on my way home. Foxy, I know you're not going to make it in by five, but I expect to see you before nine. I'm tired of covering your responsibilities until you decide to come in."

"What's up with all the sudden attitudes toward me?"

Miss "I hate to be late for anything" DéJà picked up the deposit, placed it in her tote, then said, "Let's go. We need to get out of here so we can service our fantasy clients on time."

Foxy swore DéJà was a four-star general or sergeant at arms in her previous life and Victoria was a nun. Was she the only sister living in the real world? Foxy was glad but not surprised DéJà had ended the conversation. When things got out of control, DéJà took control. When things were in control, DéJà maintained control. DéJà didn't know how to be submissive. Like most dominatrices who'd mastered being a slave before becoming a mistress, DéJà had bypassed being a follower all of her life.

CHAPTER 9

DéJà

*W*hack! *Whack!* The cold leather strap slapped against his back, his ass. Red striped marks remained. *Whack!* She'd hit him again. This time on his thigh.

Late Tuesday afternoon DéJà dominated Dr. Flannigan. He'd delivered over ten thousand of the babies born at Crème Memorial Hospital. He'd been her gynecologist for over ten years. Had heard about her being a mistress from one of his and her female clients. During one of DéJà's annual checkups, he'd asked, "May I be your slave?"

Her response was, "What is your fantasy?"

"To be your slave."

"To be my slave what?" she'd asked.

"Please?"

That day in his office she'd slapped his face. "Don't ever speak to me without addressing me properly." She slapped his face again. "From now on I'm Mistress DéJà to you." Since that visit, their relationship had been steady and confidential.

Whack! Whack!

"Yeah!" he grunted, crawling on the floor. "I've been bad this week. Beat me some more," he begged.

Her evoking pain helped relieve his frustrations. His sleepless nights curled up in hospital beds, waiting for patient after patient to dilate ten centimeters, were at times more stressful than others. Telling mothers when to push. Ordering epidurals, doing emergency C-sections. He had to have an outlet, a release from always being in control of and responsible for mothers' and babies' lives.

Whack! Whack! This time DéJà yanked the silver metal chain attached to the black leather collar around his neck. The dull spikes inside the collar applied pressure to his neck, choking him, but didn't leave any visible marks that his colleagues or patients might question. The welts on his back, ass, and thighs didn't matter to him or her.

"Don't tell me what to do. I tell you what to do." She slashed the leather across his ass. "Address me properly before I piss on you."

"Yes, Mistress DéJà," he said, bowing his head. "Oh, that feels *soooo* good."

She poured hot wax along his spine. His back arched. "Ugh . . . yeah. More," he begged. "More."

DéJà grabbed his curly hair. Yanked hard. Stooped to his level. Stared in his eyes. His eyes shifted to the corners avoiding contact with hers.

"Very good," she said, then asked, "What did I tell you?"

"Sorry, Mistress. I got excited. It won't happen again."

"Mistress who?" she asked, yanking again.

"Mistress DéJà."

"Call me Mommy," she said.

"Mommy," he repeated like a baby, leaning his head on her, against her knees.

She jerked his head away. "Did I give you permission to touch me, little boy?"

"No."

"No, what?"

"No, Mommy."

"Good boy," she said, patting his head. "You want a treat?"

He nodded.

"Lick Mommy's boot," she said. "Then I'm going to piss on you."

Dr. Flannigan's tongue extended. He pressed the tip against the toe of her black patent leather boot and licked up to her thigh.

"Good boy. Back down on all four," she commanded, straddling him. She held her thong to the side, and urinated on the wax that had stuck to his back. "Now go shower and get some rest so you can deliver some more babies," she said, removing his dog collar.

"Yes, Mommy Mistress DéJà. I will do whatever you say." This was how all their sessions ended.

DéJà peeled the wax from his back. She showered in her bathroom, changed into a fresh red tapered blouse and A-line skirt, and stepped into her cream stilettos with the 14-karat gold heels while Dr. Flannigan showered, then put on his scrubs and loafers. She followed his car off the private premises of Crème Fantasyland. Her job wasn't to judge but to fulfill fantasies. Too many wives were clueless or didn't want to know their husband's secret desires.

He went home to his wife, and she drove home to her husband.

CHAPTER 10

DéJà

Hump day, the break of dawn was too close to Sunday's morning dew.

DéJà had four days remaining to find a way to make Foxy end her affair with Dallas. Each year of fucking Dallas, Foxy had gotten more reckless. What was she thinking asking her husband to represent her man over a DUI when Dallas shouldn't have been drinking and driving in the first place? Fucking Dallas was one thing, but Foxy's fucking over Acer's partner was unacceptable. If Winton had bad press, that meant Acer would have bad press, and DéJà was not going to let that happen to her husband. Foxy was cool as long as she'd kept her shit in her backyard. Now it was time for DéJà to take charge.

And while she was getting involved in Foxy's affair, she might as well make Victoria stop fucking Rain, because if the media exposed Victoria's affair, Acer would be indirectly involved too. She'd told Victoria not to marry Naomi. She tried making her sister see she wasn't ready to be exclusive with a man or a woman. But *noooo*.

Victoria's problem was she fell in love too easily. Any man or woman who consistently displayed affection to Victoria was her friend. Any person who sexed her into cosmic orgasms was a potential husband or wife. After ten, DéJà lost count of the number of engagement rings Victoria had in her safety deposit box.

A woman either conformed to her environment or took charge of her life. She couldn't do both. If she was afraid to protect herself verbally, emotionally, or physically, she was automatically a target for abuse. If she defended those who misused her, she felt inadequate and was codependent. Regardless of how dangerous or demeaning a situation was, a woman with high self-esteem would conquer her challenges.

"Good morning, handsome. Breakfast will be ready in twenty minutes. Did you sleep well?" DéJà asked her husband, giving him a wet kiss on his lips. She smiled. Slapped him on the ass. She'd been taught by her father to marry a man with something to lose. She'd been trained by her mother to marry a good man with a better heart.

Standing behind her, he kissed her neck, then said, "I went to sleep and woke up with you. Of course, I slept well."

"Well, I can't take one day for granted," she said, thinking about her mom.

How much of a young girl's upbringing shaped her outlook on life? Reared by a perfectionist mother, every aspect of DéJà's childhood was preplanned. Learning her ABCs at two; reading at four; multiplying at six; cooking, baking, cleaning, dancing, swimming, singing, and sewing all before she turned eight was her mother's idea of what was important. Being a straight-A student and college graduate were mandatory.

Acer glanced at the items on the island. "Eggs Benedict, huh? Cool. I'm going to go shower."

DéJà slapped his ass again, watched her husband swagger out the kitchen. She placed the parchment paper inside the rimmed baking sheet, then laid twelve slices of bacon side by side before putting the sheet in the oven for fifteen minutes. She sang her self-proclaimed theme song, "I'm every woman, it's all in me . . ."

While the bacon cooked, she slid two eggs into separate skillets of simmering water with vinegar. Waiting for the eggs to poach, she thought about her mother's logic for raising her. Thanks to her mom, anything Acer wanted, DéJà did without forethought, and she knew her husband extremely well and could vow that all men were not dogs.

Her mother often preached, "Baby, cream rises to the top. A beautiful smart girl picks from the cream of the crop of men for her husband; she never scrapes the bottom of the barrel. Always do your best, DéJà, and you will never have to settle for anything or anyone. Men love intelligent women who can cook, make them laugh, keep a clean house, and keep them excited in bed. I send you to dance school not to learn how to dance, but to learn how to move your body with grace and so you will be flexible for your husband."

Turning the egg with a spoon until the egg whites were firm, DéJà wondered if her mom regretted not marrying her father when he'd proposed. She was the first woman Mason had asked to marry. He'd retired her the day she became pregnant. Other than saying Mason was a real man, DéJà's mom hadn't said much more about her father. Maybe it was the fact that

Foxy and Victoria's moms were carrying his babies at the same time her mother was pregnant with her.

Placing the eggs on a kitchen towel, she dropped two more eggs into the same skillets and put the butter and Canadian bacon in a separate skillet. A speck of butter splashed on the stove's surface. DéJà grabbed a wet cloth, then quickly wiped the entire stove.

The last words her mother spoke before DéJà went to live with Mason were, "DéJà, your father is here to pick you up. You're going to live with your two sisters. Don't forget anything I've taught you. You are not a follower. You are a leader."

She pried two English muffins apart, put them in the toaster, removed the eggs, and placed them on a separate towel. Removing the four English muffin halves from the toaster, she layered them with Canadian bacon, an egg, then topped each with hollandaise sauce.

"Breakfast ready?" her husband shouted from the bedroom.

"Almost, honey!"

Never wanting to disappoint her mother, DéJà was the best at everything she'd done. She'd done all her mother desired until the day her mother sent her to live with her dad. That was the day DéJà rebelled, defying Mason about all the things he wanted her to do. To her surprise, her dad wasn't the disciplinarian her mother had been.

Mason had told her, "Your decisions today dictate your future. I'm going to provide you with the best education you need to become successful. If you don't want to go to high school with your sisters, fine. I'll send you to whatever high school you'd like. You've got four years to live with me. But when you turn eighteen, you either go to college or you go home to your mother."

CHAPTER 11

DéJà

DéJà's dad's threat to send her back to Boston was the motivation she needed to implement the things her mother had taught her. The next morning she'd adjusted her attitude, was the first dressed for school, and was downstairs waiting for her sisters. Her father walked in the living room, and DéJà kept dancing and singing Beyoncé's "If I Were a Boy."

Mason told her, "You, my lovely queen, are a shining star. Why don't you teach princess and angel how to dance and sing like that? I'm placing you in charge." Her dad had given each of them nicknames. Hers was fitting because queen ranked above Victoria's angel and Foxy's princess.

With her father's blessings and her mother's principles, DéJà took the lead and taught her sisters how to bake, cook, sew, sing, and dance. Things had to be perfect or they had to be done over until Foxy and Victoria got it right. Sometimes DéJà made them stay up all night. When Foxy and Victoria rebelled against her, DéJà had called her mom.

Her mom told her, "You must master making them obey you. Let them choreograph a few routines. Have them perform for you. Then you must compliment them, then immediately crack your whip, and take charge by teaching them how to perform to your standards. They will learn to please you. Give it some time."

Her mother's lesson on how to get people to submit became an endless quest for control. In college, like breathing, domination came natural to DéJà. College was where she'd practiced bondage, dominance, and sadomasochism on unsuspecting students who became her slaves. Mastering being a dominatrix, controlling men and women, DéJà earned the title Mistress DéJà and started charging for her services and making her slaves write her papers, carry her books, massage her feet, and bring her food.

Acer sat at the table, tossed his tie over his shoulder.

"Honey, do you think I should make sticky buns today or honey buns?" DéJà asked, placing his plate in front him. Each morning she'd let him decide what she should bake at the shop.

"Definitely sticky buns," he said, nodding. "I like those more."

Her mother would say, "DéJà. Always let your husband think he's smarter than you, but know that you are wiser."

"Sticky buns it is. I'll bring you some home tonight."

She admired her husband. Six-four, two hundred and forty pounds with less than 5 percent body fat, he was the type of man she had to marry. Some saw her strong physical attraction to Acer as shallow. Acer had a muscular body. His midsection was thick, wide. Stomach flat and hard. His skin was smoother than a baby's. If men could pursue gorgeous, smart women, why shouldn't she have married a stunning attorney?

DéJà met Acer Dawson at the company-client social for Brown, Cooper, and Dawson that Foxy had invited her and Victoria to. That was the same day Victoria met Naomi and Winton proposed to Foxy. When things began falling apart for Foxy and Winton, Acer proposed. Their near three years of marriage was perfect. DéJà worked daily to make sure their relationship stayed that way.

Ten minutes after saying grace, Acer's three eggs Benedict and ten strips of bacon were devoured. He liked his food, his shower, and his wife, hot, hotter, and hottest.

"I'm a little horny, precious," Acer said smiling at her.

"There's no such thing as a little horny." DéJà stood, grabbed his tie, then led him to the bedroom. Undressing him, she pushed Acer on the bed, then firmly said, "Turn over." DéJà straddled her husband. She began massaging his back. Long, firm strokes from the arch of his lower back up to his spine to his neck. She jabbed his shoulder blades. Her hands circled his shoulders, traveled down his sides, and back up his spine. She kneaded his shoulders, chopped his sides, then slapped his ass. Squeezed his neck, slapped, chopped, kneaded some more, before repeatedly gripping his ass.

"Turn over," she said, rolling him onto his back.

Pouring kama sutra oil in her small hands, quickly she rubbed her palms, then gripped his dick, and began stroking him hard and fast. Up and down, she massaged her husband. Ten minutes later, right before Acer's muscles contracted to ejaculate, she tugged his balls away from his body. Bringing her husband to orgasm without allowing him to ejaculate gave him lots of energy throughout the day and stamina for her pleasure throughout the night.

"You go shower again. Get ready for work. You've got my pussy hot. Your queen is going to sex you crazy when you get home," DéJà told him. She had to be careful not to refer to herself as Mistress DéJà when with her husband.

Unlike with Foxy and Victoria's marriages, DéJà's trust and love for Acer never wavered. No person could ever replace her husband. Not even for a minute.

CHAPTER 12

Victoria

For every relationship demolished
A new one blossomed
For every child forgotten
One was conceived
For every triumph
There were obstacles
For every bleeding heart
There were unforeseen thumps of joy
Was love at first sight real or a myth?

Victoria never imagined she'd fall deeply in love with a woman. She was born straight, not a lesbian. She loved dating men. Came close to marrying several men. Was curious about being intimate with women. Had sex with a few women while she was in college and she enjoyed it. Did that make her bisexual? Trysexual? A freak? The one thing Victoria knew was that she was a woman capable of making independent decisions about her life, her body, her sexuality, and her choice of mate.

Her cell phone buzzed, startling her. Victoria slid out of Naomi's arms, picked up her BlackBerry, then quickly silenced the buzzer. Wednesday, 4:00 a.m. It was time for her to get up, but a phone call from Rain was not supposed to be her alarm. She looked over at her wife. Naomi was sound asleep. She accepted the call before it went to voicemail, tiptoed to the guest bedroom, then sternly answered, "What?"

"I want to see you, Victoria, that's what. Come over," he said.

His demands to see her were getting out of control. To Rain it was like she'd never married Naomi. His relentless behavior made Victoria wish she'd never met him at Crème City Hall. She'd gone to city hall to drop off documents for her business, say hello to her councilperson, and meet with the mayor. As she entered the mayor's office, Rain was exiting. When her meeting was over, the mayor's assistant handed her Rain's card. Victoria immediately realized the benefits of befriending the chief of police.

"I can't. I already see you twice a week in the evening. I'm not leaving my house at four in the morning to see you."

She hesitated. There were a few reasons she'd decided not to marry him. Maybe her reasons were actually excuses. Rain admired her more than he loved her. She could've learned to love him. He shared how all his childhood he'd dreamt of being chief of police. He'd fought his way through high school. Sometimes he won. Sometimes he lost. But he always had to fight. Rain's biggest battle was to prove to his parents he could do something right. He graduated from high school and put himself through college.

"Just this one time. I need you, Victoria."

She became silent.

"Please. I'm so weak for you, Victoria. Don't make me beg. I promise I won't ask to see you in the morning again."

Victoria felt sorry for Rain. He was a man with so much power, feeling helpless over their breakup. She wasn't to blame, but she did have compassion for him. To have parents that didn't love him as a child must've made him lonely. Lonely people needed someone to love and someone to love them back.

"Fine. Just this once." Victoria ended the call.

She tiptoed into the walk-in closet, put on a pair of sweatpants and a tank top and slipped on her flip-flops. Quietly stepping out of the closet, Victoria eased toward the bedroom door.

"Sweetcakes, where're you going this early?"

Victoria's heart raced. She hated lying to anyone, especially Naomi. Holding her BlackBerry in her hand, Victoria said, "Didn't mean to wake you. DéJà is running late, so I'm going to the shop to meet the delivery person. If I don't make it back before you leave, I'll call you later."

"Okay, sweetcakes. Be careful."

"I will," Victoria said.

She drove east on Shoreline Drive toward Rain's house. Bypassing Foxy's home, she noticed the lights were on. Victoria traveled twenty minutes in the opposite direction from the shop. Parking in his driveway, she turned off her engine, sat in her car. She couldn't lie. She still enjoyed the touch of his hands, the feel and scent of a man. His balls slapping against her pussy intensified her orgasms. Why couldn't she have a husband and a wife?

Rain opened his door, motioned for her to come in.

Victoria went inside. "Why are you calling me this early?" she asked.

"I woke up with the taste of your pussy in my mouth. Wanted to see you. We need to talk about your situation. Have a seat," he said, sitting beside her on the sofa. "I thought this marrying a woman thing was something you had to get out of your system. If you love her so much, why do you keep having sex with me?"

"You're my client."

"Don't give me that bullshit. I'm not your client. I don't pay to make love to you, Victoria. You keep trying to rationalize our relationship, but you can't deny our love for one another. I've thought long and hard about this, and I have a solution."

He'd come up with a solution for her situation or his?

Rain said, "Leave her. I'll pay for the annulment. Marry me. Naomi can find someone else. I can't."

Victoria shook her head. "You're funny. You know that? You know I'm not taking this seriously, right? I love my wife. I'm not leaving her for you. I'd never leave Naomi for you. What 'cop gone wild' dream did you have last night?"

Rain rubbed the back of his neck. Stretched his head side to side. Folded his arms. Bit his fingernail while staring at her. "You think I'm a joke?"

"I apologize. No, I don't think you're a joke."

Rain slid his hand inside her sweats, stuck his finger inside her pussy, stared at her while sucking her juices. "You love me too, don't you?"

"But I'm not in love with you. I've never been *in love* with you." She had to tell him the truth. Once Rain had gotten an idea in his head it was hard, if not impossible, to get it out.

"You're a liar, Victoria. You are in love with me." He parted her lips with his tongue. Kissed her as though if she could taste the sweetness of her pussy, she'd understand why he desperately wanted to change her mind. Make her admit she still loved him.

Her pussy quivered. She sucked his tongue deep into her mouth, wishing he'd shut up and fuck her so she could get back home to her wife. Victoria pushed him away, went to his bedroom, removed her clothes, threw them on the floor beside his bed like she'd done countless times during their relationship. She lay on his bed, faced down, turning her head to watch him.

Rain removed his clothes, threw them on top of hers, opened his nightstand drawer, got a condom and lube. He put a few drops of warming gel inside his condom, generously lubricated her ass.

Doggie-style was her favorite position. Rain put his dick head inside her ass. He swerved his pelvis with the motion of a snake gliding through a garden. Side to side his partially erect dick slithered inside her rectum until he made his way beyond the S-curve. She felt the blood flow to his dick extending his hard-on deeper inside her. He pushed her body flat against the bed, lay his body atop hers, French-kissed the nape of her neck while fucking her.

She teased her shaft on the cotton sheet tucked between her thighs. "Stay right there, baby. Don't move," she told him, rotating her hips to the right, making his dick hit her spot on the left. Burying her face in the pillow, she screamed, "Oh, my God, Rain, I'm cumming!"

Each time he pushed a little deeper, she came a lot harder. He pulled out. Removed the semen-filled condom, dropped it inside the fast-food paper cup on his nightstand, then lay beside her. Holding his dick, he said, "This here is the real thing, baby. A woman can't give you this. I know exactly how to hit your spots and make you cum hard in five minutes. Naomi can't fuck you like I can."

Getting out of his bed, Victoria said, "You might know how to fuck me, but you don't know how to love me. And you can't make love to me better than Naomi."

Rain frowned. "How you expect me to make love to you if I have to keep fucking you in the ass?"

She threw up her hands, went to the bathroom, turned on the shower, stuck her head out the door, then yelled, "So this is why you really called me? You're still dreaming about being my first?"

Rain entered the bathroom. "What are you saving yourself for? Give me your virginity, Victoria, so I can prove to you that I can make love to you. I'm tired of being considerate of your wants. Your asshole is only one hole away from your pussy. We can do this your way. Or my way. But I'm not going to keep politely asking for what's rightfully mine."

CHAPTER 13

Foxy

Wednesday, three o'clock, Foxy locked the door at Crème. Today the standard number of customers had come in. Fifty people had walked in and ordered pastries and beverages for office meetings, dessert, or after-school treats for their kids. Three clients had prepaid for adult fantasy services.

DéJà removed the cash drawer from the register. Foxy followed her into the office. Victoria was already seated at her desk. She'd been unusually quiet all day. DéJà too. DéJà's quietness generally meant she was up to something. Victoria's silence usually meant she had a lot on her mind. Foxy appreciated that neither of her sisters were in her personal business today.

Victoria counted their earnings. Foxy double-checked the deposit, then handed the cash and credit card receipts to DéJà who placed them in her tote. Avoiding starting a roundtable debate, Foxy picked up her purse and waited for her sisters at the front door.

They got in three separate cars, drove a short distance to Crème Fantasyland, a hidden paradise on the outskirts of the city. Their exclusive gated community was less than a quarter mile along West Shoreline Drive. The first entry gate opened to a long private road that was bordered on each side by maple trees. The branches created a canopy that overlapped high above the paved street. The end of the road forked into three long driveways that led to second gates.

To preserve privacy, each of their clients was given a single-use access code to their destination. Once on the property, they were instructed to follow the road leading to their designated house and to park inside the garage.

The first driveway led to DéJà's slave chamber, the second to Victoria's cozy haven, and the third to Foxy's dreamland. They'd invested money, time, and a lot of thought into designing their individual homes for their clients.

Foxy observed her client on the monitor. Senator Wade Pendleton lowered his tinted window, entered his code, then drove to her chocolate-tinted house with mocha trim. The pitched roof cascaded over double-paned windows on the upper level. The lower level had two-way mirrors. Foxy and her client could see out, but no one could see in. The murals of a forest, a waterfall, and Lovers' Lake coupled with seeing the trees outside her windows gave her clients an outdoor feeling while they were indoors with her.

Senator Pendleton was a once-a-month regular who billed the government for reimbursement under miscellaneous expenses for his fantasy. His having sex with her kept him happy and his being happy made him a better senator. As long as he paid her in cash, it wasn't Foxy's concern where the money came from. She was not the moral monitor of her clients' consciences. If she were, she'd have no clients.

Men came to her for various reasons. Some to fuck the way they couldn't fuck their woman or wife, others wanted her to strap on and fuck them in the ass. Then there were the men who wanted an experienced woman, and women who'd discreetly wanted the girl-on-girl experience. Some couples, both married and not, wanted a ménage à trois with a neutral person who wouldn't get emotionally attached. The list of fantasies was endless. Senator Pendleton came to her because he didn't want anyone other than his wife to know he had huge balls and a dick the size of a sweet pickle.

He entered the house through the garage, belting out, "These constituents are getting more demanding by the second I tell you. We approve same-sex marriages, now they want us to lower the legal drinking age to eighteen.

Foxy thought about Dallas's DUI, wondering why Winton still hadn't mentioned the charges were dropped. Probably too caught up with Nova.

"All the hoopla about 'If an eighteen-year-old can go off to war and die for their country, they should be allowed to drink.' Just what we need. A bunch of kids with guns drinking and shooting up every damn thing. I blame cowboys for this problem. Yep, the wild, wild West started this mess, Foxy. Ya got Johnnie ready for me?" he asked, tossing back two shots of cognac from her wet bar.

Johnnie stayed ready. She'd let the senator take his time and decide how he wanted to act out his fantasy this time. "Relax,"

Foxy said, loosening his tie. She kissed his neck behind his ear. Trailed kisses to his collarbone.

"You sure know how to make an old man feel like new money. If I weren't already married, I'd marry ya. You know that."

"Let's get you out of these clothes and into some warm, soapy, slippery water, so I can bathe you with my breasts," Foxy said, leading him to the whirlpool. Today was a day she had to take charge or the senator would waste his hour talking.

"Hot damn! Is Johnnie by the whirlpool?" he asked.

"He sure is, you hot stud, you. I can't wait for you to rub your big ole dick all over my naked body."

"I'ma do more than that. I'ma spank you with my big ole dick," he said, strapping on his male penile extension before getting in the whirlpool.

Thankfully sex was 98 percent mental. The tailored penile extension fit snugly around the senator's dick. Each time she stroked his extension the warming gel inside the dildo suctioned to his dick, allowing his sweet pickle to grow and stay fully erect until he ejaculated.

"Sure wish I could take Johnnie home. Come sit on him for me. No, wait. Stand up here, and let me see that pretty pussy first."

Foxy placed her feet beside his hips.

He spread her outer lips. "God damn! She sure is happy to see me," he said, rubbing her shaft with his finger. "I'ma eat this here pussy like you my twenty-seven-year-old wife."

Last year the senator remarried shortly after his wife had passed. He was smart to announce his engagement after his reelection. His marrying a woman half his age came as a shock to the community, but not to Foxy. There were older men who needed younger women in order to feel youthful. Foxy felt older women should marry younger, not older men and reap the same young spirited benefits. Foxy's youngest client, a wealthy eighteen-year-old, fucked her good the entire sixty minutes. He knew tricks her eighty-year-old client was too old to learn or remember.

Senator Pendleton picked up the dental dam from the poolside tray, covered her engorged shaft, then buried his face in her pussy. He licked and lapped. Foxy moaned, "Oh, yeah. You're making my pussy wet." She had a small orgasm as he continued lapping. A bigger orgasm emerged when he sucked her clit and shaft at the same time.

"Careful there," she said. "Don't swallow the dam."

"Whew, that was close," he said. "I just love this here strawberry dam . . . hot damn! I'm hard as a hammer."

He'd paid for Johnnie and could take his sidekick home whenever he wanted but told her his wife didn't like toys. "I'm ready to fuck this sweet pussy. Get down here on this big ole dick," he said.

Foxy stepped into the swirling water. He inched to the edge of his seat. She eased the dildo inside her pussy and swayed her hips back and forth, massaging his nuts with her butt cheeks.

The senator grabbed her titties, held them tight, and sucked her right breast. "These the prettiest titties I've ever seen. If I weren't already married, I'd marry ya," he said again. "Tell me you love me."

Foxy whispered, "I love you."

Some men like Senator Pendleton simply needed to hear a woman tell them, "I love you," even if she didn't mean it.

"Aw, hell. I'm cumming already. Cum with me," he said, holding her tight. "Hold me real close and cum with me."

Foxy wrapped her arms around him. Held him tight as she could. "You're making me cum on this big ole dick. I'm cumming."

The senator didn't care if she came with him. His ego had paid to believe he could still fuck a young woman into an orgasm.

He let go, leaned back, then said, "Aw, damn. An old man like me couldn't satisfy you every day. You got too much stamina."

Foxy didn't respond. He didn't need to hear her confirm or deny his feelings. At times all a man needed a woman to do was listen. It was five o'clock. Their session was over, and it was time for her to prepare dinner and her body for Dallas Washington.

En route to Dallas's house, Foxy called Victoria. "Hey, I'm on my way out."

Victoria replied, "I hope you're headed home. Your home."

"Good-bye," Foxy said, ending the call.

CHAPTER 14

Winton

Five o'clock, Wednesday. He arrived. Used his key. Entered her town house he'd paid for. He refused to put his name on the deed as she'd requested. He'd given her cash. There were no traceable cashiers' and definitely no personal checks issued in her name. He was smarter than his male clients that purchased joint property so they could reserve the right to take back whatever so-called gifts they'd given their mistresses.

The fresh scent of cinnamon greeted his nostrils at the door. The one picture she'd begged to take of him hung in a 24- x 36-inch frame on the living room wall. A 5 x 7 of the same photo was on her nightstand, and an 8 x 10 hung in her bathroom. Women had done stranger things with images of him. Posted him on their Internet pages, carried him in their purse, pent him up inside their cubicles at work.

His reputation as the best attorney made him a household

name. Why she'd showcase a married man's picture in her home was beyond him. A single man wouldn't have a picture of a married woman in any visible location in his dwelling. If she was a bragging piece and he'd fucked her and she was great in bed, he might have a snapshot of her pussy in his cell phone. Maybe.

The benefit of living in a large city was if any of his clients saw his photos in Isis's house, Winton could tell the truth and lie, saying Isis was a former client and he had no idea she had a crush on him. During their year of dating, he made sure not to leave a sock, a used toothbrush, strands of hair from his comb, or his underwear. His first mistress taught him not to trust women. She'd slipped her red thong in his suit pocket. After he finished cursing her out, that never happened again—with her or with his subsequent mistresses. What if his wife had found the cum-stained thong? How would he have explained?

Isis hugged and kissed him, removed his jacket, hung it in the foyer closet, then said, "Hey, baby. Perfect timing. Dinner is ready. Wash up while I fix our plates."

Watching her hips sway side to side, he licked his lips. She had a nice frame. Not banging like his wife's, but nice. Isis was almost five feet five and lived in three-inch heels. A woman's shoes—slip-ons, sling backs, open toe, closed toe, high heels, no heels, gladiator, alligator, leopard, zebra, snakeskin—spoke volumes about her sexuality and her inhibitions. At times all he wanted to see Isis in were high heels. He knew her well enough to know she wasn't wearing anything under that dress. Her pussy was always prepared for his dessert.

She'd taken time to style her hair, slip into a halter maxi-dress, and put on a thin layer of strawberry gloss. He sniffed the air as she walked away. "Um, so decadent," he said, appreciating she'd worn his favorite grapefruit-scented perfume. There was something about the scent of grapefruit or vanilla that instantly made him horny. That and the thought of Nova's lips on his dick.

The table for six was set for two. His seat was at the head. Her seat was to his left. The centerpiece, seven long-stemmed white unscented candles, illuminated the room. Isis's face glowed each time he saw her. She was worthy of a man that would marry and give her the two children she desired. He was selfish. Although he was married, he refused to share Isis with another man. Based on her decision to be with him, she'd delayed what was important to her, having kids.

Isis was incredibly beautiful inside and out. She'd do anything for him. He couldn't say the same about himself. Her soft skin, gentle smile, and mild demeanor attracted him to her instantly. Her spirit of pleasing him first made him feel at home in her home. She could never come to his. He seldom saw her cry but imagined there were times she had when no one was listening.

Settling for his offerings of companionship, sex; his leaving every night in the middle of the night; her waking up alone couldn't have made her happy. But he was as good to her as he could be. He stayed with her on weekends. Vacationed with her once a month. Isis was his hobby; golfing was his alibi.

She desperately wanted to have his baby. Why a single woman would want to have a married man's child was incomprehensible. Her irrational request was more of a reason why he'd faithfully worn a condom each time they made love. He did love her. He had the kind of love that cared for her but not deeply. It was time to let her go, release her to the flock of men waiting for their chance to lay between her legs. He contemplated if this was a good moment to address the inevitable.

"You're awfully quiet," Isis said. "Everything okay? You haven't touched your food."

Winton admired the feast before him. Grilled tilapia with fresh herbs and spices, whipped buttered potatoes, glazed carrots, and his favorite, mushrooms marinated in bourbon. The sourdough bread sat on a white cloth napkin inside a tan wicker basket. The porcelain dish was filled with small balls of butter. Crystal goblets half full of merlot were next to chilled glasses and a thirty-two-ounce bottle of distilled water.

You'd be an idiot to tell her now. Save the bad news for another day.

For the first time in three years, he wasn't sure why, but he wanted to go home to his wife. In between his XXX-rated fantasies of Nova, Winton recalled how his wife's tears were uncontrollable. If going home would make Foxy happy again, he could do that. Maybe he should revisit asking his wife to have his baby. He drummed on the table with his thumbs.

"It's your new client, isn't it? Do not tell me you slept with that psycho, Nova."

He shook his head, kept drumming.

"Cut that out! You're driving me crazy. What is it?"

"This isn't a good time. It can wait," he said, easing a flake of fish onto his fork. He opened wide, took his time chewing, nodded. "Um, baby, this is really good."

Isis stood, tossed her napkin in his face, stormed out of the room without responding.

He placed his and her napkins on the table beside his plate, in case he wanted to finish eating before he left, then followed her into the living room.

"Okay, fine. I was trying not to spoil a good meal, but you talk too much. Telling your family and friends that we're getting married is circulating rumors. I warned you not to do that," he said shifting the reason for him wanting a breakup to blaming her.

Isis sat sideways on her lemon suede chaise. "There can't possibly be any rumors. I only told my mom, my sister, and my best friend. Three people. That's it." She placed the leopard pillow on her lap.

"Not three people. You told three women. That's like saying it on *Oprah*. You're hardheaded. You don't listen. It's all your fault," he said, sitting on the sofa facing her.

Her eyes started tearing. "So what are you saying?"

"I care for you Isis but . . ." He paused, shook his head. "You've forced me to end a perfect relationship. I hate doing this, but I can't afford to have bad press following me. I have partners to protect. I have too much at stake. I'm sorry, baby. It's over."

"Don't say that. I promise I won't tell anyone else. And if anyone questions me, I'll tell them the rumor is a lie."

Winton shook his head, removed his key chain from his pocket.

Isis grabbed his ring. "No, don't."

He snatched his keys. "Your fault."

"So just like that you're going to abandon this," she said, untying her halter.

He stared at her succulent perfect titties. Her nipples were hard. She eased her dress down to her waist, over her ass, then let it fall to the floor. She stepped out of the dress. Her stilettos were all that remained.

"Come here," he said. "Why didn't you listen to me?" He held her hips. Positioned her pussy in front his face, kissed her pubic hairs.

She held his head.

"Don't touch me," he said, then stood. He pointed at the sofa, then commanded, "On your knees right now."

She knelt on the sofa. Looked over her shoulder.

"Don't look at me."

She turned away.

"Spread your ass," he said, taking off his belt.

Her hands curved over the sexiest ass of all his mistresses.

He folded his belt, gripped each side, placed his hands together, and . . . *snap!* Isis flinched. He snapped the belt again. She flinched again.

"Damn, that's a pretty asshole." He unfastened, then unzipped his pants. "Move your hands."

She held on to the back of the sofa. He tossed the belt to the floor.

He stroked his dick while admiring her ass. "I'm about to tear this ass up." He rubbed his dick on her shaft, teased her clit with his head.

"Baby, I'm—"

"Shut . . . up!" He stuck his hard head inside her pussy, then pulled out. She moaned. He licked his thumb, massaged her asshole, then eased the tip in, held it there. He reinserted his dick in her tight pussy. He teased her. Only putting the head in, he held it there.

She backed up.

Smack! He slapped her ass with his palm. "Keep your ass still. I'm in charge of this pussy, you hear me?"

She nodded.

"You gon' listen to me next time."

She nodded again.

He spat on her asshole, reinserted his thumb in her ass. This time he thrust his dick all the way inside her, then quickly pulled out. He stooped, pulled up his pants, retrieved a condom from his pocket. "Fuck this." He stepped out of his pants, threw them against the wall. They fell on the chaise. "I'm about to get knee-deep in this pussy, and I don't care how good it feels, or how much it hurts, you'd better not whimper or say a word."

He spat inside his condom, rolled it up his shaft, stood behind her. He reinserted his finger in her ass, thrust his dick deep in her pussy, then massaged her clit with his other hand. He slid his hand over the hole from which she urinated and circled his finger around her urethra in slow motion. He alternated from her clit to her shaft to her urethra.

He repositioned his dick two inches from the opening of her vagina and massaged his head into her G-spot. Inserted his thumb a little deeper in her ass. He pumped ten quick times deep inside her pussy, then moved his head back to her G-spot. He pushed his thumb all the way in her ass and massaged her insides while massaging her clit, shaft, and urethra.

"I'm going to—"

"Let my pussy flow," he said.

"No. Not on my sofa," she cried.

He thrust deeper with every word, "What—did—I—say? Let—my—pussy—squirt."

Ten quick jackhammer thrusts, he pulled his dick out, unplugged his thumb from her ass, lifted his finger from her urethra. He grabbed her hips and fucked her so hard his nuts banged against her clit. He pulled out again.

She cried as her fluids squirted like a fountain all over the sofa.

He had to make her squirt one last time. He'd made all his mistresses squirt for their first and probably last time. Not many men were selfless enough to learn how to make a woman squirt. Since his marriage the only woman he hadn't made squirt was his wife. He was more interested in making a baby with his wife than pleasing Foxy in bed.

Winton walked into the bathroom, left Isis bent over on the sofa. He showered. When he exited the bathroom, Isis was in her bed asleep. He left her key on her nightstand, retrieved his jacket from her foyer closet. She'd get the message. By the time she did, he'd be prepared to explain his decision to leave her was final.

CHAPTER 15

Victoria

*L*ilies float
Ships sink
Ships float
Lilies sink
People drown
In misery
Cause
Effect
Redirect
Who's responsible
When the train wrecks

No one had the right to dictate the person she shared her body with. From the men she'd left behind to the woman she married, who was asleep beside her, Victoria was true to herself. There was compassion and passion for everyone and everything in her life. All the things she'd done, all that she'd accomplished, made her and her parents proud.

Her father would say, "Girls, if your heart is in the right space, you are in the right place."

Victoria didn't have an extramarital affair like her sister Foxy or domination obsessions like her sister DéJà, but she respected their differences. She couldn't say why Foxy had married Winton but had fucked Dallas for three consecutive years. She didn't understand why DéJà had temper tantrums as a teen and why she exploded as an adult whenever she didn't get her way. "Live and let live" was Victoria's motto. Allowing others to be their authentic selves free of judgment created peace in her space.

Lying on a pillow facing her wife, Victoria smiled. She was proud to identify as a lesbian, knowing she had the right to revert to being heterosexual if she wanted. The one thing Victoria would never become was labeled. Labels only had credence if she allowed someone else to dictate or influence her choices. Her father taught her the only person that validated Victoria Montgomery was Victoria Montgomery. She was proud to have an intelligent, attractive, soft butch wife who was a partner in Brown, Cooper, and Dawson, and she was most proud to be a thirty-year-old virgin.

The relationships she had with her sisters meant more to her than the millions of dollars they'd earned operating Crème. The woman she cuddled with at night and awakened to each morning meant more to Victoria than all the men and women combined that she'd coached to orgasm.

Her cell phone buzzed at 4:00 a.m. Thursday. She rolled over, checked the display, then whispered to Naomi, "It's DéJà."

Victoria eased out the bed, went to the guest bedroom, closed the door, then hissed, "Do you know what time of the morning it is? You've got to cut this out. I can't see you anymore. I'm happily married. Please stop calling me." She sat on the bed. Waited for his response. When was he going to give up on fucking her the way he wanted?

Being a virgin had its privileges until now. Victoria's virginity made men view her two ways. Some called her a liar. Their problem, not hers. She had nothing to prove to them. Other men saw her as a conquest worth endlessly pursuing, like Rain, who was on the other end but hadn't spoken a word.

Honesty was important but didn't mean she had to reveal every detail of her life to her wife or her sisters. Whom should she tell Rain had made the ultimate demand?

He spoke. She listened. "We need to resolve this. You made me look like a fool in my city. Got my officers snickering behind my back. This is the largest city in the country, and you've humiliated me. You do think I'm a joke don't cha?"

Victoria exhaled. "Here we go."

"Here we go, my ass. You made me wait a whole year to be your first, then you changed your mind. You changed your mind, Victoria. Why?"

Why? Why was he acting like they didn't have that conversation yesterday? She sighed heavily. "I didn't tell you to brag to your friends about what's between my legs. You made yourself look foolish."

Rain had become police chief for the wrong reasons. He'd retaliated against the teenagers that beat him up back in high school. Ostracized his parents. Now he was demanding what wasn't rightfully his.

"My patience is gone. I want you right now. I took you to all the departmental functions, showed you off. Then for no rational reason, you let me propose to you."

What? Shaking her head, she rolled her eyes. He'd spoken down to her yesterday and again this morning as if she was one of his subordinates. As if what was important to her didn't matter to him. Would it have been better for her to fake it? Tell him, "Yes, I will marry you," when she didn't mean it? Accepting his proposal wasn't some sort of badge of honor and giving up her virginity to him wasn't happening. Victoria ended the call, then silenced the ringer on her cell, and went back to bed.

CHAPTER 16

Victoria

To whom much is given
Less is earned
More is taken
With little concern
For those with no power
Mercy is not their friend
To whom much is given
The less time they spend
With those who are not
Akin

She closed her eyes. In the middle of her dozing off, the home telephone rang. Victoria opened her eyes. It was 4:15.

The cordless was on her wife's side of the bed. "Hello," Naomi answered stretching her arm above her head. "Just a minute. . . . Victoria, it's for you. And it's not DéJà," she said, tossing the phone on the bed. Naomi looked at her; looked at the phone; said, "Handle it, sweetcakes"; then left the bedroom.

Victoria's eyes opened wide as she picked up the cordless. A hesitant "Hello" escaped her lips. Her stomach churned, praying he wasn't foolish enough to call her house.

"Why, Victoria? I'm not going to stop until I get what I want."

"I see why your parents disowned you. You are—" She stopped midsentence in an attempt not to meet him at his low level. What man would beg for a woman who didn't want him? "You have no right calling here. I didn't give you my home number."

"Sweetcakes, you leave my parents out of your mouth. See that's why men don't like opening up to you crazy females because the minute you get pissed off you throw our weaknesses in our face like we're garbage. You started. I'ma finish."

Victoria stared at the cordless. Was she talking to an adolescent or a grown man?

"I can legally do whatever I want, including shut down your business and send you and your sisters to jail," he said.

Victoria grunted. "I'm not your damn sweetcakes! You . . . are . . . crazy! What part of 'I don't want to be with you' don't you understand?"

He interrupted, "I don't know. Maybe your screaming 'Oh, my God, Rain, I'm cumming!' yesterday morning is hella confusing or the fact that my dick was buried in your ass while you were cumming. Help me out."

Help him out? This wasn't about him.

"I'm happily, happily married. Can't you be happy for me?" Victoria didn't want to risk having Naomi see her upset or overhear her conversation with Rain. She returned to the guest bedroom, flopped on the edge of the bed.

"Hell, no. You refused my engagement ring and dumped me for a bitch. You owe me. My patience has ended. The pussy between your legs is mine."

Ugh! Victoria's blood pressure rose instantly, giving her a migraine. For a second she'd stopped breathing. If he were close to her, she'd hit him upside the head with the phone like Whitney had done to Bobby. Was he this unreasonable as a child? "This is my pussy, and I will never let you fuck me again."

"Yes, you will. You said that shit the day before you got married and what happened?" His next threat—"If I have to, I'll rape you, Victoria. And what are you going to do? Call the police?"—made her think about shooting him with his gun, then entering a plea of temporary insanity. She was insane for loving the way he fucked her in the ass. He knew how to make her cum fast, slow, back to back. If she shot him, he'd have the law on his side and she'd have the best lawyers on hers. Who'd win? Perhaps neither of them would.

"You are one demented man. I'm going to report you," she cried. What had she done to deserve his relentless verbal attacks? Why couldn't he be content with being her client?

"Okay, I'll compromise with you. Take me on as a *daily* client," he demanded. "We'll start there. Then we'll work on getting back together."

"Over my dead body. I'm already fucking you for free," Victoria lamented. "I can't give you all of my slots. I do have other regulars." She paused, then blurted, "Oh, my God. Please say you're not serious!"

"Save that 'Oh, my God' for later when I'm fucking you. I'm dead serious."

Her stomach churned. She wanted to vomit. She hadn't made a fool of him nor did she owe him anything. The main reason she'd declined his engagement ring was he lacked the character she thought he'd had. His infectious personality had captured her heart. He used to make her laugh. His magnetic dick attracted her ass whenever she was near him. His promise to protect and serve her was convincing. But when Rain proposed to her, then said, "As my wife you'll be bound to 'the blue code of silence,'" Victoria knew there was no long-term future for them. His job was his responsibility.

Victoria knew "the blue code of silence" was an unwritten code whereby police officers refused to betray one another's errors—from misconduct to murder to sending innocent people to jail. To break the code was considered snitching, betrayal, and could cost a cop his or her life in friendly fire. And the officer who'd pulled the trigger and the officers who knew the truth would forever remain silent.

On his knees, in the middle of proposing, Rain had confessed, "I have blood on my hands. Being on the force is like having a love-hate relationship with the devil, but hey, somebody's gotta get the job done. I'm that man. I'm your man. Victoria will you marry me?"

Perhaps his confession was to clear his conscience or to let her know what she was marrying into, but at that moment, he'd proved to Victoria he had zero character. He wasn't the man she wanted to hug all night or cook breakfast for in the morning. A real police chief wouldn't abuse his authority to enforce the law. Maybe he had to. But she didn't. Victoria had politely declined his offer.

Her tears dried. He hadn't responded. If she hung up, he'd call her house again.

What had she done to make Rain want to fuck her over? Had to be more than his ego. Victoria had let him fuck her in the ass, and she'd given him the best blow jobs he'd ever had. She never sexually deprived him. If his obsession about having her virginity didn't change, Victoria would have to tell her father. Telling Mason would be worse than telling his wife. Victoria's biggest concern was Rain's threat to shut down Crème Fantasyland and prosecute her and her sisters. She prayed they'd be proven innocent. It was her fault. She should've never taken him to Crème Fantasyland.

Was the blue code of silence stronger than the truth? Yes, it was. If Victoria continued refusing Rain, she'd jeopardize the family's business. If she gave in, she'd jeopardize her marriage.

"I can ruin you in a heartbeat, sweetcakes. If you care about your wife and your sisters, stop by my house on your way to work," he said, then ended the call.

Victoria went to the bathroom, cried, washed her face, cried, washed her face again, then entered the kitchen. She sat at the table staring out the window. She had no appetite for the hot oatmeal Naomi placed in front of her.

CHAPTER 17

Victoria

Trapped inside
Nowhere to hide
Temptation winks an eye
Who me
Not me
I don't cheat
Justify the lie
Selfish gain
Beget pain
Once
No longer
Denied

Though she'd spread her legs the width of a few of her ex-men's hips, she had never allowed any man to put his head inside her vagina. Being a virgin made her better than her sisters. Like Rain, no man she'd met was worthy of breaking the tissues of her precious hymen. Not allowing him to do so made her smarter than Foxy who freely let Dallas rob her of her precious jewel. Not much to say about DéJà and Acer. If they had marital problems, they were the only two who knew.

Victoria's wife so loved the fact that she was pure, Naomi vowed at the altar never to vaginally penetrate her. "Sweetcakes, what's going on?" Naomi asked, sitting at the kitchen table next to Victoria. She placed her hand on Victoria's. Whenever possible, they sat next to, not across from, one another.

"Nothing, just plotting . . . I mean, planning my day. Thinking about the pastry specials for today. What do you think about cupcakes?" Victoria prayed that if she didn't mention the phone call, neither would her wife. Rain was probably in his bed asleep. Dirty dog.

Naomi stared at her, tapped her hand.

Victoria ignored Naomi's touch, gazed out the ceiling-to-floor kitchen window into the backyard. Orange, red, pink, yellow, and white orchids were in bloom. For a few seconds a peaceful feeling resonated within her. Why were humans the highest life-forms? Trees lived longer. Tangled roots intertwining underground could cause devastation forcing their way to the surface. The same held true for her buried secrets.

She stared in silence. Most of the flowers were a blend of orange and white or pink and red. Their exotic garden was scattered with colorful tulips and roses. Bougainvillea arched along the top of the gazebo. The sunrise peeped over the lake. The remorse for her deception was overwhelming.

Facing Naomi, Victoria curved her lips downward but

didn't part them. She was afraid of losing her wife over a few senseless acts of infidelity. Victoria admired Naomi's beautiful mixed features from her white father and black mother. Naomi's short blonde hair framed her face as her crystal blue eyes pierced Victoria's thoughts. Radiant flesh with the glaze of a natural tan—Naomi's skin was flawless. Her large breasts, small waist, and flat stomach attracted attention from men and women, but Naomi was clear about her sexual preference. She wasn't interested in men.

Oh, no. Tell me that wasn't what I thought? Victoria prayed then confirmed, it was.

Naomi's nostrils flared for one of two reasons. Either she was sexually charged or she was annoyed. The latter appeared to be the case as Naomi replied, "He's getting bolder. This time he called our house. Don't think I don't know he calls or texts your cell every day. I think you should think about what's really important to you and let me know when you're ready to discuss it. It's getting old, Victoria. And it's not too late for you to change your mind, and it's not too late for us to get an annulment. That's what I think."

Were lawyers human? She hated and loved Naomi's practical approach to every damn thing. They'd agreed not to sweat the small stuff, not to pressure one another to do or say anything. They'd also agreed their marriage was based on a need-to-know basis and what was shared inside their home stayed between them.

Victoria and her sisters had made a pact to keep the adult fantasy part of their business a secret between them and their clients and never to disclose their clients to anyone. Victoria confided in Naomi that she and her sisters owned and operated Crème Fantasyland. Victoria documented their clients and showed Naomi the daily list, and she'd briefly mentioned the Swiss account and the $1.5 million Crème yielded on an annual basis. Since Victoria told Naomi she specialized in coaching women and couples on how to improve their sex lives, Naomi didn't consider that cheating.

Naomi eased her fingers inside Victoria's white button-up collared men's shirt. She delicately grazed the nipple. "The sunrise is almost as beautiful as you," she said, pressing her lips to Victoria's. Naomi inhaled Victoria's breath, closed her eyes for a moment, opened them, and said, "I'm your friend first. I'm here for you. Whatever you want to do is okay with me. Don't feel guilty. Don't feel pressured. And do not lie to me. I love you, Victoria."

Responding would not be wise. Victoria suctioned Naomi's tongue, then sat on the kitchen table, spread her thighs, and held the middle button of her shirt. She unfastened one, two, then three buttons, exposing her mocha breasts that were the size and firmness of tennis balls. Her body yearned for her wife's touch.

Naomi dipped her finger inside her bowl of oatmeal with strawberries and cream, eased her hand between Victoria's legs, then gently traced her outer labia. Naomi scooped a handful of oatmeal, rubbed it on Victoria's titties. Dipped more oatmeal, lathered Victoria's pussy, then gripped Victoria's ass, sucked her areola, then slid Victoria's hips against the cold glass tabletop until Victoria's hairy pussy was in front of Naomi's mouth. Separating Victoria's lips, Naomi extended her tongue, deliberately flicking the tip against Victoria's clit, then pressed her lips against the shaft, holding them there until Victoria's body relaxed.

"Ah," Victoria exhaled. Sliding her hands along her wife's hair, she massaged Naomi's head, then locked her legs behind Naomi's head. Pulling Naomi closer, Victoria came long and slow but not hard the way she'd cum for Rain yesterday.

Victoria's body trembled in her wife's hands. Omitting Rain's name from the client lists she'd shown Naomi wasn't the same as lying. Something had to give. What or who should it be?

It was 4:45. Time to shower and see Rain.

CHAPTER 18

Victoria

What does it feel like
Playing in the dirt
Getting your hands dirty
Because you're hurt
Or simply playing dirty
Because you can
Negate your responsibilities
Yet call yourself a woman

Thursday morning at 5:15, Victoria reluctantly parked in Rain's driveway, turned off her engine. He stood in the doorway of his blue stucco–framed house motioning for her to come inside. His home wasn't secluded like hers. He'd benefited from "The Officer Next Door" program the government instituted years ago. He'd paid a. third of his neighbors' home values in exchange for being visible in his community.

She swore this visit was her last. Entering his home, she hoped to persuade him to see things her way. The sex was what had kept her coming back. Her pheromones instantly ignited the second she was near him. She sat on the end of the sofa closest to the door, pressed her thighs together, placed her hands in her lap.

"Get up. Let's go into the bedroom," he said, tilting his head toward the bedroom door.

Victoria didn't move. "I'm not staying. I've got to get to work." She smoothed her hands over her red skirt. Crossed one cream-colored stiletto over the other.

"Victoria you're starting to disgust me. Why are you playing games?" Rain asked, standing over her.

Dr. Jekyll had exchanged places with Mr. Hyde as Rain's personality changed. Was he waiting until after they married to expose the angry man that stood before her? His parents were in part to blame. A little boy shown hate the majority of his childhood may never learn to love himself. Impervious to compassion, he looked down on her.

Victoria's breasts heaved. Not with pleasure. The tone of his voice alarmed her. "I'm not playing games." She folded her arms over her red button-up blouse.

"Then what the hell do call what you're doing? Huh!" He bit his bottom lip, narrowed his eyes. He removed his pants, his boxers, and his shirt. "Get up." His dick drooped in front her face.

She could suck it, make him hard, make him cum in five minutes, and be out the door before five thirty. Victoria didn't move. Her heart thumped hard against her breast.

"Rain, I've got to go. Whatever I've done to hurt you, I apologize." Tears escaped her eyes. "You need counseling."

Rain moved closer. "Stop stalling. And don't tell me what I need. Today is the day, Victoria. Let's do this. Let's just get this over with, and you can go to work."

Did he think taking a woman's virginity was simple? "Please move your dick out my face." What if he raped her? How would she report him? His dick pointed at her mouth like she was speaking into a microphone. She suppressed her desire to take off her clothes and submit. "I won't come back. And you're no longer my client."

Why did he have to mess up a good thing?

"Come home, Victoria. This is your home. The only reason I became your client was so I wouldn't lose you completely. You think I give a damn about being your fucking client?"

She knew he did. The way they sexed one another was insane. The first time she let Rain put his dick in her ass, they bonded. Each subsequent time he fucked her, she'd become more emotionally attached to him. She hated the way he made her feel—out of control. They'd fucked in every corner of his house before she married and moved in with Naomi.

Rain snatched her arms away from her breasts, grabbed both her biceps, lifted her up from the sofa, then hoisted her in the air.

"Ahhhhhh," she screamed. Her feet dangled. She kicked him. Her gold-heeled stilettos plopped to the floor. "Ow! Put me down! Are you crazy!" She tried biting his face, but he was too far away.

He rattled her body. "You think I'm some fucking joke, Victoria?" he asked, carrying her to his bedroom. He threw her on the bed. Straddled her. Tugged at her red blouse, popped all her buttons. Her breasts were exposed.

"That's what I'm talking about," he said, squeezing her titties.

Victoria hurled her fist toward his nuts. He blocked her hand, then slapped her. His eyes narrowed, lips tightened. "Try that again," he threatened.

Victoria remembered when she was a teenager, DéJà made her and Foxy sit still and listen. DéJà had told them, "A woman's wardrobe is her weapon. Always have at least three items on your person that can save your life. One, have a sturdy hairpin. Do not keep it in your purse, put it in your hair. Two, wear slip-on spiked heels. No closed-in shoes. Practice grabbing the toe of the shoe and holding it your hand. Your attacker's eardrum or eyes is your target. And three, wear earrings with removable backs."

DéJà had taught them that metal necklaces, bracelets, and anklets could be used in self-defense. And as a teenager and a woman, DéJà kept a razor in a special compartment of her belt.

Victoria screamed, "Stop it! All right! We can do this but don't rape me!"

Rain stopped. His knees were straddling her waist. He inched toward her neck. His dick hung over her face like she was defeated. "Yeah. Now, you're starting to talk like you have sense. I love you, Victoria."

"You don't know what love is. As long as you get your way, you're happy. That's sick. You're sick. How in the hell did I—"

"Don't stop. Say it. How in the hell did you fall in love with me? Finish your sentence," he said, flapping his dick. "You know you want this. You know, you know you want this dick."

Once upon a time that made her smile. Not so long ago he could make her laugh.

"You know you want to laugh. Go on," he said.

Victoria smiled. She removed the back from her hoop earring, held his dick in her hand, removed her earring, then stabbed it in the eye.

"Bitch! Are you . . . fuck!" he yelled, covering his dick head.

She started to scrape the metal post deep into his balls but changed her mind when he fell onto his side. His mouth stayed open; he couldn't speak.

Victoria scurried from the bed, grabbed her keys and shoes. She left his front door open, got in her car, sped out his driveway, headed home.

He shouldn't have hit her. Maybe his plan was to intimidate her and make her give in. That way she couldn't cry rape. If he' were serious about raping her, he would've done so. Considering all the times they'd had anal sex, Rain had had lots of opportunities to try, including yesterday. Was his "I love you" supposed to make her think he cared about her? Regardless of his intent, he'd gone too far.

Rain had gotten what he deserved. Or had he?

CHAPTER 19

DéJà

DéJà entered the shop, locked the door, went into the kitchen. There was no way she could prep and bake all the pastries before opening. Yesterday they'd lost morning revenue due to a shortage of baked items. The money wasn't her main concern. Permanent reduction in clientele bothered her. If they started running out of pastries, the customers would patronize their competition. If one of her sisters didn't show up soon, today would be a repeat.

Thursday morning, six o'clock, the parking lot was still empty. DéJà had been at the shop for an hour. Tired of preparing trays of pastries alone, she sat on a stool.

"Let's see what happens if I do nothing," DéJà said, tapping her foot. Five minutes went by, DéJà called her sister's cell. Immediately she got "Hi, this is Victoria, please leave a message."

The sun was rising. Soon customers would arrive. DéJà called Foxy.

"Hey, I decided not to stop by Dallas's this morning. I'll be there in two minutes," Foxy said.

That was a first in a long time. "I'm proud of you, sis."

"Don't be. Dallas is out of town on business. He'll be home tonight."

"Yeah, if he doesn't get arrested on his way home for drinking and driving,"

Foxy exhaled heavily. "Let it go, please."

"Have you spoken with Victoria?" DéJà asked.

"No, she's not at the shop with you? I'm parking, bye."

DéJà heard the front door open. She was elated but hadn't expected to see Foxy until nine or ten.

Foxy walked in frowning. "Where do you think she's at?"

It was uncharacteristic of Victoria to be late two days in a row. DéJà's universe was out of alignment. She had to regain control. "Line up the ingredients for my popovers, Victoria's cream puffs, and your chocolate-dipped macaroons." She went to the lobby, looked into the lot, no Victoria. She dialed Victoria's home number, no answer.

"I'll call Naomi on three way," Foxy said.

"I'll do it." DéJà phoned Foxy, dialed Naomi's direct line at work, then conferenced Foxy in.

"Naomi Cooper speaking."

DéJà spoke, "Hey, Naomi. Is Victoria feeling all right?"

Naomi's voice trembled. "What do you mean is she feeling all right?"

"She hasn't arrived yet. I was wondering if she was running—"

"Hang up. I'm here," Victoria said, entering the kitchen.

"Shit! Do not walk up on us like that," DéJà said. "Naomi, never mind, she just walked in. She's fine. Sorry to have bothered you."

Victoria snatched DéJà's cell. "I had a flat tire. No worries. I'll call you later. Bye." She took Foxy's phone. Looked at the caller ID, pressed the end button, then handed it back.

DéJà snatched her phone from Victoria. "Flat tire my ass. You've been in a fight."

"A scuffle. Not a fight," Victoria clarified.

Foxy stared at Victoria's arms. Red fingerprints marked her biceps like tattoos. "What happened?"

"I don't want to discuss it. Let's hurry up and make these pastries so I can go home," Victoria said.

DéJà approached Victoria. "You're not squashing this. Like it or not, you are going to discuss it. Did Naomi do this to you? Did she find out about your seeing Rain?"

Foxy hugged Victoria.

"Naomi would never do this." Victoria cried in Foxy's arms, pulled away, dried her tears. "Rain and I had a disagreement, that's all. I'll be fine."

"It would've been better if you'd said you had rough sex. I can relate to that. But this, my sister, is beyond a disagreement. I'm calling Dad." DéJà pressed one button on her cell, placed the phone to her ear.

Victoria snatched the phone from her hand, powered it off, then said, "I need to handle this on my own."

DéJà grabbed Victoria's wrist, peeled her sister's fingers away from her phone, went in the office, locked the door, then powered on her phone.

Victoria banged on the window, shouting, "You have no right to do this! For once, can't you let me be in control of my life? I'm okay!"

DéJà turned her back to Victoria. "Hi, Daddy."

"Hey, queen in charge. How are things? I was just telling your mother I need to get by the shop and see my girls."

DéJà smiled. "Daddy, that's a great idea."

CHAPTER 20

Winton

.

Thursday evening, alone in his office, Winton mulled over Nova's case.

Their best defense would be to force a mistrial, settle out of court, or find a way to make Nova's boyfriend withdraw. His disrespecting Nova was no crime. Her hitting him with her car out of anger was vehicular assault and could get her three to five in prison. If they could prove it was an accident, her sentence would be reduced to eighteen months and parole. If they could prove she was fleeing the scene because he was trying to attack her, the fact still remained that she'd hit him with her car. Although she'd claimed he was a user, her boyfriend had no prior history of drug possession, assault, or battery, but he did have a compelling argument and witnesses willing to testify on his behalf.

Nova had no cause that the judge would consider reasonable or any witnesses Winton could subpoena in her defense, but maybe he could make the jury doubt the credibility of her boyfriend's witnesses. He had to call Nova and give her more bad news; her boyfriend was suing her for ten million dollars for his pain and suffering.

Winton laughed. Was the money compensation for the accident or the relationship? He'd charge Nova a reduced retainer of fifty thousand dollars, then bill her for another fifty grand every two weeks her case was in litigation. Life was what it was but life definitely wasn't fair. Partially billing Nova before fucking her increased his chances of having her volunteer to suck his dick. She could afford his rate, but if he were fortunate, she'd try to fuck her way into a pro bono case and he'd let her.

Wealthy men who fucked women without offering monetary compensation were stupid. That was why he'd bought Isis a house. But he'd have to handle Nova with care so he didn't end up being his own plaintiff.

Women had to choose other ways to deal with cheating men. Breaking out windows, kicking in doors, assaulting the other woman wasn't the solution. Police in Crème City were locking up all parties involved in domestic violence altercations. People should move out, temporarily leave the house, or find another mate. In most instances, men already had another woman on the side.

All of the above were difficult to do when a person was in love, but those were smart options Winton suggested when speaking to men in prison for battering their wives or girlfriends. "I don't care what she's said or done, man. . . . Step. Get out. Do not touch her ass. She's not worth your serving time."

The inmates would agree. But they'd get out, get jealous all over again, beat their women, then end up back behind bars before they found a job. Police officers weren't much different from criminals except they could justify everything including murder. Like Rain. He was the dirtiest cop on the force. So filthy no one challenged him. That was how he'd made police chief. There were some clients Winton would not represent and that included the entire police department.

Winton was in business because intelligence seldom overrode jealousy. From murder to pushing people out of cars on freeways to setting spouses on fire to shooting and stabbing them, people in love were insane. People were living with so much rage, they could snap at any second. Like Nova. She could've killed her boyfriend.

Winton could get Nova off, but he had to have more time. His immediate action for her case was to request a continuance.

Six o'clock. He shut down his laptop, locked his office, headed to the garage. A white envelope was tucked under his windshield wiper. It was a note from Isis: "Forgive me. I love you. Don't leave me. I'll listen to what you say." She was dick-whipped. His key was inside the envelope. Winton left the key in the envelope, put the envelope in his glove compartment.

He stopped at the flower shop, paid for two dozen roses. One red. One white. He told the florist, "Combine those in that lavender crystal heart-shaped vase for me."

Happy he'd made it home before Foxy, he placed the vase of flowers on her nightstand. He wasn't the best cook but he seasoned two chicken breasts, boiled the frozen broccoli, and prepared a box of rice pilaf. Winton set the dinner table for two. His presentation wasn't better than Isis's, but it was decent, he thought. He went to Foxy's bathroom, filled the spa tub with hot water and bubble bath. The water should be the perfect temperature by the time they were done eating and ready to get in.

Seven o'clock, the chicken breasts sizzled as he placed them on the George Foreman Grill. It wasn't the best combination, but he hoped Foxy would appreciate his effort. Tonight he wanted to listen to his wife and not tune her out. He wanted her to reassure him she still loved him, tell him where they went wrong, trust he was in love with her and that he'd do better.

He waited until eight. No Foxy. Winton ate without his wife. Maybe she'd stopped by one of her sisters' places. Nine. No Foxy. Ten o'clock. No Foxy.

Winton phoned Acer.

Acer answered, "Please tell me it's not an emergency and that crazy Nova woman hasn't done anything else stupid."

"No, man. That's not why I'm calling. Is Foxy there with DéJà?"

"Hold on." Acer called out to DéJà, "Baby, you still on the phone with Foxy?"

DéJà hollered back, "Just got off. Why you need me?"

Acer yelled, "Where is Foxy?"

"Where she's always at this time of night, at Dallas's house. Why?"

"Her cousin Dallas? The guy Winton got the DUI charges dropped for?" Acer asked.

DéJà yelled, "That would be him, handsome. He holds Foxy

better than he holds his liquor. Truth is, he's not her cousin, he's her ex-fiancé. Why so many questions, handsome?"

"Sorry I asked," Acer replied. He said to Winton. "Hey, man. I don't know—"

Winton ended the call. "That bitch." He washed the remaining food down the garbage disposal, took the flowers off the nightstand, then left. He headed west on Shoreline Drive, drove to Dallas's house. The lights were on. He phoned his wife.

"Hey, everything okay?" she answered.

"I need you. Where are you?" What if he really did need his wife?

She asked, "Where are you?"

"On my way home," he lied.

"Then I'll see you when you get here." She hesitated, then asked, "You okay?"

"I'm good," Winton replied. "Real good."

He ended the call, parked his car between two trees across the street facing Dallas's house. Twenty minutes went by before his wife opened Dallas's front door. He could be dead by now. She kissed Dallas, got in her car, and headed out the driveway.

Winton leaned below his dashboard. When Foxy's car was out of view, he drove to Isis's home and let himself in. Foxy was indebted to Isis. If he had followed Foxy home, what Nova had done to her boyfriend would be nothing compared to what he would've done to his cheating, conniving, low-down, despicable tramp of a wife. How dare she give his pussy to another man?

In the midst of fucking Isis, Winton stopped, then said,

"And that motherfucker was at our wedding and in my damn pictures."

Ain't that a bitch. Winton sat on the side of the bed. He was pissed the fuck off. His wife had been fucking around on him longer than he'd fucked around on her.

CHAPTER 21

Victoria

To what extent
Would you go
Out of your way
To ruin
To destroy
To condemn
A person who was once your friend
To what extent
Would you lie
Create an alibi
Deny the truth
Say it wasn't you . . . to
A person who is your lover
Liars cheat
Cheaters steal

Jealousy kills
To what extent
Do you care about your lover
Remember
Karma is a mutha

She tossed all night wishing she had something to hold instead of her wife. Victoria wiggled to the edge of the bed, turned away from Naomi. Victoria slept with her eyes opened, fearing Rain would knock on her door for attacking his dick. She didn't mean to hurt him.

She flashed back to the few television shows she'd seen about women in prison. She still hadn't told Naomi what had happened at Rain's house. Each day she felt her wife becoming a little more insensitive toward her.

If Victoria had honored her wedding vows, ceased communicating with Rain when she became engaged to Naomi, like Déjà had done with all her exes when Acer proposed, Victoria wouldn't be lying awake sweating. She flipped her soaked pillow to the dry side.

Victoria thought she could be Rain's friend without being his lover. He was a loner. Had told her she was his only friend. When he was an officer, he rode solo, no partner. As chief of police he'd schedule meetings with the mayor and other officials, but he ate lunch by himself. On occasion he'd invite her to join him. Rain's attachment was more than his wanting her virginity. The signs that his life was empty without her were clear.

Minutes felt like hours. Victoria stared at the phone, expecting her BlackBerry to ring at 4:00 a.m. It was only midnight.

CHAPTER 22

Foxy

Foxy rushed home to her husband. She searched the house. Good. He wasn't there. She'd made it home before him, took a quick shower, put on a red nightgown. She peeped into the garage. His car wasn't there.

"Hum, why did he say he needed to see me? Maybe he's taken care of his problem." She called his cell.

A woman heaved in Foxy's ear, "*Hel-lo.*"

Foxy frowned, looked at the phone, then asked, "Who is this?"

"Isis. Who's calling?" she asked, then laughed. "Stop it, Winton."

"Isis, put my husband on the phone."

"Can you call him later? We're busy." She laughed again. "Go back to Dallas's house," she said, not waiting for an answer before ending the call.

A lump lodged in Foxy's throat. *What in the hell? Busy? Go back to Dallas's.* That bitch had a lot of nerve. Foxy started to call back but changed her mind. Like with the red thong, she'd act like nothing happened. Foxy gathered her clothes for the next workday, got back in her car, and returned to Dallas.

"That was fast. Come here. Get back in bed. I keep telling you this is where you ought to be," he said, kissing her.

Foxy straddled Dallas. She sat on his dick and rolled her hips forward, up, back. She bounced deep in his pelvis, dug her hips into him, then rolled forward again. She bucked, then rolled some more.

"Damn, you should get mad at him more often," Dallas said, holding her hips.

She stroked her pussy, put her fingers in his mouth, then put the same fingers in her mouth. She pinched her nipples trying hard to forget the sound of Isis's voice resounding in her head, but she couldn't. *Can you call him later? We're busy. We're busy. Can you call him later?* Foxy tried hard to cum all over Dallas's dick. The emotional blockage suppressed her orgasm.

"Damn you! Selfish bastard!" she screamed.

"Stop it, Foxy. He's not worthy of you. Lay down," Dallas said. "Let's talk."

Tears filled with anger streamed down her cheeks. "Winton's bitch answered his cell phone."

Dallas sat up. Massaged, then kissed her foot. "I can't make you divorce him, but you knew he had another woman. What, you needed confirmation? You think he's been seeing her longer than we've been together?"

Foxy hadn't thought about that. What if Isis was a woman

Winton was supposed to marry but didn't? Softly she said, "I don't know what I need."

"Yes, you do. Men don't get rid of their exes," he said. "At least not the good ones."

"How many good ones do you have?" Foxy asked. Were all of Dallas's business trips business or pleasure?

"You know how I feel about my girls. Getting their mothers pregnant were my mistakes. But my daughters are no mistake. Would I have preferred to have kids with you? You know I would have. Still do. A number of women can complement my life. But Foxy you complete me. I'm patiently waiting for the day when I can complete you."

Maybe she completed him. Perhaps she was convenient. Who in the hell was Isis?

Dallas took her in his arms, pressed his lips to her forehead. "Have no doubt that I love you."

Men could love, be in love, make love, and still fuck other women. Her mind drifted, wondering what her husband was doing to Isis.

"Turn around." Foxy wrapped her arm atop his waist. Pressed the front of her breasts against his back. She was tired of thinking. In four hours she'd make love to Dallas properly, shower, and go to work. From now on, Isis could suck Winton's dick morning, noon, and night. If the roles were reversed and someone was fucking her husband, Isis would trip. Isis was probably another lonely woman so desperate she'd give all she had to get what another woman has got on lock.

Desperate trick!

CHAPTER 23

DéJà

Thank God for Fridays.

Five o'clock, DéJà arrived at work. Victoria was sitting at her desk in the office with the lights off. They sat in silence facing one another. DéJà held Victoria's hand. DéJà preferred her sisters to listen to her rather than be sympathetic and stuff. Dominatrices were not the caring kind, but her father taught the girls to stick together. DéJà couldn't treat her sister like she treated her clients, but she wanted to beat sense into Foxy and Victoria.

Moving her hand, Victoria said, "He didn't take my virginity. He tried but it didn't happen. I have to find a way to make Rain stop calling me. Naomi isn't so understanding right now. That's why I'm here early. I couldn't sleep." Victoria started sniffling.

"Don't think I feel sorry for you. I told you a long time ago to stop fucking his retarded ass, but no, you want to point fingers at Foxy and Dallas when Rain is the crazy one. There is something wrong with a man that believes everybody owes him something. His mama disowned him. His daddy hated him. The kids at school picked on him. Victoria won't give him any pussy. Give me a break, sis, and admit that retarded-ass dick has got you going dumb. You have no one to blame but yourself. You're my sister. I love you. You could've come by my house. You didn't have to go to his house or come here," DéJà said.

Victoria stopped sniffling. Shook her head. "This was yesterday. I didn't go to his house this morning."

"Before or after the flat tire? You brought this on yourself," DéJà said.

"It's your fault that I'm here. Why did you call my wife at work looking for me? I am your sister. Your blood. You should've called me, not Naomi."

When was Victoria going to grow up and accept responsibility for her shit? "My fault? I did call you. You didn't answer. What was I supposed to do? Nothing?" Was Victoria for real? DéJà wondered if both of her sisters were suffering from acute anxiety.

Victoria said, "Just admit that you're jealous of me and Foxy. You've always been jealous of us ever since we were kids. All you've done was try to boss us around."

Foxy turned on the light. "Forget jealousy." Foxy stood over DéJà. "Did you tell my husband about my relationship with Dallas?"

DéJà stood. "This is the thanks I get for trying to help you two."

"Help?" Foxy grabbed DéJà's hair. *Slap!*

Whack! DéJà hit, then shoved Foxy out of the office and into the kitchen. Foxy was lucky she was her sister or DéJà would've chopped her in the throat, banged her head against the wall, slammed her on the floor, and made her apologize then beg for mercy.

Foxy stumbled. Regained her balance.

Victoria stood between them.

Foxy dug in her hair, pulled out a hairpin. DéJà slipped two fingers inside her belt and revealed her razor.

"Cut it out!" Victoria cried. "We're sisters. What are y'all doing?"

Foxy heaved, then agreed. "She's right. I'm sorry y'all," she said, then flung a handful of flour in DéJà's face. "I'm sorry DéJà opened up her mouth. You did that shit on purpose."

Victoria threw powdered sugar at both of them.

DéJà grabbed two containers of honey.

Foxy and Victoria conceded.

DéJà said, "We'll talk this through on Sunday, but some serious changes have to be made in your personal lives. And I'm not asking, I'm telling you, if I can't help both of you, I don't need your permissi—— father."

—— le said he needed to stop

—— ound a way to keep my

—— me of night or day, was

—— else's life better. DéJà

CHAPTER 24

Victoria

A midst bliss
There is sorrow
Both self-inflicted
To know not pain
Is to know not joy
Dying with no addictions
No love
No dreams
No happiness
Is a spiritual confliction
The road chosen is bleak
For often those who make decisions
Do not think
Before they seek

Tell Naomi or keep it all in was Victoria's tremulous dilemma. She could boldly march in the bedroom, blurt out the truth, and pretend she'd never said a word. As she vacillated, her heart rate increased. Was she betraying Naomi? Maybe she was making a big deal out of something her wife could help her with, if she knew. Perhaps she was doing the best thing by waiting for the perfect moment. None of her options felt like the right thing to do. It was Friday night. Victoria didn't want to ruin their weekend. She decided to wait another day before confessing.

She stood at the kitchen sink staring at the faucet. Turning on the water, she rinsed a colander full of blueberries loaded with antioxidants that would purge toxins from her body. What about her conscience? What could expunge her guilt?

The small steps she took only prolonged the inevitable. Entering the bedroom with a bowl of fresh blueberries, Victoria cleared her throat, then asked, "Any good bedtime stories?"

"How's your arms?"

"Better. They're not hurting anymore," Victoria said. She had a lot on her mind, but the fading marks on her biceps were furthest from her thoughts.

"And you? Are you hurting?" her wife asked.

"I'll be okay."

"Want to discuss what happened? Why your sister called me looking for you?"

"Hurting my arms was an accident. I'd forgotten about them until you mentioned it." Victoria asked, "What's happening at the office?"

Not focusing on the playlist selection she made from their iPod, Victoria eased her naked body atop the covers beside

Naomi. She placed the bowl between them praying tonight would be better than last night. Hopefully Rain had taken her attack as a sign to back off.

Neither Victoria nor Naomi wore pajamas or cared to rest under covers that restricted their freedom of movement. A soft melody resonated throughout the room. Naomi turned off the television.

Rachmaninoff's "Lilacs" trickled through the air like a musical waterfall, like background confession music in a love story. Not a good choice. Victoria's body became tense. She fluffed her pillow, shuffled her legs. The classical piano rhythm strummed her emotions like a harp, making her want to sing like a canary. "Tell it all," her subconscious said, tapping her on the shoulder. Exhaling, she remained silent.

Those crystal blue eyes looked at her. "You probably have an idea, sweetcakes. Your sister's marriage . . . I don't know all of what's going on, but I'm confronting Winton in our next partners' meeting. You know I'm not the type to get involved in other people's business, not even yours, but his fucking Nova could jeopardize our practice. That woman is dangerous. Potentially lethal. She's the type that will hold us liable if she loses her case," Naomi said, scooping a handful of blueberries.

Victoria had forgotten about the bowl of berries that were in the bed. She picked a few, not to eat right away, but to help calm her nerves. "How do you know for sure he's fucking her?"

Naomi opened her mouth, dropped in a few blueberries, then answered, "Try my walking in on them with his dick buried in her pussy."

Oh, no. Healthy or unhealthy, penetration created an emotional bond. Being sexual with Rain had taught her not to be penetrated unless she was prepared to accept the emotional attachment. The more Victoria thought about Rain, the more clearly she realized she didn't know the man inside the man. DéJà was right. Rain did believe everyone was indebted to him.

"Why didn't you say something when you saw them?"

"Sweetcakes, when I'm at work, I'm in lawyer's mode the entire time. If I had said something, I would've become an identifiable witness if she filed a case." Naomi continued, "This morning, I'd left my notes in our mock courtroom. Walked in at lunchtime to get them, and Winton's pants was below his knees, Nova had on a judge's robe, nothing else from what I saw. Her legs were wrapped around his thrusting ass. How stupid can he be?"

"Are you sure she didn't see you?"

Naomi shook her head, ate more berries.

"Is that no, as in she didn't see you, or are you not sure if she saw you?"

"She didn't see me, sweetcakes."

Victoria knew her sister would be outraged if she found out. "Don't tell Foxy." Foxy deserved to know the truth but her knowing would complicate Victoria's situation. Victoria questioned herself: *And Naomi doesn't deserve to know the truth about Rain?*

Naomi replied, "Of course not. You know I wouldn't do that. But like I said, I am going to confront Winton."

Temporarily escaping the spotlight of her own drama, Victoria didn't want to betray Foxy. But she didn't think telling her sister was a good idea. Not right now. Foxy would fire back with questions about Rain. Fearing her marriage to Naomi might be in jeopardy, Victoria didn't want Foxy to confront

Naomi. And she didn't want to be the one to give Foxy a reason to ask Winton for a divorce.

Winton was a good man. His marriage to Foxy . . . could be better, but who was Victoria to judge. What if Winton were to lie and say, "Victoria and Naomi are lying. I did *not* fuck Nova"? Then what? Sometimes silence was golden. Especially when it came to getting involved in other people's relationships.

Victoria placed the bowl of berries on the nightstand. She kissed her wife's lips, her neck, her breasts, then her stomach. With each kiss she moved a little lower until she buried her face in Naomi's sweet pussy. Opening her wife's thighs, Victoria kissed Naomi's clit. When she inserted her finger inside Naomi, her wife's pussy was hot and wet.

Victoria contemplated giving her virginity to Naomi. If her wife made love to her, if her wife was the first to penetrate her, then Victoria could let Rain know she was no longer a virgin. But would Rain be satisfied, disgusted, or think her to be a liar? He hadn't called since she'd left his house. What was he up to?

She looked up into Naomi's eyes.

Naomi was teasing her own nipples. "Strap on for me, baby."

Victoria shook her head, then said, "Not tonight. Tonight I want you to strap on for me . . . and I don't want you to fuck me in the ass," Victoria said, handing Naomi the seven-inch dildo and harness.

Naomi patted the bed beside her. "Come here, sweetcakes. We need to talk."

"I don't want to talk. I want you to fuck me. Now."

CHAPTER 25

DéJà

Around noon, soccer moms, nannies, husbands, and singles—some clients, others oblivious to the adult fantasy menu—piled into Crème to buy pastries, iced coffee, hot coffee, breakfast beverages or to pay for a satisfaction-guaranteed trip to Crème Fantasyland. After two, the shop would become quiet with only a few stragglers or travelers passing through town.

Seven o'clock Saturday morning and the first customer standing outside the shop was Rain, suited up in his police uniform. His SUV patrol car blocked the entrance to the parking lot. His siren blared. Blue and red lights swirled atop his car. Customers slowed, stared, then kept driving.

It was too early for this nonsense. DéJà unlocked the door. "You need to move that damn car. You're deterring our customers."

"You don't want your customers to hear what I have to say. I'll move my car when I get ready. Be glad you're not in the backseat."

"What, Rain? What do you want?" DéJà sternly asked. He needed to earn his salary, get on his job, get away from hers.

"I need to speak with Victoria's trifling ass right now," Rain insisted, adjusting his crotch.

DéJà did not believe in giving respect where it wasn't due. "Your ass need to back up outta here. She's not available to you."

"Tell her to make herself available. . . . Victoria!" he shouted over DéJà's shoulder, bypassed her, walked behind the register like he owned the place. "I know she's here. Her car's outside."

"I never said she wasn't here. I said she's not available to you. She doesn't want to see you. Can *I* help you with something?"

Rain was silent. He sucked in his teeth, put his hand on his gun.

"If there's nothing *I* can help you with, then you need to get out. Now!" she yelled, then mumbled, "Your parents sure did fuck you up."

Rain's eyes turned red. Hate oozed from his pores. He tightened his fingers around the handle of his gun. "What did you say?"

DéJà shook her head. She'd told Victoria not to date his dysfunctional ass.

"Don't talk crazy to me. I'm not your husband or one of your slaves. I will put your ass facedown and slap these on you if I have to," he said, fingering his cuffs.

"And you're not Victoria's husband," DéJà sarcastically replied. "She has a wife."

Rain nodded. Stared down at DéJà. "Victoria also has something that belongs *to me.* Tell her if I don't get it soon, I'm shutting this place down, and . . ." Rain paused, released his grip on the gun, then left without completing his sentence.

What in the world? DéJà wanted to beat his arrogant ass for acting an ass. She'd never seen that side of Rain, but he was no fool and his idle threats about shutting down the shop had grown old. If he were serious, he would've closed them down already. Thankfully no customers were in the shop. DéJà didn't care about him. She locked the door behind Rain and went into the kitchen.

The terrified look on Victoria's face was clear. Rain had overstepped his boundary. But if Victoria wanted help, she was going to have to open her damn mouth and confess everything.

"Give it to us straight," DéJà said, then asked, "What the hell is happening between you and Rain?"

Foxy ran cold water on a paper towel. Handed it to Victoria to wipe her face. "We are waiting for an answer this time."

DéJà commented, "Yeah, and don't give us that 'He wants my virginity' line again. That's old. Rain's threats are old. He can't be that outraged over your pussy. And I'm tired of it! Say something dammit."

Sighing heavily, Victoria said, "Nothing is happening between us. That's the problem."

DéJà said, "Fine. Keep the truth to yourself, Miss 'I don't lie to anybody,' but when the shit blows up in your face, you'd better pray he's not serious about shutting down what I've worked my ass off to achieve. Speaking of work, I'm getting to work."

DéJà returned to the front. Unlocked the door and greeted

her regular Saturday morning client. "Let me guess. You want the off-the-menu hot-and-sticky bun?"

"Ou, I like the hot, saucy attitude," he said. Then whispered, "We should get started now."

DéJà glanced at his hard dick, shook her head. "No. Not now."

"Calm down. I was just kidding. You know what I want," he said, grinning as he followed her to the register.

"One or two?"

"One hour today. Gotta get home early. Today is my wife's birthday," he said, then winked.

"That'll be the usual," DéJà said, extending her hand. "Flogging or verbal?"

"Wish I had more time 'cause I'm loving your jalapeño energy. Better stick with the verbal today. Don't want to get caught up. See you at four," the dean said, then left.

Their meeting place for the last two years was the same. She'd meet the dean of Crème University at the house he owned on the lake. The dean's five-thousand-square-foot house was on a quarter of an acre. His cottage, what some called an in-law unit, the two-bedroom dungeon, was a good walking distance from his big house. She'd park behind the cottage so no one would see her car.

Men were at times more clever than women. Knowing his wife was terrified of snakes, the dean had brought two eight-foot boa constrictors home as pets. His wife screamed, "Get those things out of here!" His response: "I'll keep them in the cottage."

His plan to make the cottage all his had worked. His wife hadn't gone near the cottage in over two years. The dean wasn't interested in cheating on his wife, but his fantasy to be dominated by a gorgeous woman led him to Crème. The first time DéJà had tied him up, beat his ass to his satisfaction, he'd become her regular customer.

Not him again. DéJà accosted Rain in the parking lot before he'd gotten out of his car. "What is your malfunction? I told you she doesn't want to see you."

"I suggest you get out the way before you end up behind bars," Rain said, silencing his ignition.

"Fine." DéJà stepped back from his car. "But you enter Crème, and I'm personally going to file a complaint against you."

He leaned his head back, laughed from his gut. "In case you forgot, sweetheart, I am the chief of police. Who're you gonna call? Me?"

"How about I contact the Office of Citizens' Complaints, Internal Affairs, the Citizens' Police Review Board, the *Crème City and County News*, and the mayor for starters? You are not God, okay. And you can shove that badge up your ass. Keep away from my sister and our business."

He hesitated, then replied, "I can shut down this little pastry shop anytime I'd like."

"Yeah, yeah, yeah. You are fucking with the wrong one. I am not Victoria. Do something or shut the hell up. You have no idea who we service here, but let's just say you're not the top dog on our list. We go down, I'm dragging your pathetic behind underneath us."

What Rain didn't know was she wasn't bluffing. His boss, the head person at the Office of Citizens' Complaints, was DéJà's personal client.

Chapter 26

DéJà

Four o'clock, Saturday afternoon, DéJà parked behind the dean's cottage, grabbed her bag. As usual the door was unlocked. When she entered, the dean was on his hands and knees.

Black leather shorts suctioned against his body like a second skin. The suspenders strapped over his bare chest and back.

DéJà dropped her black travel bag at her feet. She spoke down to him with authority, "Slave."

"Yes, Mistress DéJà."

"Up on your knees now." She walked around him, stopped in front of him, tapped his pubic area with her finger. His plastic groin cup was under his shorts. "Take that shit off. All of it," she said.

"Yes, Domina DéJà."

"And lick my bag," she added.

She removed her red skirt and panties. "Don't look at my pussy unless I tell you. Look at my pussy again, and I'm going to punish your ass." She removed her shirt and bra. Stood before him.

"Yes, Mistress DéJà." The dean's head hung low. He stared at her feet. His tongue stroked the side of her bag as he removed his shorts.

"Now, lick my toes like a good little boy. Lick all my toes!" She grabbed the back of his head. Shoved his head to her foot. "Do it now!"

"I don't want to," he said.

"Oh, you are going to," she said. "Hand me my rope. Hands out in front!" She looped the black nylon rope in a figure eight, secured the middle with an extra loop and a knot.

Standing naked in front him, she jerked the rope, then said, "You think I'm playing. I told you not to look at me. Get your facemask."

"But, I," he said, hopelessly looking at his wrists, then up at his mask that was suspended in the air. "I can't." The mask was attached to a metal-link chain that hung from the ceiling. The center of the living room was where she had chained him for flogging during previous sessions.

"You are pathetic. Down on all fours. You're a bad dog. And bad dogs need to be disciplined."

"Thank you, Mistress DéJà. I am pathetic," the dean said, hanging his head lower. He placed his bound hands on the floor.

DéJà removed his mask from the hook. Retrieved a black patent leather corset, thong, thigh-high boots, and her cat-o'-nine-tails whip from her bag. Stepping into the thong, she put her ass in front of the dean's face, then inserted the string between her cheeks. "Do I have a pretty ass?"

"Very pretty, Mistress DéJà."

"Kiss my ass," she demanded.

The dean did as instructed.

The silver metal links of her corset overlapped until her titties sandwiched tight together. "Put on my boots," she said, standing over him. "And don't touch my pussy."

With his hands tied, the dean struggled to put on the thigh-high boots.

"Hurry up! I don't have all day!" she yelled.

The dean was an obedient slave.

Her boots were on, but crooked. She shoved his facemask over his head. "If you can't do it right, you don't deserve to see!" She slapped her whip against his naked ass.

"Mistress DéJà, please, no flagellation. Remember? My wife's birthday is today," the dean pleaded.

"Don't you ever make the mistake of telling your mistress what to do," she said, thinking about how unappreciative, disrespectful, and disobedient Foxy and Victoria were this week.

"Sorry, Domina DéJà."

DéJà opened the lid on the snakes' aquarium. Two brown-and-red boa constrictors crept over the top, then zigzagged in her direction. Their tongues slithered in and out of their mouths. She picked one up, draped it over her shoulders. The smooth underbelly felt sensual against her bare arms.

"Mistress DéJà, may I go to the bathroom? I have to pee," the dean said.

"You'd better hold it," she said, feathering her cat-o'-nine-tails over his back.

The snakes fascinated her. She watched the one on the floor crawl toward the dean. "What's that! You didn't . . . ahhhh!" he yelled.

DéJà laughed as the snake crept up the dean's thigh and onto his back. The girth of the boa constrictors were the size of cantaloupes. The snake in her arms started coiling around her shoulders. She stretched it back out. The constrictor on the dean's back slowly coiled around his waist.

"Mistress DéJà, I don't think this was a good idea," the dean said. "This snake could crush me to death. Please untie me."

"Shut up. Speak when you're spoken to."

"Yes, Mistress DéJà," he said.

The lower body of the snake wrapped his inner thigh. The dean reached between his legs and fell on his head. "My nuts. She's crushing my nuts." He tried to grab the boa but couldn't.

"Stop whining," DéJà said.

The dean was speechless. DéJà realized he was serious. She knelt, let go of her snake, got on her knees. While DéJà unwound the snake's tail from the dean's inner thigh, the snake on her shoulders slowly coiled around her neck. The struggle to save her life before the constrictor crushed her was more immediate and more difficult than she'd imagined.

The dean was still speechless. The snake was tight against his dick and balls.

Okay, DéJà, you will not be defeated by no damn snakes. What were you thinking? "Ugh, ugh. Ha, ha." She managed to get the snake from around her neck and back into the cage.

She struggled to unwrap the other snake from the dean's thigh and groin. She grabbed the tip of the snake's tail. Its mouth opened wide, head reared back, fangs protruding. "Oh, shit." DéJà backed away. Regrouped. *Okay, DéJà. Snakes will strike if they feel threatened. Take your time.*

Sitting still until the snake closed its mouth, she unwrapped the upper half, placed it over her left shoulder. The snake slowly transitioned from the dean's body to hers. DéJà put the snake in the aquarium and secured the latch.

The dean's hands were cupped over his dick and balls.

DéJà untied the rope. "Are you okay, slave?" she asked, slapping his face. "Say something."

The dean whispered, "That was the best session ever. I feel great."

DéJà never knew what would excite her clients, but the snake episode would not repeat. Not with her.

CHAPTER 27

Winton

Sometimes a woman had to confront her husband head-on when her talking, crying, begging, having an attitude, and withholding sex hadn't gotten his attention. His wife was miserable, lonely, on the verge of an emotional breakdown, and he hadn't cared for three years. Not once had he asked Foxy, "Baby, are you okay?"

Nothing Foxy had done had gotten his attention until he'd learned she'd made a fool of Winton Brown. Lied to him about Dallas being her cousin. She was engaged to that motherfucker. Giving his pussy to a man she'd convinced him to represent . . . for free! Men were sleazy. Women were scandalous.

Thursday night he'd made it home before ten o'clock, not to appease his wife, but to see if she'd have the decency to bring her cheating behind home at a respectable hour. Women. Her lying ass actually said, "I'll see you when you get here," like she was at home. No wife of his was going to fuck around on him.

It didn't matter if he was irrational. If he had another woman. If he was being vengeful. His wife should've realized she married a man and not just any man. Foxy Montgomery, a waitress at a pastry shop, snagged Winton Brown, the number one attorney in the damn country. She should've realized her place. And she should've kept her legs closed. Even if he wasn't fucking her, that was still his pussy. The rock on her finger, the license filed at city hall, the house she lived in all meant she belonged to him.

He clenched his teeth. Flinched his jaws. Winton needed a strategy. Could a love lost be renewed? Maybe if he tried dating his wife like he'd done before he proposed, he could learn to be the husband he once was. What had made him stray? Oh, yeah. No kids. Her refusal to have his child was the demise of their marriage and solely her fault.

For the first time in years, Winton entered his house on a Saturday night. The living room was dark. He flipped the light switch. The first order of business was to remove the four white wedding photo albums from the living room mantel. He stacked them in his arms. If the fireplace was lit, he'd have burned the albums to a crisp.

Winton glanced around a room he hadn't stood in for months. He checked to make sure the DVDs of the wedding and the CDs with all the pictures were in the back sleeves. The photo album opened up to pages with pictures of Dallas with Victoria, DéJà, and Foxy. He'd feel better if Dallas was an ugly man, but the brother was handsome.

"Fuck Foxy and her family, keeping this shit from me."

A dim hallway light led the way to the dark bedroom. Entering his wife's bathroom, he considered moving her to one of the guest bedrooms. Or he could put her ass out. Winton turned up the track lighting, sat the photo albums on the vanity, removed his clothes, filled the spa tub with warm water. He went to the wet bar, got a bottle of cognac and a snifter. He brushed his teeth without toothpaste. Didn't want to ruin his palate for the alcohol. He sat in the tub. Wow, when was the last time he had relaxed at home? Sitting in his wife's bathtub alone, he actually enjoyed being there. A peaceful energy floated in the air.

The more liquor he consumed, the more his stomach tightened. Sharing time with his mistress was rewarding. His marriage was not. Isis made him happy because she was happy. Foxy was miserable when she was with him. But she wasn't always miserable. She used to be happy.

Winton reflected on the day he first saw Foxy. She was strutting her stuff through the mall, laughing with two women she'd introduced as her sisters. They were beautiful too, but Foxy stood out. Her big booty, large breasts, sexy pouting lips, and confident yet cool attitude let him know she was the one for him. He knew the moment he saw her, she'd become his wife. He leaned back in the tub and smiled.

When she looked into his eyes, he saw the brightest light, and then she smiled at him and said, "Hi, Winton Brown. I'm Foxy."

The way she'd said "Foxy" excited every nerve in his body. Those were the days when he couldn't get enough of Foxy. Had to see her every moment he wasn't working. He'd had the highest-quality diamond flown in from Africa and set in platinum.

Her engagement ring had to outshine every woman's engagement ring. He took a week off from work. Took Foxy island-
hopping in the Caribbean. Unlike other women, she never
asked him for anything. Appreciated all he'd done. She fully
supported him. Was a great listener and gave intelligent advice
on some of his cases.

"Hmm." Winton sat up.

There was a technicality in Dallas's case. From a speeding
ticket to being sentenced to death, every action in law required
processing paperwork. Incorrect documentation, failure to
submit proper documentation, and Dallas could have a war-
rant issued for his arrest.

Winton had approved the paperwork for filing, but if he
could get it back from his assistant first thing in the morning,
then he'd file Dallas's paperwork in his bottom drawer. Winton
smiled. He reserved the right to change his mind. See if Foxy
goes running down to central lockup to bail her cousin out.

He stepped out of the tub, rubbed body oil on his wet skin,
toweled off the excess, then admired his physique. His dark skin
glistened like that of a bodybuilder ready for competition. His
big dick and sagging nuts should be an exclusive playground
for his wife like they were during their first year of marriage.
As he stared in the mirror, a visual of Nova's lips flashed, causing his dick to rise. *Damn that Nova was good.* Could he make
love to his wife and not think about Nova? Isis? He'd try.

It was impossible to make love to his wife when his bed was
empty. He went to his study. No Foxy. Opened the door to the
garage; Foxy's car still wasn't there. He called her phone. No
answer. Called again. Got his wife's voicemail again. He ended
the call. He was not sitting outside another man's house to re-

confirm what he already knew. Winton was not losing his wife to Dallas. *Fuck!* Foxy was winning this round, but he refused to give up the fight.

That's what he got for coming home early. Three years of sleeping in his mistresses' beds, and the one fucking night he decides to come home, what the fuck happened? Now again tonight. It wouldn't happen a third time. Winton put on his pajamas and went to sleep alone at eleven. Awakened by his phone, Winton checked his caller ID. It wasn't his wife. It was Nova.

"Hey, you okay?" he asked

She whispered, "Yeah, baby. I'm okay." Then she moaned, "I need you to come over and let me suck your dick."

Instantly, his dick got hard as a damn brick. He stood to make sure he wasn't dreaming. "Um. I don't know how to answer that?"

"*Pleeease*, baby. I want to empty those huge succulent nuts, swallow your cum, then feel your balls slam against my forehead while you lick my pussy."

Whew! Had he died and gone to heaven? Winton turned on the lamp, sat on the edge of his bed. Going to visit Nova at—he glanced at the clock—midnight wasn't smart. "This is Winton," he said.

"You don't think I know who I called?"

"Look, why don't I see you in my office first thing Monday morning. You'll be okay. Good night," he said, ending their call before he changed his mind.

His phone rang again. This time it was Isis.

"What happened? I thought you were coming over," she said sleepily.

Isis's timing was impeccable once more. His life would be miserable without her. If all he had was Foxy, they'd be divorced by now.

"I'll be there shortly."

Winton stepped into a pair of sweatpants, slipped on a T-shirt and his sandals, grabbed his wallet and keys, and left.

CHAPTER 28

Foxy

To thine own self be true.

Foxy jiggled her ass, swung her hair, sang out loud. If she had more space, she would've bounced her booty to the floor like Beyoncé. Dallas danced with her.

"These front-row seats are amazing!" she yelled, gyrating harder.

Dallas received lots of perks from the CEOs he represented. Foxy was anxious to utilize their VIP backstage passes, but she was more concerned about Winton and Isis. Plus her feet were throbbing from standing and dancing the entire time Beyoncé performed.

Before the last song ended, Dallas said, "Here's the moment I've been waiting for." He rubbed his hands together like a child in a video-game store. Reminded her of Winton's excitement for Nova.

"My feet are killing me! I don't want to go backstage!"

Dallas stopped dancing. "Are you serious?"

"Go without me. I'll take a taxi to your house."

She knew he wouldn't put her in a cab. The ride to his house was quiet. They showered. Dallas massaged her feet until she fell asleep. Foxy awakened in Dallas's arms. She glanced over his shoulder at the clock, midnight. It was time to go home. She had to figure out where this Isis woman lived. What she looked like. Foxy hated admitting the woman had gotten to her.

Tapping Dallas on his chest, she said, "Baby, give me a kiss. I'll see you in a few hours."

"You're going to make things worse. Nothing good can come out of you tracking Winton. Stay," Dallas said, hugging her tighter.

"You never tire of asking me to stay?" she said, squirming away from him.

"Never have. Never will. But it's Saturday, and you always stay with me on Saturday nights. We've had a great evening. Dinner, concert, plus I gave away my VIP passes to be here with you."

Foxy sat on the edge of the bed. Tonight she was more concerned with where her husband was. Softly she said, "I want to stay," not knowing if Winton would come home. Had she asked for more of her husband's time than she wanted? Maybe her timing was off for asking him. She'd assumed her request went unheard. Wasn't sure what she'd do if Winton stayed at Isis's all night again. Not knowing was better. She could pretend her husband wasn't cheating. Knowing the truth hurt. Dallas was right.

"Dallas?"

"Yes, baby," he said, massaging her back.

"Make love to me."

She didn't have to ask twice.

Dallas gently laid her body down. He caressed her feet, kissed her arches, licked the ball, then sucked each of her toes. Tears escaped Foxy's eyes. Tears of joy, pain, love, and sorrow connected as they flowed into her hair. Why was love a complicated emotion to grasp? Love definitely wasn't everlasting.

Hate was hate. If someone said, "I hate you," their feelings were clear. If someone said, "I'm happy," happiness was happiness. When Foxy said "I love you" to Dallas or confessed to herself "I still love my husband," the meanings manifested the greatest love and the deepest hate.

Why couldn't Winton love her the way Dallas had?

Dallas raised her leg, pressed his lips to the back of her knee. His tongue danced in the groove. Lowering her leg, he trailed his fingertips over her pubic hairs, between her thighs separating them.

His movements were slow and deliberate as he passionately kissed her clit. He nestled his tongue in the upper left side of her crevice next to her shaft. His tongue stiffened. The tip flickered in her left groove.

His hands slid up her stomach to her breasts. He teased her nipples, suctioned her shaft into his mouth. Foxy came and cried at the same time. This time she didn't say, "I'll see you in a few hours." Foxy eased out of bed and went home.

Opening her eyes, Foxy rolled over. Her husband's side of the bed was neatly tucked. Not because he'd tucked the sheet as he'd normally do when he got out of bed. Two nights in a row, Winton hadn't come home.

She sat on the floor, exercised, stretched, then went to her bathroom. The tub was filled with used water and their four wedding albums.

"Fuck you, Winton! Stay with that tramp-ass bitch!" Foxy cried. "I hate you!"

Why hadn't she kept walking that day in the mall? Why had he done and said all the right things to win her heart? She drained the tub, sat on the bathroom floor, placed her hands over her face, and cried. "He used to hold my hand in public. Open doors. Surprise me with red and white roses. He told me, 'The white is for our everlasting friendship. Red is for the love I have in my heart for you, baby.'"

Foxy cried louder. It dawned on her. She'd lost her best friend. She tossed the photo albums in a hefty black garbage bag, then tossed them in the trash.

Maybe her sister DéJà was right. Foxy should choose before she lost her man and her mind. She'd been so consumed with her situation, Foxy had forgotten to check on Victoria. No need to call now. Today was sisters' day, and they'd see one another at church.

CHAPTER 29

Victoria

Pray
  Listen
  Wait
  Sit still
  Fast
  Meditate
  Do unto others
  Parents
  Siblings
  Lovers
  Breathe
  Repent
  Confess
  Give thanks
  You are
  Blessed

Victoria arrived at church before Sunday school. She sat in the third pew with her purse on the bench to her left and her Bible to the right. Other adults sat in front, beside, and behind her. Victoria's purpose for arriving early was to reserve seats close to the altar for Foxy and DéJà to join her in prayer during service.

"Be faithful unto the Lord. What does that mean?" the teacher asked, standing before them.

Victoria hadn't answered or asked questions of the pastor's wife, who was also the teacher. She wondered if the pastor's wife was faithful. What was her definition of faithful? Her sins? Had her husband slept with any members of the congregation?

The woman seated next to Victoria's Bible said, "That means we must adhere to our duties to the Lord and not put our needs . . . sexual needs or our desires . . . before His, and we must keep our promises to Him. We must fast and pray to cleanse our souls for Him. And we should yield not to temptation."

"Anyone else want to add to that?" the teacher asked.

Victoria listened to the other comments. Each person had their own interpretation of what faithful meant. Were their definitions tailored to suit their lifestyles? Victoria hadn't dwelled on the meaning until now. She had an obligation, a duty, and a responsibility to do right by Naomi. Her not doing right by Naomi also meant she wasn't doing right by the Lord.

As Sunday school ended, DéJà and Foxy walked in and sat on opposite sides of her. Foxy wore a beautiful red and gold sleeveless dress. DéJà had on a basic black dress with short black lace gloves. They hugged. Teary-eyed, Victoria said, "I love you, guys." They might not have agreed on certain things, but Victoria was happy her father had made sure his girls were close.

"Love you too," they said in unison.

The pastor preached about the Sunday school message: being faithful. Foxy quietly stood, went to the altar, and knelt during the sermon. People stared. Victoria held DéJà's hand, stood. They knelt on opposite sides of Foxy.

Silently Victoria prayed for her sisters, her mother, their mothers, their dad, and their spouses. She prayed for Rain, his parents, and she prayed for herself. Tonight she'd tell Naomi the whole truth.

CHAPTER 30

DéJà

"The sermon was fitting for you two," DéJà said, unlocking her car.

Foxy sat in the front passenger seat. Victoria sat behind Foxy.

"I'll admit that," Victoria said.

Foxy replied, "No comment."

DéJà drove east along North Shoreline Drive to their favorite spa. "Church always makes me feel high-spirited. I can't wait to take off my clothes and get on the massage table for two hours." She'd soon tell the masseuse, "Harder, faster, deeper, harder, faster, deeper."

"I'm getting a mani, pedi, and a facial," Victoria said. "Foxy, what are you having?"

"A coffee ground thigh wrap, a brown sugar body scrub, and massage," she said.

"Oh, that's what I should've gotten," DéJà said.

White gauze soaked in coffee, then lined with wet coffee grounds was the best treatment for eliminating her hard to get rid of cellulite on the backs of her thighs. The first time she tried the coffee ground thigh wrap, DéJà had immediate results. She threw out her expensive cellulite creams that didn't work.

"So what moved you to the altar?" DéJà asked, looking over at Foxy.

"You want to hear me say you were right? Is that it?" Foxy asked, staring at her.

"No, that's not it. I just asked you a question."

"Yes, it is," Victoria chimed in. "Admit you want to hear both of us give you credit."

"Okay, I admit it. But am I wrong for wanting what's best for my sisters? You're both married to good people. If you change your ways, you can work things out. I want you two to have happy marriages like Acer and I."

Foxy adjusted her seat belt. Stared out her window. "I prayed for peace. I do want my husband back. And," she paused, then said, "I'm ready to have a baby."

Victoria shouted, "That's what I'm talkin' 'bout! Let it be a girl. I'ma name her Precious."

How dare Foxy try to give their father his firstborn grandchild. DéJà hadn't considered having a baby, but she'd bet that would make Acer happy. Her too. Starting today, she'd stop taking her birth control pills.

"Too much estrogen in the family already. No girl," DéJà said. "I want you to have a son. We will give him a nice, strong name like Solomon Brown. People will look up to him all his life. You have to dig deep in your gut and add bass to your voice to pronounce Solomon."

The name Solomon was a suitable first name for Foxy's last name. DéJà would name her son Adam Acer Mason Montgomery-Dawson. Adam would always come before Solomon, with his birth, in the Bible, and with their father. Naming her son Adam would give him his own identity. The name Acer would make her husband happy. Ending his name with Montgomery-Dawson would allow him to know how to identify with both sides of his families.

"Listen at you, guys. I'm not close to getting pregnant. I haven't had sex with my husband in three years. I have to stop taking the pill, then wait three months to get the contraceptives out my system. I have to talk to Dallas. And I have to see where Winton's head is. If we can't work things out, I'm not having his baby."

Good. Foxy's procrastination would give DéJà the time she needed to get pregnant first. DéJà said, "A woman has the power to salvage her marriage. You can do this. But by the time you do all that, that just means you'll get pregnant on the first try."

They all laughed as DéJà valet parked at the spa.

DéJà's prayer at the altar had been answered. She'd prayed that her sisters turn away from the negativity and darkness in their marriages, embrace what was right, and see the light. Victoria and Foxy honestly had good-hearted spouses who needed their help in order to have a change of heart.

CHAPTER 31

Foxy

The scrub and massage were exactly what Foxy needed. She drove DéJà's car from the spa to the mall. They started their shopping spree in their favorite store, Spectacular Stilettos.

Foxy picked up a pair of yellow leather slip-ons with brown and red snakeskin-covered heels. "I have to have these."

"Let me see the heel," DéJà said, getting a closer look. "No, you don't. Put them back. The snakeskin is too thin. You'll only wear them once, maybe twice, before the heel starts to peel. And you can never wear these while driving." DéJà reached for Foxy's shoes.

"I protect my heels. I wear flats while driving; you know that. This is a battle you will not win," Foxy said, handing the shoes to the clerk. "I'll take these in a size eight."

Victoria held up a pair of clear open-toe stilettos with cherry metallic heels and the same style in green apple. "Which ones?"

Foxy and DéJà both pointed at the green apple–colored shoes.

DéJà bought a pair of bright purple and green stilettos with a shimmering gold heel. She didn't solicit her sisters' opinions. She said, "Omega Psi Phi and Mardi Gras rolled into one, baby. You can't beat that."

It was customary for each of them to buy one pair of stilettos each week, and their next tradition was to split up for an hour, shop on their own, and buy something special for one another.

Foxy headed to the jewelry store for her hour. She picked out diamond-encrusted Xs and Os charms that represented the love she felt for her sisters. "Gift wrap three of these for me, please. Separately," she said.

She stopped outside a kids' clothing store. Watched mothers shop for their babies. Strolling the mall, she noticed babies in beautiful carriages and pregnant women. She loved the way the expecting mothers glowed and was especially fond of the men holding hands with the pregnant women. Foxy glanced down at her flat stomach wondering if she'd get stretch marks.

Arriving at their favorite restaurant in the mall, Foxy joined DéJà and Victoria who were already seated. She placed her gift bags on the chair beside her. After lunch and before ordering dessert, they would exchange presents.

"The usual, ladies?" the waiter asked.

"Yes," DéJà said. "And bring a bottle of champagne. We're celebrating."

Foxy and Victoria frowned at DéJà. "Don't ask," Foxy said, looking at Victoria. She picked up her bags, handed DéJà a black bag and Victoria a white one. She kept the red one. "I don't want to wait. Open your gifts now."

DéJà covered her mouth, then removed her bracelet from the box. "Foxy, this is beautiful." DéJà extended her arms for a hug.

"Foxy, what in the world were you thinking?" Victoria asked. "This is too much." Victoria leaned toward Foxy with open arms.

"From my heart to yours. I have one too. We'll wear our bracelets to symbolize our sisterhood and everlasting friendship." DéJà fastened Victoria's bracelet. Victoria fastened Foxy's and Foxy did DéJà's.

"Okay, I can't wait either," Victoria said, handing Foxy her gift.

Inside a small pink box was a small pink crystal baby bootee with a gold bow.

DéJà stared at Victoria. Narrowed her eyes. "No, you didn't."

Victoria frowned. "Didn't what? She wants a baby so I got her something special."

Inside the box DéJà gave Foxy was a small sapphire crystal baby bootee with a platinum bow.

"Great minds think alike," Victoria said.

DéJà stared from the corners of her eyes at Victoria. "We do not think alike. What is in those other bags you have?"

"None of your business," Victoria said, moving her bag to the chair beside Foxy.

"Okay, you two," Foxy said. "This is the easy part. I love both bootees. And regardless of what I have, I'm covered on both ends."

While the waiter poured three glasses of champagne, Foxy's cell phone buzzed. She said, "I have to take this, it's Dallas."

"Don't answer it," DéJà said, grabbing Foxy's wrist. "He'll ruin our celebration."

Victoria crossed her fingers, placed them over her heart, shook her head, then mouthed, "Do not answer the call." She jingled her bracelet.

"I have to," Foxy said, excusing herself from the table. "Hey."

Dallas sighed heavily in her ear, "I need you to bail me out."

"Bail you out of what? What now? Not another DUI," she said, scanning for a semiprivate area to talk in the crowded mall.

"Jail. That's what. I'm in Crème City Jail."

"I'm on my way," she said, rushing inside the restaurant.

Foxy picked up her purse, placed the two baby bootees back in their boxes, then in her purse. "Thanks for the gifts. Can't stay for lunch. Gotta go."

DéJà stood, blocked her exit. "Foxy, no. When are you going to let go of Dallas? He's a grown man. He can take care of himself. Sit down." DéJà handed Foxy a glass of champagne.

"Your prayer at the altar, remember that?" Victoria added.

Foxy ran out of the restaurant. She had driven and fortunately the keys to DéJà's car were in her purse. Her sisters would have no problem getting home. They shouldn't drink and drive anyway. Acer or Naomi could pick them up. Foxy rushed downtown.

Dallas had never been arrested. Why was he in jail? "Oh, my God, no." Almost running a red light, Foxy slammed on the brakes. She thought about the soaked wedding albums. "Winton wouldn't have."

CHAPTER 32

Foxy

One curveball after another, Foxy had no control over Dallas's actions, but she'd never leave him in jail. There were too many black men already incarcerated. Dallas was a good man, a loving father, and had never been to prison.

She sat in the bail bonds office shaking her left leg. "Please hurry."

"These things take time," the bondsman said. "Calm down. It's just an attachment for a DUI." An unlit cigar dangled from his lips. "I need five thousand dollars cash, and what are you going to use for collateral?" he asked.

Her leg shook faster. "Cash? Collateral?" She hadn't thought about that. It was Sunday. The banks were closed. She couldn't use her house. She refused to use her business. "I'll be right back," she said.

"I'll be right here," the bondsman said.

Foxy walked a block to the automated teller machine. The only debit card in her purse was for her joint account with her husband. She had no choice. Take the money or leave Dallas in jail overnight. She keyed in her pin number, then withdrew five grand. She'd redeposit the funds first thing Monday morning.

Returning to the bondsman's office, she handed him the money and the registration to her car. "Here. This ought to do."

He glanced at the make and model of her luxury car. "Sure will," he said smiling.

She paced while he typed on his computer. He handed her a paper. "Take this across the street."

She'd done as he'd instructed. Had to wait in line. Wait for more paperwork to be processed.

"Number two twenty-seven," blared over the intercom.

Almost three hours had elapsed between the time Dallas had called her and for her number to be called. She hurried to the counter, spoke to the clerk behind the glass window. "How much longer before I can bail out Dallas Washington?"

The clerk smiled, then said, "Wow. Are you sure you're here for Dallas Washington? This is a first."

"What's a first? What? Don't tell me I'm in the wrong place?"

He shook his head.

"Stop procrastinating," Foxy said. "Tell me what's a first. Did I do something wrong? I haven't done this before."

Four years married to Winton plus the one year she'd dated him, Foxy hadn't been to a city, county, federal, or state prison. Had no desire to be in the environment. The closest she'd come was serving jury duty.

The clerk smiled. "He's already been bailed out."

Had she heard him right? What he'd said made no sense. "Who bailed him out?"

"Attorney Winton Brown. Can you believe it was an error on his part? His assistant forgot to file the paperwork so the courts issued an attachment on his client."

"Forgot my ass," Foxy said. "If DéJà would've kept her mouth shut, none of this wouldn't have happened. And Winton, that bastard. He didn't have to do this."

The clerk frowned. "Hey, aren't you Brown's wife?"

"Depends on who you ask," she replied, storming off. Foxy drove to Dallas's house, let herself in.

Dallas met her at his front door. He hugged, then kissed her. "I love you."

"You don't love me! What the hell just happened here?" Foxy asked, throwing her purse and DéJà's car key on the sofa. "I waited forever to bail you out to find out you were already out. Why didn't you call me?"

He laughed. "At first I was ready to kick Winton's ass. But sitting in that cell gave me time to think. I can't be mad at you or him. Now, if I were Winton, I'd be disappointed in myself if I were mistreating a woman as good as you. But I know how men think, and regardless of how screwed up our relationships are, we do not want another man sticking his dick in our woman. After all the years we've been together." Dallas frowned, hunched his shoulders. "You think he knows about us?"

Foxy hadn't told Dallas what her sister had said. She figured Dallas didn't need to know. Foxy followed Dallas to the bedroom. "He knows for sure now. Big mouth DéJà told him. This is her fault."

"What?"

"Well, she told Acer and Winton overheard."

"Your sister needs to mind her own damn business," Dallas said, sitting on the bed.

"Don't go there. DéJà is going to be DéJà."

"Yeah, and you can talk about her but I can't. And you're going to defend her to the end. What she did was intentional. But none of that matters now. Today you proved again that you are my lady for life. Let's go out and celebrate."

Foxy scratched the back of her neck. Was her relationship with Dallas destined? The moment she felt she wanted to have a baby for her husband, she was sucked into a tornado of emotions that flung her to Dallas. "Celebrate what?"

"Never have I had a more loyal friend than you. This is my way of saying thanks. Can't hang a price tag on what you won't do for me. I feel great! Let's go."

She had Dallas follow her to DéJà's, parked her sister's car in the driveway, left the key under the mat, got in his car. They dined at the top of the Marquis, sat in a booth with a rotating floor. Every twenty minutes Winton's building came into view. Foxy wondered if her husband was in his office working or fucking.

Dallas ordered the best of everything on the menu, way too much food for them to eat. They sampled sushi, sashimi, lobster, steak, crab cakes, calamari, and the food kept coming along with bottles of wine.

Making it back to Dallas's house was a blur for Foxy, but she managed to slur, "Thanks for dinner."

Dallas kissed her, picked her up, stumbled to the bedroom with her in his arms. He dropped her on the bed, fell on top of her, then said, "Tonight, I'm gonna fuck you like you're my woman and make love to you like you're my wife."

Anxious to have his body intertwined with hers, Foxy removed his clothes. "I'm going to suck every last sperm out your dick or get lockjaw trying."

Dallas grinned as though he were posing to have his picture taken.

Foxy sucked his soft dick into her mouth and swallowed. His head slid past her tonsils. She hummed, gurgled, moaned. "Ummm." Bobbing, she tightened her jaws, suctioning blood into his dick, then released. His dick stood at her attention.

Dallas stripped away her clothes, frisked his fingers through her hair, slapped her ass. "Down on all fours," he said, pointing to the floor.

Foxy got on her hands and knees, then smiled. She wasn't into BDSM like DéJà, but she enjoyed what Dallas had introduced as free play—impromptu moments where one of them initiated something out of the norm and the other immediately played along, no questions asked. They didn't have to be naked or in the bedroom to express themselves.

Free play could start at the restaurant with them feeding one another with their fingers or his finger fucking her under the table. She could motion to whisper in his ear, then stick her tongue inside, and say, "Come fuck me in the restroom."

Crawling behind her, Dallas circled her like he was a lion in the jungle and she was the lioness checking him out. He slapped her titty, stood tall on his knees, swung his dick side to side. Foxy turned her ass to him, glanced over her shoulder, then nodded.

"Come and get it," she said.

He held her hips, penetrated her pussy, then like a wild beast he fucked her fast. Instantly she came. He pulled out, put it back in. Pulled out. Put his dick back inside her. "I am one lucky man," he said, ejaculating on her ass. Dallas massaged his sperm on Foxy's booty.

She rubbed her ass, then sucked each of her fingers. "Got more?"

He eased his dick back inside, then said, "There's a lot more. I'm just getting started, baby."

Foxy placed her hand on Dallas's chest. "Stop."

"What's wrong?"

She sat on the edge of his bed. "I don't understand why one minute I'm so in love with you. Then I feel guilty for being with you. All these years you've been an emotional outlet for me but is this—" She paused, sighed, then continued. "Is what we have love? Or are we two people who don't want to be alone?"

Dallas exhaled. Held her hand. "Come here," he said, leading her to the living room. He powered on his iPod. "All the Man That I Need" by Whitney Houston resonated from his Bose speakers.

He hugged her. Lay her head against his chest. "Remember, you dedicated this song to me on our first anniversary? Please don't tell me I'm not all the man you need. Other than my girls, you're all I've got."

Tears streamed between her cheek and his chest. "I'm scared of letting go. I'm afraid to keep holding on."

An eclipse of her heart resurged. Once again Foxy was confused. Dazzling baby bootees in her purse. Her man fucking her doggie-style. Her husband, only God knew where, probably wouldn't come home again tonight. Fair exchange at this point in her marriage was necessary for her to maintain her sanity. Foxy decided to stay with Dallas until midnight, then she'd go home.

There was next Sunday to try and share time and her new-found desires with her husband. And no matter what happened tonight. She could pray about it tomorrow.

CHAPTER 33

Winton

Midnight. Sunday. Winton stood in front of his wife. He folded his arms to keep from choking her. He looked down at her. His wife's hair was gathered in a mangled ponytail. She had on a red and gold sleeveless dress and stilettos. He sniffed the air above her head. The stench of stale cum disgusted him.

"Where in hell have you been?" he asked, already knowing.

He wasn't sure what made him stick his finger in her pussy, then sniff her scent but what he wanted to do next would get him life in prison. He motioned to clench his fingers around her throat, cut off her oxygen, strangle her to death. His hand stopped an inch from her neck. Refraining from killing Foxy, he smeared her juices on her jaw.

"You didn't have the decency to douche?"

Foxy shoved him aside. "Fuck you, Winton."

"Fuck me? No, fuck you! You're out all night with your

what, your fucking cousin. Got me bailing that"—he paused, refraining from using the word *nigga,* then said—"bailing his ass out."

Foxy's ponytail whipped in front, then behind her, as she faced him, stepped up to him, stared up at his face. He'd never seen his wife give him a look that projected she could kill him too.

"You come home before midnight for the first few nights in three years and what? Expect me to be home waiting on your selfish, inconsiderate, cheating ass while you're fucking some other woman with the dick that should be inside this good pussy every day? You're the one who forgot you were married, Winton Brown, big shot attorney-at-law, not me. Ya still got that nasty-ass red thong from three years ago? Who was that bitch? Who the fuck is Isis? Don't blame me for having a stunt double, do your damn job. Go thank Dallas for saving your marriage. If it weren't for him, I would've divorced you a long time ago.

"When you want your wife back, you know where to find me. Until then, go live with that bitch Isis. I'm sleeping in, let her suck your dick in the morning. I'm tired. Tired of being alone in this marriage. Tired of being ignored by you. Tired of your ass, period. Now get and stay the fuck out my face!"

He watched his wife's booty jiggle down the hallway and into the bedroom. *Slam!* The doorknob fell off. This wasn't a good time to continue arguing with her, but the conversation wasn't over.

Winton got in his car. Dallas could have his wife. Against his better judgment, he drove to Nova's and rang her bell. Nova opened her door. He expected her to look ordinary and not so attractive in the middle of the night.

"Hey, I didn't expect to see you. Come in," she said.

Nova was more beautiful without makeup. "Thanks." Her place was ultrafeminine with porcelain dolls displayed throughout the living room.

"What brings you here?" she asked.

"Came by to see if your offer was still good." He needed his dick sucked. The unforgettable stench of another man's sperm was still on his finger and in his nostrils. He exhaled hard through his nose.

"Let's take a shower," Nova suggested.

"Great idea."

She stepped in the shower with him. Winton pressed his lips to hers. Her lips felt amazing and he couldn't wait for her to give him head. As he stepped out of the shower behind her, Nova exuded sex. His dick hardened like it had done the first day she sat in his office. She handed him a bottle of oil, then led him to the bedroom.

"I want you to massage my body. I want your hands all over me. Fast and firm. Nice and slow. And I want you to spank this pussy, finger fuck the shit out of me, then I'm going to take that big-ass dick and let you stick it wherever you'd like." She opened her legs, spread her pussy. "Look at her. She's so damn hot for you."

Winton admired Nova's Brazilian wax. He wondered if Foxy had said those things to Dallas. Winton wasn't gay, but Dallas was a great-looking man and he was single. The background check he'd done on Dallas revealed he was, like Foxy claimed, a headhunter for corporate executives of the top companies in the country. Well, at least that part about Dallas that his wife had told him was true. But what made a handsome, successful bachelor want Foxy?

Maybe it was time Winton confronted Dallas.

CHAPTER 34

Victoria

Precious moments
Whisk by
Conjugating lies
Truth unfolds
Beauty beholds
In eyes
That are brave
And wise

Victoria opened her eyes at four in the morning. Another restless night fearing her BlackBerry would alarm her. Naomi was sleeping peacefully. She had to talk to her wife before their day was interrupted with clients, customers, and things unforeseen like Rain showing up at their front door.

She nudged Naomi. "Honey, wake up. I'm ready."

Naomi yawned, stretched her arms. "Ready for what?"

"To talk."

"Okay." Naomi yawned, propped the pillow behind her head, leaned against the headboard. "I'm listening," she said, yawning a second time.

Victoria hesitated, cleared her throat, faced Naomi. She folded her legs like a chicken wing, placed her hands in her lap. "Regardless of what happens based on what I'm about to tell you, know that I love you and I never meant to hurt you."

Naomi exhaled, yawned, nodded.

"I haven't been honest with myself or you. I've never stopped seeing Rain."

Naomi interrupted, "Seeing or fucking?"

Victoria swallowed the lump in her throat, remembered her prayer at the altar to tell Naomi the truth. "Both."

Naomi's body tensed. Her lips tightened. "Keep going."

Covering her mouth, Victoria fought to hold back her tears but couldn't. "He's angry because I won't—"

Naomi shouted, "Don't tell me about how he feels! How do you feel?" Her wife readjusted her pillow. Leaned back.

Victoria flinched. She'd never heard Naomi yell. The feeling was horrible. Made Victoria want to disappear. "I don't know what I feel. There's a part of me that's sexually drawn to the way he penetrates me, and—"

Smack! Naomi's hand landed across Victoria's face. "I've heard enough!"

Victoria cried, not knowing if she deserved that or not. She understood Naomi's frustrations. Felt responsible for hurting Naomi. She slapped Naomi's face. "Don't ever hit me again. What I did was wrong, but that does not give you the right to abuse me."

"You're right. I'm sorry," Naomi said, hugging her. "But I

don't understand why you didn't come to me. I never expected your desire to be with men to go away overnight. Victoria, I married you because I'm crazy about you. I love you. But I know you're human. I hit you because you lied to me, not because you had sex with him."

Was Naomi justifying her action? Was she justifying hers? Which was worse? Lying, cheating, or fighting? "I'm so sorry," Victoria cried.

"Look at me," Naomi said, holding Victoria's hands. "Tell me the truth. All I want to know is do you want a divorce?"

Victoria shook her head. "No. No. I love you."

"Then let's put this behind us and move forward. Kiss me," Naomi said.

Their tears blended. Was it possible to forgive and forget that fast? Victoria caressed, then sucked her wife's breast. She opened the nightstand drawer, removed the dildo and harness from a satin pouch. She attached two gold bullets to the strap-on. Victoria sat Indian-style with her back against the headboard.

Naomi mounted the dildo, wrapped her legs behind Victoria. Victoria eased one bullet into her rectum and the other into Naomi's ass, then brushed her nipples against Naomi's stomach while sucking Naomi's nipples.

Hugging Victoria, Naomi ground her hips onto the dildo until her body trembled.

Victoria prayed a silent prayer that Naomi would never let her go. Good sex with Rain wasn't a good reason to go back to him. Victoria would rather be loved by a woman than be tolerated by a man.

CHAPTER 35

DéJà

What made Acer faithful?

DéJà knew there were women who'd done all the right things for their husbands and their marriages failed. Their husbands cheated and disrespected them. Which was harder, staying in a bad marriage or leaving? DéJà imagined Foxy and Victoria stayed because they were the ones cheating. Even when she'd watched *Cheaters* on television, the cheaters never wanted to leave. The person who'd done the right things in the relationship felt betrayed and ended the relationship. Cheaters begged, cried, and pleaded for forgiveness. DéJà had no reasons to and would never cheat on Acer.

"Handsome, breakfast is ready," DéJà called out to her husband.

"Coming, precious!"

Two steps forward, hopefully only one back. Foxy had

dashed out of the restaurant yesterday like her life depended on it, the hell with how she and Victoria were getting home. DéJà hadn't heard from Foxy or Victoria. Not good, but she'd see them this morning, hopefully on time.

"Morning," Acer said, sitting at the table.

DéJà placed a plate stacked with three piping hot cinnamon pecan pancakes and another plate with scrambled eggs and bacon in front of her husband. Her plate had one pancake, two scrambled eggs, and two strips of bacon.

"Honey, this looks good," Acer said. He leaned over the plate and inhaled. "Um, um, um," then drowned his pancakes in buttery syrup.

"Thanks for picking us up from the mall," DéJà said. "I honestly didn't want Winton to find out about Dallas. Not from me. Not like that. My sister thinks I'm trying to force her to end her affair."

Acer chewed, swallowed, then said, "I'm not concerned with Winton. He might be the top attorney, but he's a despicable husband. Whether he overheard from you or found out from someone else, he got what he deserved. I'm more concerned about Foxy. She was the happiest, sexiest . . . not sexier than you, precious, but your sister was so full of life when she married Winton. How he destroyed that beautiful woman is inhumane."

DéJà was quiet. She reflected on how Foxy was the life of every party in high school, in college, and after they'd graduated. Foxy used to make her and Victoria laugh. Her sister was confident, sassy, and sophisticated. Before Foxy married Winton, men literally begged to date Foxy. Her clients took her on all-expenses-paid vacations. One man, the man who should've uplifted her sister, burst her sister's bubbling personality.

"Hadn't thought about it like that," DéJà said. "Good point. Thanks."

"No problem, you still need me to drop you off at Foxy's to get your car?"

"Yes, I do. Handsome, do you think I'm too involved in my sisters' lives?" DéJà asked.

"Uh, no. Not at all. That's what family is supposed to do. Look out for one another."

"How are you feeling this morning?"

Shoving a strip of bacon in his mouth, he said, "Good."

"Do you think I'm too bossy?" she asked.

"Nope." Acer's plate was half empty.

Her husband ate faster. He knew regardless of his answers, she'd make her own decisions. She just needed him to listen to her.

"Breakfast was great," Acer said, kissing her forehead. "I'd better get going. If you want to talk later, call me at noon. Love you," he said, excusing himself from the table.

"Honey, wait. Come back," DéJà said. "You forgot that fast. You're dropping me off."

"Oh, yeah, throw on something quick," he said.

"Sit down for minute," DéJà said to him.

Acer frowned. Sat in his seat. Covered her hand with his. "What is it?"

"I want us to have a baby," she said. DéJà was serious 'bout not letting Foxy have the firstborn.

A smile stretched across her husband's face. He loosened his tie, carried her to the bedroom. Undressed her.

"I have to get on the bottom," DéJà said, holding her legs in the air, praying they would get pregnant soon.

Acer stroked deep inside her.

"When you cum, push all the way in," she told him. Gripping his ass, she pulled him toward her, tilted her pelvis, held his ass tighter. "We're going to have to do this a lot. It's going to take time for me to start ovulating but I want this baby as soon as possible."

Her husband hadn't ejaculated in the morning for years. Now, he'd have to cum deep inside her at least twice a day until she became pregnant. "Go shower and get dressed. We're late. Never mind. Don't wait for me. I'll figure out how to get my car back," she said, holding her legs in the air.

Her husband showered, then danced out the door. "I love you."

"Love you too, handsome."

DéJà waited twenty minutes giving the sperm time to find an egg that wasn't there. Practice would one day, hopefully soon, produce the positive results she wanted. She cleared the table, cleaned the kitchen, called her dad.

"Hello, my queen," he answered.

DéJà said, "Don't give me that. Where have you been? You need to come see us."

Mason laughed. "That's my girl. I will, promise. Working on some things first. Give your sisters a hug for me, and Daddy will see his three favorite ladies real soon . . . kisses."

DéJà sighed, then said, "Kisses, Daddy. Bye."

At the pace her father was moving, she'd be pregnant before she saw him.

Acer called.

"Hey, handsome."

"Your car is parked in the driveway," he said. "Have a nice day."

When had Foxy dropped off her car, and why hadn't she called?

CHAPTER 36

Victoria

Summer breeze
Carefree whispers
Is early dawn your lover
Do you steal her breath away
Heat and moisture
Blend into humidity
Dancing throughout the day
Night falls
Humidity crawls
Back into the arms of dawn
For peace and comfort
Summer breeze
Hot
So cool
Yet never cooler than dawn

Like dawn, early Monday morning at Crème was quiet. Regardless of her personal issues, Victoria had to work. Working was better than sitting at home, soaking over problems she had no control over.

A thin man entered the pastry shop. He looked around, swiped his forehead with a white handkerchief, then stuffed it in his back pocket. Three tables, five chairs. No waitress stirring around. He avoided eye contact with the tall mocha-complexioned woman standing behind the counter. Had his friend given him the correct address?

Rectangular coffee bean–colored wooden tables were lined up against the wall. Padded armless chairs the same rich color appeared comfortable enough for him to sit a while at the one unoccupied table, but he wasn't there for coffee. He wanted the special pastry his friend told him about.

Red velvet curtains stretched across the windows, low enough to let the sunshine in, high enough to shield seated patrons from outsiders' views. What if one of his coworkers drove by and saw him standing in the doorway? He'd have to make up his mind or risk further embarrassment.

To his right, two women sat chatting at the second table from the door. They sipped from mugs, giggling like teenagers. The opposite side of the café, one table, one chair, a man in a dark suit sat in the corner, one hand on his coffee mug, the other holding his electronic device.

Above the counter, a flat screen was illuminated with vibrant colors. The words *Today's Special* flashed above three scrolling pictures of pastries that made the thin man's mouth water:

Banana Crepes with Chocolate Drizzle
Sticky Bun

Cream Cheese–Filled Spice Cupcake

His friend had told him to order the cupcake. His friend had said, "Man, the sticky bun is for people who enjoy being dominated. You know, getting their ass beaten. And the crepes are served up by a bootylicious woman that does it all, but she's too much woman for you and your wife put together, man. Take cash and buy the cupcake. If they try to charge you less than a thousand, you've ordered the wrong thing. Just to be safe, take three gs. They might charge extra for couples."

The thin man scratched his head, faced the glass door, placed his hand on the steel bar.

"Excuse me, sir, may I help you with something?" Victoria asked. She stood behind the counter smiling at him. She should've offered him assistance five minutes ago but didn't want to scare him off. Behind Victoria's smile were no worries about Rain. She'd left those concerns at the altar yesterday, and Naomi forgave her last night.

Pivoting his body in her direction, his feet still facing the door, the thin man prepared to leave. His voice trembled, "This place is too nice. I must have the wrong address."

Victoria motioned for him to come closer.

Slowly he approached her, glanced up at the screen, then at the three items in the pastry display case. "I'd like *the* cupcake," he said, hoping the way he'd enunciated the word "the" would confirm he'd come to the right shop.

"Okay, let me get one for you. I'll be right back."

She went to the kitchen, removed a cupcake from the tray Foxy had just placed on the rack. "We have a potential," Victoria said.

"Are they sure they want a cupcake?" DéJà asked, handing

Victoria a cream-colored box with a red ribbon and a gold bow. "You okay?"

"Yeah, why wouldn't I be?" Victoria frowned, then said, "That's what he ordered, but I'm not sure exactly what he wants yet. I'll find out." She returned to the counter. "Here's your cream cheese–filled spice cupcake. The best stuff is always in the middle, not on top." She smiled at the thin man who peered into the pastry display as if wanting to make a different selection. She tapped on a few keys, then said, "That'll be five dollars."

The thin man's head rattled. "That can't be right. I was told I could get a special cupcake for my wife's delight," he said.

CHAPTER 37

Victoria

Victoria smiled, hoping to comfort him, as she confirmed, "You can. I have one more cupcake available. If you'd like it for your wife, you need to fill out the top of this catering request." She continued, "And that'll be two thousand dollars cash." Victoria wondered if she should call Rain and apologize for assaulting his dick. And to find out what was brewing in his wicked mind.

The man's short narrow fingers unfolded his wallet. He counted out twenty one-hundred-dollar bills, laying them on the counter, then picked up the form.

Victoria softly asked, "What's your fantasy?"

He hunched his narrow shoulders.

She rephrased the question. "What catering services would you like?"

"Oh," he said. "An orgasm for my wife."

Victoria slid a white card under the red ribbon on his pastry box. "Bring her here."

Nervous, he nodded, then asked in a low trembling voice, "What time should I bring my wife to"—he looked at the address on the card Victoria had given him—"this location?"

He was a new customer; he wouldn't have known the number noted in the lower right-hand corner of the card indicated his start time. Victoria pointed, then said, "Your appointment promptly starts at four and ends at five o'clock sharp. I'll be ready for both of you."

"Wow, a whole hour." The thin man rubbed his palms on his pants. Glanced over his shoulder, around the shop, leaned closer to Victoria, then whispered, "I've never done anything like this before, but my wife has never had an orgasm and I want her to share the pleasure she gives me."

Matching his tone, she replied, "Relax. She'll have one today, or I'll refund your money. See you in a few hours."

Victoria's surefire secret had helped nonorgasmic women experience their first. Explosive orgasms depended upon a person's timing and how well they knew their body. Since not all orgasms were explosive, some of her clients had had them but weren't aware. The same held true for women who unknowingly squirted. Some women actually ejaculated retrograde into their bladder because they didn't understand when to contract, relax, or push. Kind of like a man overly anxious to ejaculate experiencing blue balls. Victoria enjoyed educating couples and singles on how to reach a higher spiritual and orgasmic state.

"I'll sit in my car and fill this out," he said.

Victoria picked up a freshly brewed pot of caffeinated coffee. "Refill?" she asked the ladies. She glanced over the curtains and saw the thin man in his car writing while talking to a woman, presumably his wife, in the passenger seat.

"No, thanks. We'd better get on the road," one of the ladies said.

"Yeah, got a long ride ahead. But this is a quaint spot. We like it. And your banana crepes are delicious."

The man seated in the corner placed his electronic device in his pocket, followed the women out the door to the black limo. The thin man returned, handed Victoria his form, then looked at his feet.

"You can change your mind if you'd like," Victoria said. "Our catering services are fully refundable, no questions asked."

The thin man said, "I don't want my money back, but can we get together now? That would be better because if I wait I might not show up later. I'm really nervous."

"Is that your wife in the car?"

He nodded at his feet.

"I don't normally do morning appointments. Wait here," Victoria said, placing the coffee pot on the warming station, then entering the kitchen. The thin man was a welcome mental departure from the memory of Rain hoisting her in the air. She told Foxy, "I need to make a special accommodation. I'll be at my place, and I'll be back in ninety minutes. Cover for me."

Looking at the monitor in the kitchen, Foxy said, "Not so fast. Let me get a closer look to see what this new client looks like." Foxy followed Victoria, picked up his form from the counter, walked outside, and wrote the thin man's license plate number and the color, make and model of his car. "Ninety minutes you'd better be back," she told Victoria. "No backsliding to you know who."

"You first," Victoria said, then left the shop.

CHAPTER 38

Foxy

Foxy took over the register for Victoria.

Standing behind the counter, Foxy rewound her conversation with Winton in her mind, then replayed it like an audio podcast. She was definitely the star. Winton, her costar. She hated verbally attacking her husband, but if she hadn't acted crazy, slammed the door with the intent to break it, he would've gotten more aggressive. His sticking his finger in her pussy was awful. His leaving was good for them both. When Victoria returned, Foxy would go to Winton's office. Maybe if they talked in a semiprivate place neither of them would yell as they'd done last night.

"Where is Victoria?" DéJà asked.

"With a client."

DéJà frowned. "Who?"

"The man who bought the cupcake."

"I'll be back," DéJà said. She went into the office, returned with her purse.

"DéJà, don't," Foxy said. "She's fine. Really, she left with a client. Here's his receipt. You want to check the register too? Damn, can't you relax for one minute?"

The customer seated at a table became quiet, stared at Foxy. "My apology. Sisters' quarrel. Nothing serious. More coffee?" she asked. Picking up the pot of caffeinated coffee, she handed it to DéJà, then said, "I have to leave too. I'll be back."

Foxy's emotions were eating at the lining of her stomach. She couldn't wait until Victoria returned. She had to go talk to her husband now.

CHAPTER 39

Victoria

M issionary yes
Mercenary not
Pheromones
Endorphins
Contribute a lot
For happiness
Health
Emotional wealth
Happily bust from the gut
Orgasms are a must

Victoria got in her car, motioned for the thin man to follow her. She entered the gates of Crème Fantasyland. Escorting
the couple inside her home, Victoria led them to the lavish
bathroom equipped with a steam and dry sauna, Jacuzzi, and
shower for two.

"Remove your clothes. Shower. Put on robes. Meet me here in the bedroom when you're ready."

Victoria closed the door, lit cedarwood- and clover-scented candles, sprayed lavender freshener in the air to heighten their senses, opened the patio door, turned on the cascading waterfall headboard, selected Mozart from her iPod playlist, and neatly folded the white comforter to the edge of the bed.

She opened her pleasure chest drawer beneath the bed, fluffed the pink feather that sat atop the crystal bottle filled with edible cotton candy dusting powder, then set the bottle on a silver platter beside the bed. Surfing through the chest again, she selected a G-spot vibrator, a lipstick clit stimulator, then placed them on the platter. Since most women experienced clitoral orgasms first, Victoria had a special collection of items for the clit.

"Hmm, I want one more thing on the platter, but what?" She dug deeper into the chest. "Perfect." She retrieved a tin of strong peppermints and opened it.

The woman entered the room with her husband close behind. "Wow, this is like being in paradise," she said, checking to see if the water was real or a mirage. "It's real, honey. Touch it."

Victoria smiled at them. "Keep your robes on for now. I want you to lay sideways across the bed," she told the man's wife. Victoria slid a satin pillow underneath the woman's shoulders and head, then asked, "Are you comfortable?"

The woman reached for her husband's hand, then said, "Yes."

Victoria handed her husband the crystal bottle. "I want you

to slowly open her robe, then dust a little cotton candy on your wife's breasts, stomach, and her kitty hairs. Is that okay?"

Her husband nodded.

The woman squeezed her husband's hand. "Okay."

Victoria asked the thin man, "Do you like cotton candy?"

"Oh, yeah. Loved it ever since I was a kid," he said smiling. Meticulously he dusted his wife like she was precious china. His enthusiasm exposed the vulnerable little boy inside him.

Men were fragile because their sensitivity was suppressed. Taught not to cry, to silence their pain, act like they didn't need love and affection. Women reared boys to be men, who were groomed to be grooms, who were expected to know but were seldom taught how to love. The thin man wanted to please his wife. Having the desire to please was a good place to start in any relationship, but Victoria wanted to find out how manly he was.

"Look at how beautiful your wife is. Tell her you're going to make her cum."

His brows rose. "Who? Me?" he asked, tightening his robe.

"Tell her what I said, and tell her you want her to tell you what feels good and to let you know right away if anything doesn't feel good."

The thin man mustered up the energy to speak directly to his wife.

"Kiss your wife. Inhale her breath. Hold her close . . . good. Now, stop touching her and admire her body, then I want you to spread her lips and look at her pussy."

"Wow, that's my wife?" he said. "We usually have sex in the dark, or if the lights are on, we do it under the covers. Honey, you are beautiful all over," he said without being coached.

While he was mesmerized, Victoria handed him the pink feather. "Now, tease her body."

The thin man took the crystal bottle from the tray, dumped the cotton candy powder on his wife's body, then dusted her.

Victoria laughed. "Okay, there is no wrong way to do this."

His wife laughed. A sense of humor was good anytime, especially during sex.

"Trail kisses from her neck to her breasts. Lick her nipples."

The man went wild with long, wet strokes all over his wife's body, lapping up the cotton candy like he was at a carnival. He hadn't noticed that his wife's body had tensed, her hands were clenched, and she'd started moving away from him.

"Stop," Victoria commanded. "Look at your wife. Does she look pleased?"

He frowned. "I thought she was supposed to tell me if it didn't feel good."

"Lay back down," Victoria told the woman. "And you, I want you to ease your hand over her stomach down to her shaft. Insert your middle finger inside her vagina. Is she wet?"

"No."

"Then you're not exciting her. I want you to suck your middle finger and rotate it on her clit and suck her nipples at the same time.

"Ou," his wife moaned. "That feels nice."

The man went wild again, then settled himself.

"Okay, that's good." Victoria instructed, "Now, I want you to kiss her shaft."

"I don't do that," he protested.

"I thought you wanted your wife to have an orgasm."

"I do, but I don't do that."

"Let this moment be about her, not you."

The thin man placed his face between his wife's thighs, took a really deep breath. He started off lightly licking his wife's pussy in an upward motion with the tip of his tongue.

"Ou, yes," his wife moaned again.

He placed the center of his tongue over her clit and dragged his taste buds up her shaft. "Honey you taste so sweet," he said, lapping faster.

"Slow down. Go back to using the tip of your tongue. I like that better."

He did, and his wife moaned louder.

Softly, Victoria said, "Now gently suck the tip of her clit . . . and I want you to insert your middle finger into her vagina but don't stop sucking. Is she wet?"

"Yes. Yes, baby you're wet," he said.

It didn't matter if she was wet from his saliva or if her juices had started flowing. What was important was that the couple was excited about making love. "Good. Now curl your middle finger toward you and keep sucking."

This time his wife screamed "Oh, my!" repeatedly. Her breaths were shallow and closer together, her back arched.

"Excellent. See how much fun that was. Look at your—"

Before Victoria finished her sentence, the woman ripped off her husband's robe, pulled him to her, and said, "Penetrate me. I'm going to make you cum, and I'm cumming with you."

"Well, my job here is done. You have twenty minutes remaining. Enjoy. There are hot disposable towels in the warmer next to the bed. When you're done, you can freshen up."

When the alarm sounded signaling their hour had ended,

they quickly showered. The thin man buckled his belt, hugged, then kissed his wife. "We did it, honey!"

She giggled like a little girl. "I'm not done yet."

Their smiles were wide and genuine. Victoria put the vibrator, stimulator, mints, and a special pink and purple vagina pillow in a gift bag. "Y'all enjoy these at home. If you need instructions on how to use them, call me." She escorted them to their cars, got in her car, and followed them to the main road.

CHAPTER 40

Winton

M r. Brown your client, Ms. Scotia, is here."
Winton hoped his spending the night with Nova wouldn't complicate her case. Had enough obstacles in his personal life, a nasty wife for starters. He closed the interior blinds to the hallway windows, left the exterior shades partially open, tilting upward.

"Send her in," he said.

She entered his office. Closed, then locked the door. He reached for the knob to unlock it. She grabbed his hand, slid it across her breasts, then under her skirt between her thighs, all the way up to her vagina, then pushed his middle finger inside her.

"I can't believe how big and fabulous your dick is. I masturbated all morning thinking of you. I had several orgasms on the way here each time I fantasized about your huge thick dick and how it felt inside my hot pussy. I have to have you inside me right now," she said, squirming on his finger.

His hand was still attached to the knob. He removed his other hand from her pussy. Ten o'clock, Monday morning. Quietly he pushed her away. "Please, stop. We have to get down to business." He unlocked his door, opened it about an inch. She closed, then locked it again. She swiped his moist finger over her lips, then kissed his.

Again he said, "Please, stop. This is inappropriate."

Nova retorted, "So you can show up at my house whenever you like, fuck me, then leave, and I can't get this good dick when I want it. Don't make me scream for this dick."

Winton scratched his brow. Now he understood why her boyfriend was suing her. Nova wanted everything her way. Wished he could tell her he was dismissing her case, but that would further complicate his life.

She inserted her finger into her pussy, shoved it in his mouth. "Eat me like you did last night. I want to cum so bad all you have to do is put the head in and I'll shoot fire like a rocket."

Nova's pussy cream was sweet. His dick hardened. Who was he fooling? He wanted more. He checked the knob. The door was locked. She had him hard and hot. His dick leaked pre-cum. He could hit it right quick, then get down to business.

Winton unbuckled his belt, shoved his pants and boxers below his knees, then carried Nova to his couch, sat her on his lap, lowered her blouse. He sandwiched her breasts. His mouth pivoted from nipple to nipple.

"Put it in," he commanded.

Nova protested. "Wait. But you're not wearing protection. Last night you had a condom. We need one. You got one?"

"No. You?"

She shook her head.

"It's okay. Just this one time we don't need it. Don't you have somewhere in your contract no babies allowed? Put my dick in your hot pussy. I'm going to fuck the shit out of you." She was the one who'd walked in seducing him. Now she wanted to stop? Was she joking? Well, he wasn't.

When Nova eased his head inside her, Winton grabbed her skirt. Crumbled the soft cotton material against her ass, then thrust his dick deep inside her. Nova tried backing away.

"No, baby. Don't pull away from me," he whispered, squeezing her ass tighter.

"Winton, please. I can't risk getting pregnant. I don't take contraceptives. They make me gain weight. Please, stop. I'll lose my modeling contract."

Oh, now she was asking him to stop? Why did women initiate sex, then change their mind after the dick was inside the pussy? This wasn't about her. He had to pay back his wife and Dallas.

"You're fucking fantastic. Your pussy is the best baby. I can get you out of anything. No worries." Winton inhaled through his mouth, then exhaled. "I'm cumming for you, Nova."

The pulsation of his dick felt incredible. His entire body tingled as his cum squirted inside her. If Foxy had sucked him off and swallowed his cum this morning instead of bringing her pussy home full of some other nig . . . He couldn't say the word even in his mind, he wouldn't have had to fuck Nova. It was his wife's fault for not fulfilling her duties by satisfying him. He had the right to fuck Nova and wished Foxy could see them in action.

Nova stood, gapped her legs. His cum drizzled down her thigh. She looked a mess. She wasn't the same woman on the covers of sports magazines. She wasn't the supermodel he'd dreamed and fantasized about. Nova was just another woman with more issues than he cared to address, including her case. But he wasn't stupid enough to share his opinion of her with her.

Between heavy breaths, he gasped, "You are so beautiful. Thanks. Let me get you some paper towels for that. Don't move."

Knock. Knock. Aw damn. What other person wanted him?

Hoping they'd go away, Winton ignored the knock, handed Nova the paper towels. "Hurry up," he told her.

She held up her skirt, pointed at the front. "Look what you've done." Their cum had created a huge wet stain on her mint green skirt. She held up the back. There was a larger stain.

Knock. Knock.

Fuck. Think, Winton, think.

Nova picked up her purse, unlocked, then opened the door before he'd finished buckling his pants. "I'm going home to bathe. I'll be back in two hours."

Foxy's eyes roamed from Nova's smeared red lipstick down to the stain on Nova's skirt.

Nova looked down at Foxy and said, "Excuse me."

Foxy watched Nova walk away. She pointed at Nova's ass. "I see you took me up on the offer to let her suck your dick, but with a wet ass like that you took it all the way."

He wanted to say, "Fuck you, Foxy," to get back at her. Let her see how it felt to have him dismiss her. But he didn't. "Foxy, wait. It's not what—" Why should he give a damn what his wife thought? Wasn't like she cared about him.

"Find yourself someplace else to live, Winton. You can have your assistant fill out our divorce papers," Foxy cried. "I can't do this anymore."

Winton pulled his wife inside his office, closed the door. "So your coming home with a wet ass doesn't mean anything to you? Can't you see this is all your fault. You were the one who told me to let her suck my dick. Remember?"

Foxy sniffed the air around him, stared up at him, patted his chest. "I said let Isis suck your dick, but what difference does it make who it is, as long as it's not me. You're right, baby. I did say that. Good job." She opened the door. "I came to tell you I was ready for us to have a baby, but I wouldn't birth a child into this madness to save your life. Enjoy the rest of your day."

His wife calmly walked away. "Foxy! Come here, baby. I apologize."

Foxy jiggled her booty out the door. Naomi caught the door before it closed.

"We need to talk," Naomi told him, inviting herself into his office. "As soon as Acer gets in. He's parking right now. Meet us in the conference room in ten minutes. No, on second thought, we'll come to your office." She sniffed. "It stinks in here. Back to plan A, meet us in the conference room."

CHAPTER 41

Winton

This was not how Winton anticipated his Monday starting. He'd had the best pussy a man could get, and less than five minutes after ejaculating, his high was low . . . Aw, damn. He got a whiff of what Foxy and Naomi had smelled. Winton exhaled, closed, then locked his door before Acer came by.

Winton opened the windows, sprayed deodorizer, snatched paper from the printer, and began fanning the air. Why did he have to ask Nova to come into his office? Since he wasn't having dinner with his wife, dinner with Nova would've worked in his favor. He needed to call Nova and apologize. Needed to call his wife and explain. Or vice versa. He frowned. Looked around. Had his wife said she was ready to have his baby?

Okay, Winton. Handle this situation like you're preparing for trial.

Knock. Knock. Winton tossed the printer paper in the trash on top of the soiled paper towels, then unlocked the door. "Plan C," he said. "I thought we were meeting in the conference room."

Acer entered his office first followed by Naomi.

"What's up?" Winton asked, sitting behind his desk with his hands clamped over his dick.

Naomi sniffed twice. "Good job. You clean up quick. Based on what I'm getting ready to say that could work to your advantage. You've created a messy situation that's potentially damaging to the outstanding reputation that Brown, Cooper, and Dawson has earned."

Acer frowned.

His name came first. His reputation carried the firm. They were just two more attorneys trying to make it big before he partnered with them. Since he'd let them in his circle, he had to be honest with them. Winton explained, "It won't happen again. I'm having some marital problems. I admit fucking Nova in my office was a mis—"

"Nova? In your office?" Naomi interrupted. "I thought you and your wife . . . never mind. I'm here because I saw you fucking Nova in our courtroom. Exactly how many times have you fucked Nova Scotia?"

Winton's eyes met with Acer's. Acer's left jaw flinched repeatedly.

Acer spoke for the first time. "You know I stay out of your business, but I don't understand men like you. You have a great wife and you treat her like shit. You single-handedly took a beautiful, intelligent, vibrant woman to the altar, then nailed her to your sacrilegious cross. I don't know why she tolerates you, and I don't blame her for having another man. What in the hell is wrong with you? You're the smartest attorney in the country but have the dumbest dick in the world."

Winton's lips tightened. He stared out the window. There was no correct answer outside of beating Acer's ass. Fighting was for animals less intelligent than humans.

Acer continued, "If this tarnishes our reputation, we're removing you from the partnership."

Naomi commented, "We may remove you anyway. This isn't your first affair. But it is the first one that might bite all of us in our asses."

"More like remove yourselves," Winton lamented.

"Power play any way you'd like, but the end results would be the same," Acer said.

Winton was more concerned with Acer's comments about Foxy. Acer was unquestionably committed to DéJà. All this time Winton thought he was the man, and it took another man to turn on his light.

Was Foxy tolerating him?

CHAPTER 42

Victoria

olden touch
Power of the hands
A simple touch
Could heal so much
A broken heart
Sad friend
Failing marriage
A loving touch
Can mend
So you can
Start
Again

His wife's orgasm was worth every penny the man paid.
Victoria laughed wishing more couples would invest time in

learning what pleased their mates. She entered the pastry shop, smiled, then called out, "Foxy, see I'm back with two minutes to spare. It's not even noon yet."

DéJà entered from the kitchen. "Foxy isn't here."

"Then who's watching the register and helping the customers?" Victoria asked.

"Y'all want to be in charge. You are," DéJà said. "Offer your customers fresh coffee and take over everything until Foxy gets back." DéJà shouted from the kitchen, "I'm going to meet my husband, then I'm going to call my father. I'll be back when I get back. Do not call me for anything."

Victoria shouted back, "He's my father too." *What is up with DéJà,* Victoria thought, picking up the pot of caffeinated coffee. DéJà never left work to meet Acer. Was she having an affair? "Why are you going to see Acer? You never go to his office."

DéJà stood in the doorway behind the register. "I'm not going to his office," DéJà said. "I'm meeting him at home for a late lunch. We're working on having a baby."

The customers stared at DéJà.

Victoria followed DéJà into the kitchen. "No, you are not. You are wrong for this. You didn't want a baby until Foxy said she wanted to get pregnant. You will not have a baby before Foxy."

"Your customers are waiting," DéJà said.

Foxy was going to blow when she heard what DéJà was up to. This time Victoria was not getting involved. "More coffee?"

"Finally," the man said.

Victoria picked up his cup. Glancing out the window, she smiled, picturing the thin man's new attitude about his wife. Her smile vanished. A quiet storm brewed in her stomach. Victoria's eyes widened. Her jaw dropped as Rain parked his SUV in the parking space next to her car.

"Foxy, come here. I mean, DéJà, come here!" Victoria shouted.

The coffee pot and cup slipped from her hand. Victoria jumped backward. The glass pot crashed on the cream-colored marble floor. "Shit!" Hot coffee splashed on her shin. "Ow! I'm so sorry," she said to her customer. "Are you okay?"

The man pushed away from the table, escaping the splash, got up, then walked out the door. DéJà flung open the kitchen door, stood in the doorway. Victoria ran toward the kitchen as Rain entered the shop.

DéJà blocked Victoria's entrance into the kitchen. "Naw, you've got it under control. Go talk to him."

Victoria's eyes watered. "Please, sis."

DéJà told Victoria, "Just what I thought." Then she said, "Rain, stop right there. I need to clean up Victoria's mess."

"Not you again," Foxy said to Rain as she entered the shop. "This is harassment, Rain. You need to leave and not come back." Foxy took over sweeping up the broken glass. Victoria stood behind the register.

Victoria watched her sisters. Why did she have to be the sensitive sister? Why couldn't she be in control like DéJà? Rain didn't intimidate DéJà. DéJà began taking pictures of Rain.

"Take all the damn pictures you want," he said, flashing an evil grin. "Victoria, come here."

DéJà said, "Victoria, get in the kitchen."

"I'll go back there with her," Foxy said. Then she snapped at Rain, "Join FaceBook. Request some friends, and stop coming here with your foolishness."

Victoria closed the door, sat on a stool in the kitchen. Holding her knee to avoid touching her shin, Victoria cried, "My leg feels like it's on fire. Get me something cold. Quick." She fanned her leg as tiny blisters emerged on her shin. "Damn, that bastard made me mess up my leg."

Foxy got a bowl, filled it with water and ice cubes. She soaked gauze in the freezing water, placed the bowl under her sister's leg, then squeezed cold water over Victoria's burn. "You made peace with this yesterday. Let it go. You don't even care why he's here. His problem is not yours."

Yes, she did care, but she was tired of dealing with him.

DéJà entered the kitchen. "Move the gauze, let me see." DéJà moved closer to Victoria's leg, looked at the burn. "That bastard is nuts. Your burn probably feels worse than it looks. It's not that bad. Foxy keep putting cold water on her leg, she'll be fine."

"Please, DéJà," Victoria cried. "Get rid of him."

"Oh, now you want DéJà to take control. Whatever. You two are confused."

"How'd I get in the middle of this?" Foxy asked.

DéJà stared at Foxy's stomach, then at Victoria. "Like I said, whatever. He's gone, and like it or not, I'm going to make sure he stays gone. And Foxy, so you don't have to hear this from Victoria, I am going home to make love to my husband so I can have a baby before you."

CHAPTER 43

Winton

Monday evening Winton left his office, sat in his car. Should he go to Isis's house first or Nova's? Nova was supposed to return to his office in two hours, but he hadn't heard from her since she'd left this morning. He decided business before pleasurable disappointment. Visiting Dallas was third on his list.

Winton drove to Nova's house, rang her bell.

"You are so crazy," she said, opening the door. "I forgive you for what happened earlier. Come in here."

Forgive him? She had things twisted. He stared at her ass as she led the way to her living room. Nova's orange boy shorts separated her butt cheeks like a Georgia peach. She sat on the sofa sectional facing him. The spaghetti strap tank top barely covered those nipples he loved to suck.

"Was that woman your wife?" she asked.

Winton nodded.

"Then you are crazier than my boyfriend. Did you know she was coming to your office?"

Her nipples screamed, *Bite me!* Winton scratched the nape of his neck. "I didn't stop by to discuss my wife. I came over to let you know I cannot represent you," he said, sucking in his lips, staring at hers. The ones spilling out the sides of her shorts.

"What am I supposed to do? I need you. You're the best," she said. "All you men are alike. I know what'll change your mind." She licked her lips, kissed him.

Winton carefully held her arms. "Please, don't do that." His dick disagreed. *Come on, man. Hey, down here. Don't I have some say so?* His dick hardened.

Why, when he tried to do right by his wife, did women entice him to do wrong? Was self-preservation the law of the pussy? He let go of her arms.

Nova left the room, then quickly returned. "Look what I have for my friend," she said, waving a black and white XL condom packet. "Is that a smile I see?"

He shook his head, squeezed his dick, wondering which of them was her friend.

Nova frowned. "Let him go. Don't treat him like that. That's not nice."

Yeah, that's not nice, his dick repeated.

What the hell? Since she was giving her pussy to him, he'd take one for the road. Winton unzipped his pants.

Nova smiled.

He stood, removed his clothes. Her lips devoured his head.

"Um, um. I love the way your dick tastes like mango, papaya, pineapple," she said, slobbering her juicy lips all over him.

Winton fantasized they were filming a porno flick and he was the star. His daily consumption of fresh fruits and eight ounces of pineapple juice used to make his wife love the taste of his dick. At least Nova confirmed his ritual still worked.

"Suck that dick, girl. Take it all in. Spit on the head. Yeah, like that," he said. Interlocking his fingers behind his head, he spread his thighs wide, slid down, got more comfortable, and a better view of Nova polishing his dick with her tongue.

"Ou, yes! This is the best big black dick I've ever sucked. I'll suck your dick anytime," she said. Her head bobbed up and down on his.

He watched her. No doubt she was having a good time sucking his dick. She gripped his shaft, held his dick tight, then teabagged his balls like a big-mouth bass feasting.

He'd guessed he was wrong. He was a lucky man. He could get for free what lots of men had to pay for. But nothing was truly free. Would Nova demand he keep her on as a client? Maybe he was her rebound, just a good dick to take her mind off her boyfriend until her case was settled. Or perhaps she was getting all the good dick she could before going to jail. Hopefully she wouldn't have to serve time. As good as he was, Winton wasn't sure he could get her off as good as she was getting him off.

"Suck it, girl, suck it. Do your thang. Sandwich my dick between those titties and suck the head," he said.

She did. He watched closely, so he could replay the images whenever he masturbated. Man, she had beautiful titties.

"Come here. Ride this dick," he said.

"Ou, yes." She squeezed his dick from the base to the head, then sucked all his precum into her mouth.

"You gon' fuck around and make me cum down your throat." Briefly he thought about how he missed his wife's morning blow jobs. *Pa-yah!* He slapped her ass, then said, "Saddle up on this horse."

Nova placed the condom in her mouth, put her mouth over his head, and rolled the condom down his shaft with her lips.

"Ou, girl." He finished securing the condom down to his nuts, held his dick at the base. "You sure know what to do with that mouth and this dick."

She smiled. "I sure do."

The second Nova mounted his dick, she started moaning. "Ou, yeah. Uh, yeah. Yeah. Yeah. You feel so good. Fuck, yeah. I love this dick." She grunted. "I love this big black dick." She yelled, "Fuck me. Fuck me. Fuck me."

Her mouth gaped open. Her breathing became sporadic. Fast. Short. She inhaled. Held her breath.

"Breathe, baby," he said, slapping her on the ass.

"Umm! I'm cumming," she said. "Slap me again."

Winton massaged her clit to help her cum harder.

"Ughhhhh!" he grunted from the pit of his gut. "Fuck! Yes! Ugh!" He shook his head, then kissed her forehead.

Denying himself the pleasure of what he knew was incredible sex was not working when Nova was in his presence. Tomorrow he'd mail her a letter.

Winton leaned back on Nova's sofa. He had to regroup before getting dressed. Guess he'd done wrong for so long it was harder than he'd realized to do right. Now that his nuts were milked, it would be easy stopping by Isis's on his way home to give Isis her key back again, but it wasn't a smart idea to stop by Dallas's.

Fuck that. Isis had that voodoo pussy too. He'd just mail the damn key to her.

CHAPTER 44

Foxy

Six o'clock, Monday night. No husband. And she was not cooking dinner.

The house was quiet. Peaceful. "This is a good thing," Foxy said. "I'm going to enjoy me some me time. I'm going to take a nice hot soak in his Jacuzzi with a bottle of merlot and read *Sexaholics*. Maybe my problem isn't my husband. Maybe it's me. Should've kept my mouth shut."

Foxy turned on the bathwater, removed her clothes. "Whew! Sure feels good to be naked."

Walking in on Nova smelling and looking like a tramp as she left Winton's office, Foxy had indeed asked for more of her husband's time than she wanted. She'd interfered in his game.

He wasn't supposed to surprise her by messing up her rotation, coming home earlier than usual. She wasn't supposed to catch him with that bitch in his office. How many times had he fucked in his office? Foxy had assumed her request for more time went unheard. If he had come home *after* midnight as he'd normally done, she would've had time to douche and bathe as she'd always done. Whose fault was it that her husband discovered Dallas had ejaculated inside her?

Thinking how screwed up her marriage was, Foxy consumed the entire bottle of wine, tossed the erotic novel to the floor beside the tub. The hot and steamy sex in Pynk's book had her heated. She placed her pussy in front of the jet and stroked her clit. Good thing Winton wasn't home; she'd take her dick tonight. She came quick and hard.

Foxy rested her head on the inflated pillow, continued playing with her pussy. She spread her lips, clenched her shaft with one hand. Imagining Dallas was making love to her, she stroked her pearl with the other hand.

"Why, oh, why does masturbation feel so good?" She sped up her rhythm.

"Oh, yes!" She closed her eyes, concentrated on her clit. "This shit does not make sense," she said as her back arched. "Forget holding back," she said, releasing herself a second time. She yelled, "Goddamn!" Thank goodness for Dallas or she'd have a serious case of carpal tunnel from getting herself off.

She picked up the book, tossed it on her husband's vanity. "I'm definitely no sexaholic. The freaks in that book are in fuck mode 24/7. When they're not having sex, they're thinking about having sex."

Lifting the lever inside the Jacuzzi, Foxy placed a cap over her hair, stepped in the cold shower to sober up. The pulsating water carried her tears down the drain. "I hate you, Winton Brown!" she yelled.

Where did we go wrong? I should've talked to my husband three years ago. Is it too late? As wonderful as Dallas is, God knows, I don't want him on a permanent basis, and I am not trying to find another husband. Not with all the miserable men I get paid to service.

She exited her husband's shower. Midnight had arrived. Foxy dried, then moisturized her body, and went to bed alone. She tossed and turned for six hours. Opening her eyes, she saw her husband's side of the bed was neatly tucked. Winton hadn't come home again.

Foxy texted DéJà and Victoria. "I'm taking the day off. Please don't call me."

DéJà texted back, "I'm running late. Be there at eight."

Draping a blue, white, and gold strapless maxidress over her head, she adjusted her breasts, then lowered the dress to her ankles. Foxy slipped on a white thong and her blue heels. Checking her appearance in the full mirror, she saw that her hair and makeup were flawless. Foxy eased her sunglasses on top of her head.

As she walked past Winton's study, she saw he was seated in his bourbon-colored chair with the newspaper in his lap. He must've heard her footsteps. Peeping inside the door, she scanned from his feet to his face to his feet again, then back to his face. His reading glasses were on the tip of nose. *Damn, he is fine.*

She stood tall, giving him an unobstructed view of how good she looked. She knew it. She didn't need his confirmation. "Have a good day at work," she said smiling. No need to confront him about what happened. She wanted a day of peace, alone.

"Foxy, we need to talk," he said. "Come here, gorgeous."

Sarcastically, she replied, "We can talk tonight. That is, if you'll be home. If you're not here, I won't be here either."

"What in hell has gotten into you, woman? I asked you to come here so we can talk."

Foxy glanced at her husband's face. Veins protruded on his forehead. Staying in control, Foxy left.

She drove west along Shoreline Drive. Bypassed Victoria's house, cruised by Dallas's home, and sped past DéJà's place. Driving and thinking, she must've circled the city twice before parking at the pier.

She wanted to cry but was tired of crying. She had so much to give thanks for. She was frustrated but clothed in her right mind. She was sad but had so much to be happy about. Family. Food. Clothes. Money. Good health. At times she forgot how many millions of dollars she and her sisters had. She opened her purse, placed the bootees side by side in her palm.

A part of her felt like driving to her dad's. Another part just felt like driving. Then there was the part of her that felt like doing nothing at all.

CHAPTER 45

Victoria

Didn't come this far
To stop being the star
Made my own decisions
Sink or swim
Succeed or fail
The blazing trail
Is rugged
Struggle
Strife
Deception
Confessions
Are all a part of life

Tuesday morning it was Foxy's day to work the register. Victoria busied herself prepping a tray of raspberry strudel for

Foxy's clients, blueberry scones for DéJà's clients, and apple dumplings for her clients.

Victoria smiled thinking about the thin man and his wife. She hadn't heard from them, but surely he'd run out of cotton candy body dust by now. She had a one o'clock appointment with a soccer mom. A recently divorced fifty-year-old mom with a five-year-old daughter and a seven-year-old-son who wished she had remained married to their father.

Divorce wasn't the woman's decision. She loved her kids more than life but never envisioned she'd have to rear them alone. Her body hadn't changed much on the outside. She exercised regularly, enjoyed playing with her kids. What she didn't enjoy any longer was sex. Her libido was zapped, and she wanted it back.

Interrupting Victoria's thoughts, DéJà texted, "So how are things between you and Rain?"

She texted back, "I'll answer that in a minute."

Exiting the kitchen, Victoria entered their office. Since she was the only one there, she left the office door open, picked up her cell phone, and dialed Rain. She hadn't heard from him and DéJà's inquiry was confirmation that it was time for Victoria to make a call. His unannounced drop-ins had driven her mad. His silence scared her more.

Things with Naomi were better but not perfect. Once Victoria totally purged her thoughts of Rain, she was confident her marriage would thrive.

He answered, "Took you long enough."

"So is no news from you good or bad?" she asked. "We cool?"

"Hell, no, we ain't gon' be that until it's a done deal. And if you try that shit again I'ma beat your ass for real. You know you owe me. I didn't call you. You called me. You know you want this dick. I've got the real thing, baby, and you know it. You know what you owe me or you wouldn't have called. Right?"

How could she help him? Convince him to get professional help? "Wrong. You're a sick man. I don't owe you anything. But I know someone who can counsel you. I think if you deal with your childhood issues, you won't be so bitter."

"Fine, then there's no need for me to delay what I have to do. The women in prison are going to love—"

"Stop it, dammit! Just stop it," Victoria cried. Rain acted as though he hadn't heard her offer to help him. He probably thought counseling was for weak or crazy men. That wasn't true.

With the emotions of a lion going in for the kill of a deer, Rain said, "If I were you, I'd save those tears for later. You'll need them."

"Go to hell! Dirty bastard!"

"I've been called worse. Since you called me, meet me at one o'clock. My place," he firmly said.

"I have a client at one," Victoria explained.

"Cancel."

"For you? Never," she said.

"If I don't see you at one, you'll see me."

Victoria exhaled. "I'm so damn sorry I ever met you."

"No, you're not. You're sorry you didn't marry me." He repeated, "One o'clock."

"I can do three after my appointment, but promise me all I'm going to do is talk. I'll do whatever necessary to protect myself." Victoria was desperate to make him stop harassing her. She turned her back to the glass window.

"See you at one. Don't be late," Rain said, then ended the call.

Victoria placed her cell phone back on the desk and entered the kitchen. Quietly she resumed tending to the pastries, only this time she slammed the pastries onto the baking pan.

"Throw those away," DéJà said.

"Oh! Shit. You scared me," Victoria said. "I didn't hear you come in."

"Kind of difficult to hear when you're talking stupid. I called Dad. This time I gave him details so he's coming for sure," DéJà said. "He'll be here at one. I made the decision. You left me no other choice. You know whatever problems we have with men Dad takes care of it, and it's time for him to step in."

Victoria gripped the sides of her pan, banged it on the stainless steel table. The raspberry strudels popped up. Some landed on top of one another, others smashed on the floor. Victoria cried, "You had no right to call Dad! I don't want to talk about this. Is that so bad? I stay the hell out of your business, and I haven't mentioned anything lately about Foxy's fucking Dallas. Why me, DéJà? Why?"

DéJà hugged Victoria. She pressed her sister's head on her shoulder. "Because I love you. And sometimes family have to step in. I'd rather step in than stand by and let Rain keep hurting you."

"Then why haven't you said something to Foxy lately?"

"Because Foxy can handle Dallas. And Dallas isn't homicidal. Rain is. You, my sister, are not in control of your situation. If you don't want me involved, then you need to tell Dad about Rain."

"You don't understand. I can't tell Dad. If I do, he might kill

Rain. You called Dad, you talk to him. I'm leaving," Victoria said, walking into the office. She picked up her purse and her cell phone.

Slam! Victoria turned around.

DéJà rolled a metal pastry stand with eight shelves in front the office door. Locked all four wheels. "It's for your own good. You're not leaving until Dad gets here."

Victoria opened the door but couldn't get out. Her narrow body was too wide to slide between the bars. One at the time, Victoria shoved the pans off the rack. Each time a pan fell, DéJà picked it up and put it back before Victoria could maneuver her legs between the bars.

"Satisfied? You've ruined all the pastries. We can do this for the next four hours if you want, but you're not leaving until Dad gets here."

"Fine! Forget it! You still can't make me talk to him," Victoria yelled. Plopping on the ivory desk with her back to DéJà, Victoria dialed her dad.

Clank, clank, clank.

Victoria looked over her shoulder and exhaled. DéJà had placed another pastry rack in front of the pastry rack that blocked the door.

"Hey, sweetheart. How are you?" he asked, sounding chipper as usual.

Had DéJà really called their dad this time or had DéJà overheard she'd planned on seeing Rain today? "Hi, Daddy. You coming to see me today?"

"Yes, my angel. Be there at one o'clock sharp just like DéJà insisted. What are my girls up to? Are you planning another surprise party for me?"

Victoria's cell phone beeped. She glanced at the caller ID. "Daddy, hold on a minute," she said, then answered the other call. "I can't make it for one. Is three okay?"

"Hell, no. I've already made arrangements."

Victoria's eyes widened. "Arrangements?"

"You're not going to fool me twice. You try that shit again, and I've seriously got something for you. Today is going to be special for me," Rain said, then laughed.

"You're sick! You need a woman of your own."

"Had one of my own. She turned out to be a pussy licker. I'd rather beat my shit than deal with confused women like you."

Victoria was furious. Naomi had refused to penetrate her. Victoria would rather fuck herself than give her virginity to Rain. "What if I told you I'm not a virgin?"

"You don't want the answer to that. One o'clock," he said, then ended the call.

DéJà was in the kitchen talking to Foxy. Foxy was not properly attired for work. She really had taken the day off. DéJà never knew when to quit. *Whatever.* Victoria spread a sheet on the leather sofa and lay down. Her cell phone rang. Exhaling, she walked to the desk. It was her dad.

"Hey, angel, you forget about your old man?"

"No, Daddy. Can you come now?"

"I'm on my way."

CHAPTER 46

DéJà

An hour later DéJà and Foxy greeted their father in the lobby of Crème. DéJà hurried to hug him first. Foxy wrapped her arms around Mason and wouldn't let go.

"It feels good to hug you too, princess." Their father embraced Foxy as long as she held him.

This was a rare moment when DéJà could not interfere or overrule Foxy. Mason did not allow any of his girls to interrupt the others' hugs. And he'd taught them a man never let go of a woman first.

"Daddy, it's so good to see you," Foxy said.

DéJà stood behind their father's back, mouthed to Foxy, "Let go," then pointed toward the back.

"I love you, Daddy," Foxy said, releasing her embrace.

"Follow me, Dad," DéJà said, leading the way into the kitchen.

Mason laughed at the racks in front the office as DéJà unlocked the wheels. She rolled the carts to the side.

Their dad chuckled. "Is my angel a prisoner in her own office? What in the world is going on?" he asked, standing in the center of the office.

Victoria awakened to the sound of rolling baking racks and her dad's voice. "Daddy?" she said. Her eyes widened. "Daddy!" Victoria sprang from the sofa, dashed to her dad, held him tight.

Mason hugged Victoria.

"Daddy, it's a long and short story," Victoria said, squinting at DéJà and Foxy.

"Well, I've got more time than money when it comes to my queen, princess, and angel." He waited for Victoria to release her embrace, then said, "Let's all sit on the sofa, and angel, you start from the beginning."

DéJà hurried to sit on the opposite side of their father. Foxy sat next to her. Victoria sat on the edge next to Mason.

DéJà noticed their dad hadn't asked Victoria to summarize her story or give him the shortest version and he hadn't told her to start at the end and explain the story backward as he'd done numerous times when they were teenagers. Start from the beginning meant her dad had as much time as it would take to listen to Victoria's problem.

"Y'all already know but do not interrupt me," Victoria said, staring at DéJà.

"Wait," Foxy said. "Don't start without me. I need to lock the front door."

"We have customers," DéJà said.

Foxy whispered, "I'll give them a twenty-dollar coupon and

politely ask them to leave." Foxy was back in the office in less than five minutes.

Victoria exhaled. Her dad held her hand. Mason placed his burly arm around her shoulder. Tears streamed down Victoria's cheeks as she began to explain. "Rain is upset with me."

"This is about him?" Her daddy laughed, then asked, "He's still soaking about your marrying Naomi?"

"It's more than that, Daddy," Victoria said, watching her sisters cling to every word coming out of her mouth.

"I'm sorry, angel. I never really knew him, but each time I saw him on television, he seemed a little off. Like something was always troubling him. Tell Daddy what's bothering my angel."

Victoria swallowed air, took a deep breath, then said, "Rain told me my virginity is his and—"

Mason Montgomery stood. His nostrils flared, eyes watered, lips twisted to one side. He balled his fingers into fists, rubbed his knuckles together, then interlocked his fingers and cracked all his knuckles at the same time. "Keep going."

Victoria closed her eyes, then said, "If I rape you, Victoria, what are you going to do, call the police?"

"That's it!" DéJà yelled. "Rape you? You've been keeping something like this from us? You've been passively acting like all he wanted to do was have sex with you, and that fool threatened to rape you?"

Tears of anger flowed down Mason's face. "DéJà, get your gun. I need to pay this Rain man a visit."

DéJà hurried to their safe, unlocked it, retrieved her .45 caliber, then handed it to her dad.

Mason commanded, "Victoria, let's go."

"This was what I was afraid of." Victoria looked at DéJà and said, "Satisfied?"

DéJà said, "You thought you could handle something like this on your own? Sis, what's wrong with you? Don't worry. I got your back. Remember that. I'm going with you guys."

"Me too," Foxy said.

Victoria couldn't say no to their dad so she got her purse and followed Mason out the door with her sisters trailing. The ride to Rain's house was quiet. They all knew when their dad was outraged, it was best for them not to talk while Mason was thinking.

Victoria sat in the front with her dad, wondering what Naomi would say when she found out about this episode. Maybe Victoria could swear her sisters to secrecy. What was she thinking? Depending on the outcome, Naomi might hear the news before Victoria got home.

Mason parked in Rain's driveway. "Angel, come with me."

It was as though they were all nicknamed Angel, because Foxy and DéJà followed Victoria and Mason to the door. Mason stood at the front door beside Victoria. Victoria stood in front of the peephole, rang the doorbell.

Rain opened the door, opened his mouth.

Bam! Mason's fist landed in the center of Rain's face. Rain tried to slam the door. *Bam!* The second punch caused Rain to stumble, then fall in the doorway.

"Get your punk ass up, or my foot is coming down there to get you," Mason yelled.

Victoria stared at her father's cowboy boots. Her sisters remained quiet. Victoria did not derive pleasure from seeing her dad beat Rain. Honestly, she was afraid of what would happen after the fight was over.

Rain scrambled toward the coffee table.

"His gun!" Victoria screamed.

DéJà beat him to the table, kicked the table over on Rain, then kicked his gun under the sofa. Rain stared at Victoria. If looks could kill, she'd be the one on the floor fighting for her life.

Mason stomped Rain in the chest, left his foot there, applied so much pressure that Rain tried weaseling his way out of the fight but couldn't.

"I'm sorry, Mr. Montgomery. I wasn't serious. Victoria, tell your dad I'd never hurt you."

Mason looked at his daughter. Victoria remained quiet.

Mason placed his other foot on Rain's chest. He pushed his heels into Rain's chest.

Rain wheezed. Tried to speak but couldn't.

"You come see Mason Montgomery when you want to be a man. Do not man the fuck up against any of my girls. If you go near any of them again, I will kill you. That's a promise. And when Mason Montgomery makes a promise, he keeps it. And when your sorry punk ass is dead, who you gon' call mother-fucker? Who you gon' call? Dirty ass cop. I see why your parents disown you."

Mason stepped off Rain's chest and said, "Girls, let's go."

CHAPTER 47

Foxy

There was rage inside every man that could unexpectedly explode at any moment.

Come clean or walk away dirty? Witnessing her father crush Rain's chest, Foxy understood DéJà's concerns. How would she feel if Winton had lied to her, claiming his ex-fiancée was his cousin? Had invited her to their wedding? Allowed her to stand with his family in their wedding photos?

Her dad was so mad he could've killed Rain. Whether Rain was serious or not about raping Victoria, there were near-casualty consequences beyond Rain's imagination for his actions. If Rain knew the type of man Mason was, he would've never threatened to rape Victoria. But Rain hadn't known. And Foxy didn't know what would break her husband, but it was time to squash the love triangle. She had to work things out with her husband or divorce him.

Tuesday night her frustrations had again led her to Dallas's house. She couldn't continue the emotional tug-of-war. Foxy had made her decision. She lay in the bed beside him with his head on her breast. She stroked his hair.

Foxy whispered, "Baby."

"You ready?" Dallas asked, gently biting her nipple.

Foxy slid her hand between her nipple and his mouth. For the first time since she'd known Dallas, his touch irritated her. Foxy wasn't upset with Dallas. She was irritated with her situation; therefore, everything agitated her, including him.

Maybe talking about her problems would help. "I walked in on Winton and Nova yesterday morning."

"He was bold enough to bring a woman to your house?"

Foxy shook her head.

"Yesterday?" he repeated.

Foxy nodded. "Yeah."

"Where? Weren't you at home or at work? How could you walk in on him, if you were supposed to be someplace else?" Dallas leaned his back against the headboard. Scooted a few inches away from her. Folded his arms.

Foxy hadn't seen him behave like an adolescent. She snapped, "I was supposed to be wherever I was. I went to my husband's office."

Dallas stared at her. Disgust coated his eyes. His right eye squinted. "Why?"

Something in the air had folks borderline hostile. Was there a full moon? Her dad beat Rain. Rain acted like a madman. Winton was angry. DéJà was up in arms. Victoria was trying to get in Naomi's good graces. She was heated, and Dallas was pissed off.

Foxy wasn't explaining why. "Forget it, Dallas," she said, hitting him in the face with a pillow. She went to the bathroom, turned on the shower.

Dallas entered the bathroom. "I asked you why. Why did you go to his office?"

Foxy stepped inside the shower, closed the glass door.

Dallas opened the door, stood in front her, closed the door. "Foxy, you are going to tell me why you went to his office. Say it."

She felt cornered by his relentless questioning. Didn't want any sudden outbreaks. "I want my husband back. I mean. I love you, but . . . we can't go on like this forever. It's time for me to make a decision. I decided. That's why I went to his office. Satisfied?"

Dallas stepped out of the shower, left the door open. "No regard for me, huh? If that's what you truly want, I'll help you," Dallas said. "You've made my decision for me. If you go back to him, I'm selling this house and moving out of state to be closer to my girls. I was hoping to surprise you with the house I'd bought for us. Maybe you're right. Maybe it is time to make a change." Dallas blinked away his tears. "Leave my key on your way out, and don't come back unless you're moving out of state with me."

Foxy stepped out the shower too then stared in his eyes. She swallowed hard. Tears streamed down her cheeks. When was he going to tell her he was moving? He hadn't left, and she was already feeling lonely with the thought of not seeing him and jealous of girls she hadn't met. They'd have Dallas and she wouldn't.

"I'm sure you've made the right decision," she said, praying she'd done the same. "I'm gonna miss going out on Saturdays and stopping by in the morning and—" Foxy stopped in the middle of her sentence then stepped back in the shower.

"I'm going to miss you too," Dallas said, closing the shower door.

Foxy placed her hand on the glass. He was too far away to hear her say, "I will always be here for you and I will always be your friend."

CHAPTER 48

Victoria

Butterflies
Orchids
Women
Blossom into beauties
Spreading wings
Peeling leaves unfold
Harvesting colorful wonders to behold
Taken for granted
Oblivious to nature's tenderness
See?
Not
Most precious to the world
The essence of existence
Will cease to exist

When women stop producing
Little boys and little girls

Roaring thunder, darting lightning, darkness overshadowed the day. Victoria stood in the lobby, staring out the window. She'd forgotten to visit the fifty-year-old soccer mom yesterday. She apologized and tried refunding the two thousand dollars the lady had paid, but she insisted that Victoria keep the money and rescheduled the appointment.

A streak of lightning bolted through the dark clouds illuminating the sky. "Y'all ready," Victoria asked her sisters.

Foxy's tote bag was on her shoulder. DéJà's purse was in her hand.

"Maybe we should give it a few more minutes for this downpour to ease up," Foxy said.

"I can't cancel on my client twice. She desperately needs this appointment." Victoria slid her chair to the table with her sisters. "Besides, what am I going to do at home until Naomi gets there?"

"You're still afraid to be home alone?" Foxy asked, then offered, "I'll go home with you and wait until Naomi gets home."

Victoria was afraid. She hadn't seen or heard from Rain since her dad had beaten him. But she felt in her gut that the question was not if but when would Rain seek revenge. "Nah, I'll keep the appointment. Besides, her house is en route to mine and servicing my client will take my mind off of him. Well, looks like it slowed down enough for us to make it to our destinations."

"I'm following you to her house," Foxy said, locking the front door.

"And I'm following you," DéJà said to Foxy.

Victoria hurried to her car in time to beat the next downpour. She started her car, flipped the switch for her windshield wipers. Frantically the blades swept back and forth but still not fast enough to keep pace with the gusty winds slamming rain against her windshield. Victoria drove fifteen miles per hour along Shoreline Drive until she came to Lakeview Pike.

Foxy's headlights flickered, then Victoria's cell phone rang. She tooted her horn at Foxy, ignored her phone. She'd be okay. Victoria pulled into the soccer mom's driveway and waited for the rain to subside, so she could make her way to the woman's front door without getting drenched. She checked her caller ID. "Blocked" appeared on her display. She'd assume it was Rain or the wrong number as no one called her from blocked numbers. There was no message to check.

Victoria opened her car door, screamed, then slammed it shut. "What the hell was that?" Her heart pounded in her throat. She sat staring into what was now moderate rainfall. "Okay, Victoria. You can do this. Get out of the car. You can see her lighted porch from here and you're twenty minutes late."

She opened her car door again, placed both feet on the ground, then closed her door. An overstuffed, soaked baby doll was on the ground beside her car. "Why do parents buy these things for their children?" Stuffed animals had no useful purpose, and parents needed to boycott dolls. What child needed to pretend she was a mother before she learned to read and write?

Knocking on the door, Victoria waited for the woman to answer.

"Hey, I assumed you weren't going to make it in this horrible weather. My kids are home. I picked them up early. Would you like to come in?" she asked, opening the door.

"Sure," Victoria said. "We can talk about whatever you'd like."

The truth was with no window coverings and not being able to see what or who might be outside, Victoria didn't want to be home alone. She didn't want to sit at DéJà's house, and she refused to go with Foxy to Dallas's place. Victoria followed the woman to her living room.

"Let me get you a towel to sit on. I'll be right back."

Victoria stood in front the mantel. *What a lovely family photo.* The man was bald, dark, handsome and had a smile that showed how happy he was in that moment. His eyes beamed. The children clung to him, and he held tight to his wife. Victoria wondered if there was a chance for the soccer mom to remarry her husband.

"Would you like a cup of tea?" the woman asked, handing Victoria the towel.

"Oh, that would be perfect. Nice picture."

"Yeah, I leave it there for the kids. If it were up to me, I'd throw it out," she said, leaving the room.

Victoria wasn't convinced the woman meant that. Her bitterness was in part responsible for her low libido.

She returned with two cups, a white pot with hot water, tea bags, honey, and spoons on a tray. The woman set the tray on the coffee table.

Waiting for the woman to sit, Victoria spread the towel next to her, then settled in on the sofa. She gave the woman time to get comfortable with her presence. "We can talk about whatever you'd like."

She cried. Wiped her tears with one of the cloth napkins from the tray.

"It's okay to grieve over your husband leaving the family. But it's more important to have hope that he'll return. If that's what you want."

She sniffled with the roar of the thunder, then nodded. "I do still love him. I do want him back, but I'm so angry with him."

Victoria was selfish for a moment, reflecting on her marriage. She didn't want to live her life without Naomi.

The woman exhaled. Took a deep breath, then sighed. "I thought I could handle it all, you know. But now that he's gone I have time to think about how he must've felt. I was Mom first. Nothing came before my kids, not even my husband. I was supervisor to thirty employees dealing with their family problems. I came home and cooked because I refused to feed my kids fast food." She chuckled. "See, I'm still programmed. I said my kids, not my family. I cleaned. Checked homework."

Victoria placed her hand on the woman's hand. "Everything you're saying is I, not we. Did you let your husband help?"

She shook her head, closed her eyes. "I assumed I was supposed to do it all. That's what a mother does you know. And when he tried to help, well he was always in my way. I could do it faster and better without him."

Looking into the woman's eyes, Victoria asked, "What does a wife do?"

A flat smile stretched across the woman's face. Tears glazed her eyes but didn't fall. She nodded, rocked. Sat there as if she feared giving the wrong answer.

Victoria changed the topic. "Let's focus on your sex life."

The woman chuckled. "What sex life? I don't have one since he's left. That's why I called you."

She obviously didn't have much of a sex life when her husband was there, but Victoria didn't educate her clients by making them feel guilty. Why had this woman waited until her relationship was over to make a change? If she had exerted this energy while her husband was home, he'd probably be the one sitting on the sofa next to her.

Victoria said, "There's something that I refer to as G-spot genocide or sabotage."

"Huh?"

The storm had quieted. Victoria was ready to go home.

"Mommy, we're hungry. What's for dinner?" the little boy asked.

"Go keep an eye on your sister. I'll be there in a moment."

"But I'm hungry now," the child wailed.

Victoria said, "Another five minutes, okay?" wanting to tell the kid to obey his mother. But the child made Victoria realize the woman had no control over her son.

"I'd better get him something to eat," she said.

Victoria placed her hand on the woman's hand. "Before we meet again, that is if you'd like to continue this session, I need you to do three things. Reconnect with the woman you were before you got married. I want you to expand your sexuality through self-exploration. And I want you to reunite with your husband by inviting him out on a date. But not before you do the first two things I mentioned."

The woman exhaled, stood, escorted Victoria to the door. "Thanks for coming. I mean that."

CHAPTER 49

Winton

Hump day. Winton had to slow things down. Too much happening too soon.

He powered off his computer, stood in his office, looked down at the west side. He sat on the edge of his desk, one foot planted on the floor. "Six point nine million people." If he had to guess, he'd say one out of every ten thousand were truly happy, most of them being children. Not many adults appreciated life. Men were busy trying to get over or stay ahead of whomever they deemed competition. Women sold themselves on corners or over a hot meal at a decent restaurant.

Men like him were defined by money and material possessions. Money equated to success. The underlying definition of success meant a man was worthy of having whatever woman he wanted, especially a younger woman or a beautiful woman. Acer was a real man, and he was right. Winton had nailed

Foxy to a rugged cross. Not caring about any of the women in his life, Winton had a cross for Isis and one for Nova. What he didn't understand was why?

Why had the women in his life cared enough to bear the burden of his bullshit?

Knock. Knock.

"Come in," he said, glancing over his shoulder at Acer and Naomi. "What now? More bad news? Found a way to get rid of me?"

"Depends on how you look at it," Naomi said. "Have a seat."

"I'm good right here," Winton said, sitting on the corner of his desk facing them. Winton didn't take orders from Foxy, and Naomi would not dictate to him where he sat. Winton had more respect for Acer than he had for any woman.

"I think I can help your marriages and mine," Naomi said.

Winton smirked. "Yeah, right."

Acer said, "Leave my marriage out of this."

"Sorry, Acer. I meant marriage referring to Winton. Go along with me," Naomi said. "Acer, what does your wife do for a living?"

Acer frowned. Stared at Winton, then at Naomi. "She works at a pastry shop with her sisters."

"Winton, what does Foxy do?" Naomi asked.

Winton closed, then opened his eyes. "The same as Acer said. Why? I'm not comprehending your point. You do have a point?"

Naomi stood. Her eyes scanned Crème City. She faced the west side. Pointing, she asked, "What's the brightest area on the west side?"

Acer pointed. "That section over there."

"That section over there my partners is Crème Fantasyland," Naomi said, sitting in Winton's chair.

Shaking his head, Winton said, "Fantasyland? Our wives work at the pastry shop. Crème is down the street to the left. Over there." He pointed toward the bakery.

"Correct. Let's see. How can I put this? Our wives are multimillionaires."

Winton laughed. "No disrespect, but they're not multimillionaires from selling five-dollar pastries. That's ridiculous. After overhead and taxes, their annual net is about two hundred fifty thousand tops."

Naomi wasn't making sense. But there were moments in the courtroom when it appeared she was headed down a dead-end road and miraculously she'd present evidence to persuade the jury in her favor.

"Yeah, that would be ridiculous if that were all they were selling. Gentlemen, our wives sell sexual fantasies to the tune of one point five million dollars a year."

Acer frowned. "What exactly does my wife do?"

Naomi smiled. "I'll give you one guess."

"Massages," he said.

Winton shook his head. "Massages would translate into ultimate fighting for your wife. She's too rough."

"Nah, not at home. She's firm. Not rough," Acer explained.

"Acer your wife is a domina, a mistress, a dominatrix," Naomi said.

Acer's eyes enlarged with fascination. He smiled, then bit his bottom lip. "Aw, damn, that's hot. I could see that."

Winton had to know. "And my wife?"

"Let's just say you've been missing out on a good thing. I've booked each of us appointments with our wives. The only question you'll have to answer is, 'What is your fantasy?'" Naomi said, then continued, "The real reason I wanted to talk with both of you is, we need to have the chief of police transferred to another city in a different state. I tried not to get involved, but I'm not going to stand by and let him ruin my marriage."

"Yeah, that was cold how you stole his almost fiancée," Acer said. "Guess you've got skills on and off the case."

"Rain? He's still soaking over your stealing Victoria from him?" Winton added.

Naomi replied, "His attitude would be easy to deal with. It's his actions I don't approve of. Rain desperately wants my wife's virginity and I'm sick of it. He's threatening to send Foxy, DéJà, and Victoria to jail for operating Crème Fantasyland, but he won't because he was Victoria's client after she married me."

Winton was intrigued. Acer listened attentively to Naomi. They agreed to book appointments with their wives and to give Rain an ultimatum to transfer out of state or quit and move out of state. Either way Rain had to move out of Crème City quietly and quickly.

After the meeting with Naomi, Winton was relieved. He wasn't angry or disappointed in his wife. Foxy was wise. She'd married him and maintained her financial independence. Winton had a newfound respect for Foxy and her sisters. His wife was gorgeous, a multimillionaire, and a freak? That was every man's dream. It was time for Winton Brown to wake up and reclaim his wife.

CHAPTER 50

DéJà

Thursday, 4:00 a.m. Acer nudged DéJà. "Precious, you asleep?"

"Huh?" DéJà stretched her arms, hugged her husband.

He cleared his throat, then said, "Mistress DéJà, you asleep?"

Her eyes flashed open. "What did you call me?"

"My apology. Should I say Domina DéJà?"

DéJà sat up. "How'd you find out? It was Foxy, wasn't it? She is miserable in her marriage and mad at me. I never thought—" She stopped speaking midsentence. Retrieved her cell from the nightstand. "I'm calling her right now."

Acer smiled. "Honey, your sister didn't tell me. Naomi did."

DéJà was more furious. She paced the bedroom floor. "So Victoria is the one. Okay. All right. I'll deal with her. But why didn't you say something before now? How long have you known? I can explain."

Things were not going to fall apart in her marriage. The harder DéJà worked to help her sisters, the more jealous they'd become. She sat on the bed next to her husband. "I'm sorry. I should've told you. But it's not like I have sex with my clients."

He touched her hand. "Honey, it's okay. Why don't you prepare breakfast and tell me more while we eat?" He smiled. Kissed her.

DéJà frowned. Her husband was too happy to say he knew. She waited until Acer was in the bathroom, went to the kitchen with her cell phone in hand, called Victoria.

"Not again. What do you want?" she answered.

"It's me. Wake up," DéJà hissed into her Bluetooth, then programmed her oven to four hundred degrees. "I need to speak to you."

She overhead Naomi ask, "Sweetcakes, who is it?"

"It's DéJà. I told you she'd call. And she'd be upset. I'm sure it's about what you told me last night," Victoria replied.

"So, it is true. Naomi told Acer I'm a dominatrix?" DéJà placed twelve strips of bacon on the parchment paper, poured two cups of milk in a pot, then placed the pot on the stove. She added two pats of butter and a teaspoon of salt to the milk, turned the knob between low and medium.

Victoria told her, "And she told her partners about my situation with Rain."

"You need to be at work at five sharp," DéJà said, then hung up.

"I don't smell anything cooking," Acer belted out from the bedroom. "Are you feeding me cereal?"

"Of course not, handsome." He knew she'd never feed him

anything cold. DéJà wanted to call Foxy but didn't have time, so she texted, "Be at work five o'clock sharp."

No time for a fancy breakfast. She put the bacon in the oven, scrambled four eggs, dropped four slices of toast in the toaster, then stirred the grits into the bubbling milk. In ten minutes, everything was ready. She stirred cheese into the grits, then prepared her husband's plate.

Acer sat at the table, ate his grits first. DéJà was quiet. "You know, I'm proud of you, honey," he said.

DéJà kept quiet. Waited for the *But*.

"I understand why you didn't tell me about your business. But . . ."

Okay, this was the part that mattered most. DéJà listened attentively.

Acer continued, "I'd be a fool to end our marriage over your choice of profession. And I understand why you didn't tell me. What man wouldn't be intimidated by a dominatrix?"

"My sisters and I promised not to tell anyone. Our dad doesn't even know. He thinks we own the bakery he bought us. Victoria broke our promise." DéJà stirred her grits but hadn't eaten anything. "I have to talk to her."

DéJà became quiet again wondering what was next. Would their spouses ask them to close Crème Fantasyland? Victoria had no right to do this.

"Honey, don't be upset with your sister. Only a few married people have our kind of love, but Victoria loves Naomi, and like it or not, your sister did what was best for her—"

"What about me?" DéJà asked. "Family is supposed to do what is best for family."

"Hold on. She did do what was best for you."

DéJà shook her head. "No, she didn't."

Acer nodded. "We know about Rain's inappropriate behavior. Happy to hear Mason kicked his ass. Wouldn't look good if we had to do that, but today we will have him removed from his position."

DéJà stared at her husband. "Good." She wouldn't have to solicit help from her contacts. "How?"

Acer shook his head. That meant their plan was confidential.

"Now back to you," Acer said, stuffing the last piece of toast in his mouth. "I want to be your slave, Mistress DéJà."

DéJà smiled at her husband. "Be careful what you ask for." He was going to get it really good. Could she be a great mistress and the perfect mother?

CHAPTER 51

Victoria

True love
Cannot be broken
Every man has flaws
Before you judge someone else
Take a moment
Pause
Consider your mistakes
True love
Can withstand
The toughest tests
When people in love
Do their best . . . to
Understand
Forgive
And
Live and let live

Thursday morning, five o'clock, Victoria stood in the kitchen with Foxy and DéJà. "Forgive me," she said. "I didn't know what else to do."

Foxy stopped kneading dough. "Now, what did you do?"

DéJà told Victoria, "She must not know."

"Know what?" Foxy brushed her hands on her apron. "You're pregnant?"

DéJà said, "That would be great news. I am going to have Adam before you have Solomon."

"Enough baby talk." Victoria summarized what she'd told Naomi, hoping Foxy would understand.

"You told her what!" Foxy yelled. "As if I don't have enough problems in my marriage. Great, Victoria. Save your ass by sacrificing mine!"

DéJà kept kneading her lump of dough. "Calm down, Foxy. I've given this some thought and although what Victoria did doesn't seem like it, it is a good thing."

Victoria's brows rose. DéJà was siding with her? *Whoa.*

DéJà continued, "Let me explain. We, as wives, are more empowered in our marriages than we've ever been before. Nothing changes at Crème or Crème Fantasyland unless we make that decision. We no longer have to hide from our spouses what we do. Winton will come around, and when he does, do not forget my sister. You are in control. Not him."

Victoria's cell phone rang. She wiped her hand, then pulled her phone from her apron pocket. "Hi, Daddy."

"Hi, angel. How are you?" he asked, sounding chipper.

"Great, Daddy. At work with my sisters," she said, winking at DéJà and Foxy.

"Hi, Daddy," her sisters said.

"Tell princess and queen I said hello . . . and . . ."

Victoria's eyes grew larger. "And?"

"Take Saturday off because I'm sending a limo for my girls. I need to find out what's happening with each of you. Y'all have a beautiful day. Love you, angel."

"Love you too, Daddy." Victoria ended the call, then screamed, "Daddy is sending a limo for us Saturday!"

"That's what I'm talking about." Foxy tossed her dough in the air, caught it, then gave DéJà a high five. Foxy asked, "Does Dad know about Fantasyland?"

"No way," Victoria said.

"Great," Foxy commented.

DéJà stared at Victoria, then said, "And let's keep it that way."

CHAPTER 52

Foxy

Thursday evening, Foxy serviced her client, shopped for groceries, bypassed Dallas's house. She missed him already. Had he left yet? Foxy closed the final chapter to their book. Regardless of what happened with Winton, Foxy promised herself never to return to Dallas. She entered her home at six o'clock, sat the groceries on the island.

"Let me help you with dinner," Winton said.

"Ou, you startled me," she said, holding her hand to her breasts.

Winton took a few steps in her direction until they were face-to-face. "Foxy, I'm sorry for hurting you. Baby, please. Forgive me."

Tears streamed down her face. Her husband kissed them away.

"Please, let me start over. I want my wife back," he said.

In her heart and mind, Foxy wondered but didn't ask *Where is Isis? Where is Nova? When would her husband slip into the arms of another woman? Today? Tomorrow?*

"I can't do this by myself. You hurt me so bad," she cried.

"I know, baby. We hurt each other. But I never want to hurt you again."

She wondered how much he knew about Crème Fantasyland. What were his thoughts about her? Foxy hugged her husband.

"I apologize for hurting you. Winton, I love you so much it hurts."

Those were the same words she had spoken to Dallas. She thought about him for a moment. Wondered how he felt now that she was out of his life. A woman didn't fall out of love overnight. A part of her would always love Dallas. Was her husband in love with another woman? Other women?

Winton said, "Go relax. Let me cook dinner for my wife."

"That, I can do," Foxy said.

"Gorgeous?"

"Yes." She paused in the doorway.

"Were you serious about us starting a family?"

Foxy smiled, dipped her hip, jiggled her booty, then said, "Very serious."

CHAPTER 53

Victoria

Smart or clever
Witty or wise
Funny or charming
Deception or demise
Beauty or brains
Heart or courage
Wicked or wild
Tame or tenacious
Bold or cold
Aggressive or aloof
What are the things
That matter to you
The most

Friday morning, three o'clock, Victoria eased out of the bed careful not to wake Naomi. She tiptoed to the guest bedroom, sat on the edge of the mattress. Thanks to Brown, Cooper, and Dawson and her father, there was an interim chief of police for Crème City.

Victoria entered the walk-in closet, turned on the light. The lingerie she'd bought last Sunday hung in the closet. She removed the green and gold bustier, adjusted the lace tie in the back, fastened the three hooks in the front. She eased on the gold thong with green trim, stepped into her green apple heels.

Opening the package from the pleasure store, she cleaned the six-inch green dildo, then removed the harness from the box. Victoria curled her hair, brushed on apple-flavored lip gloss. Took a deep breath before returning to their bedroom.

She straddled her wife, placed the dildo in Naomi's hands, then whispered, "I'm ready."

Naomi smiled. "You sure you want to do this?"

"Positive," Victoria said.

"You look beautiful. Stand up. Let me look at you."

Victoria stood, posed, dropped her ass to the floor, pushed her hip to the side, then slowly stood. "You better act like you want this new pussy," she said, then laughed.

"Hold that pose. Let me get my camera," Naomi said.

Naomi powered on the video recorder. She must have taken a hundred photos.

"Enough," Victoria said, holding her hand in front the camera lens.

She watched her wife strap on. Victoria lay on the bed, lifted her legs in the air. Closed her eyes. She felt the tip of the dildo press against her hymen. Victoria inhaled, held her wife's shoulders. "Keep going," she said.

Naomi penetrated her a little more.

Victoria's eyes closed tighter as she clenched her teeth. Her nails dug into Naomi's shoulders.

"We can stop if you'd like," Naomi said.

Unable to speak, Victoria shook her head.

Naomi continued taking her time penetrating Victoria until the dildo was completely inside. Victoria exhaled. The stinging sensation wasn't pleasurable. She could've used a clit stimulator or put a bullet or butt plug in her ass, but Victoria wanted to experience her first time with her wife without enhancements.

Naomi kissed her lips. "Sweetcakes, you are more beautiful than the sunrise."

"Is this what I waited thirty years for? I sure hope this vaginal penetration feels better next time." Glad the mystery was finally over, Victoria kissed Naomi. "I love you."

CHAPTER 54

DéJà

Friday morning, three o'clock, DéJà stood in front of Acer. She stared down at him. She adjusted her black patent leather knee-length trench coat. She wore nothing underneath. Her thigh-high boots were six inches short of touching her pussy.

"Lick my boot."

Acer smiled, flicked his tongue. "Yeah." He held her boot in his hands, then licked the toe, the sides, and the ankles as if giving her a spit shine.

"Do not speak unless I give you permission," DéJà said, not believing her husband was enjoying being her slave.

"Yes, Mistress-wife-precious DéJà," he said.

Hmm. She liked the way he said that. She suppressed her smile, resumed being serious. "Stick out your tongue and crawl behind me," she said, walking into the living room, through the kitchen, then back to the bedroom.

Whack! She couldn't resist slapping his incredible naked ass.

"Harder, please, Mistress-wife-precious DéJà," he begged.

"You feel it this time," she said, hitting her husband a little harder. "Open my coat," she commanded. "Then I want you to suck my nipples."

"Yes, Mistress," he said untying her belt. "Oh, my God. Look at this," he said like he hadn't seen her naked before.

Passionately he cupped her breasts together and sucked like a baby breast-feeding. He played with her nipples, kissed them, sucked, then buried his face in her breasts.

"That's enough. Down on all four," DéJà commanded.

Acer knelt before her.

DéJà placed her fists on her hips, spread her feet. Her naked upper body, trench coat, and boots made her feel like a sexy porn star. "Lick my pussy. Slow."

"Ou, yes, indeed, Mistress," Acer said, sucking her shaft.

"I said lick, not suck," DéJà commanded.

"Forget this," Acer said, throwing her on the bed. "I've gotta have my pussy."

DéJà tried to get on top and he playfully slammed her back onto the mattress. "I'm in control now," he said. "Suck my dick, precious."

DéJà frowned, then said, "All right."

"All right, what? Call me Master Acer."

"I believe I've created a monster," DéJà said. Obeying her husband's command, she joyfully sucked his dick until he came in her mouth.

There was no rush to have kids. She'd give her husband a child, but DéJà was no longer interested in having a baby before Foxy.

Chapter 55

Foxy

Friday morning, three o'clock, Foxy awakened in her husband's arms.

Last night, dinner was perfect. Not the food Winton prepared. Dinner was perfect because they talked like a husband and wife should. He spoke, she listened. She talked, he heard her and responded. They agreed to start anew. Promised not to dwell on or discuss their infidelity.

Foxy glanced at the bootees she'd placed on the nightstand. "Definitely the blue one." She wanted a boy first, then a girl. She peeled away the covers to reveal the most attractive man alive. She wrapped her mouth around his dick.

"Gorgeous, wow. Good morning to you too," he said, pulling her on top of him. He kissed her lips, her cheeks, her forehead and chin. "Gorgeous?"

"Yes," Foxy said, straddling her husband.

He flipped her onto her back, pressed her legs together, raised them in the air, bit her cheek, then licked her pussy.

Foxy came on his tongue, parted her legs so her husband could get closer. His mouth covered her lips. His tongue roamed over her pussy. She clenched her PC muscles.

Winton braced himself on top of her. His dick was fully erect. Her shaft completely engorged.

She felt his head penetrate her. Tingling on the inside, her entire body responded to him. Tears of joy, not sorrow, flowed. She curled her arms under his, held him with passion and compassion.

Her husband stroked deeper. He moved his ass the way he had when they used to slow dance. A slow grind. He dipped, then pushed. Dipped, then pushed his dick deeper inside her.

Foxy prayed the moment would last forever. She rolled her pussy onto his dick each time he dipped. She gripped his dick with her vaginal muscles. He pulsated to her beat. She'd forgotten how in sync they were.

"Look, honey," she said, pointing at the bootees. "Which one do you like more?"

Winton rubbed her ass, then said, "This one." Her husband pressed his lips to her ear. He whispered, "I want you to cum for me, gorgeous. Then I'm going to make you squirt."

The tone of his voice, the touch of his hands, the conviction of his love made Foxy gush like she'd never done before.

EPILOGUE

Mason

Let the boys be boys . . . and men be men.

All men should be man enough to educate their daughters. Tell them the truth about the scandalous ways of lying and cheating men. Tell their girls, "Never fall for the bullshit, and stop falling so easily in love with men who don't deserve you." Teach their daughters how to man up by marrying up and staying one up on their mate.

Marrying up didn't always mean marrying a man with more money. A wise woman saw the added value in extending her hand to a judge, a notable attorney, the CEO or COO of his corporation, a scintillating athlete, a brilliant nerd, a geek on the cutting edge of technology, or any man of power and good character who would benefit her and their children.

Fathers should squash their egos, claiming, "No man will ever mistreat my daughter." Men who stroked their egos were straight up trying to impress women with false pretense. Women should recognize that the men who boasted the loudest did and owned the least. Most men hadn't kept a guarantee of respect for the next man's daughter.

Their lame intentions didn't mean much to their daughters, especially if their daughters seldom saw them. The man who'd brag about his manhood, then bail out on the mother of his child—financially and emotionally—transforming himself from a sperm donor to an absentee dad should keep his dick to himself. Why should any woman respect a man who doesn't respect her? Words without actions were a waste of everyone's time.

Lounging poolside at his mansion, Mason smiled, admiring the three beautiful women playing under his waterfall, his three girls. Foxy had his no-nonsense attitude and her mother's voluptuous body. Victoria possessed his sensitive side and her mother's slender frame. And Déjà, like him, was protective of her sisters and she had her mother's sexy athletic build. The family bond he instilled in his daughters was unbreakable by their mothers and by him. By his design, Mason's girls genuinely loved one another more than they loved their spouses.

Honesty was his virtue. Real men didn't lie to women. Weak men (afraid to face their own truth) lied to themselves and the women in their lives. Despicable men used women, beat women, degraded women, cheated on women. Mason never worried about how men should treat his daughters. He focused on teaching his girls how to detect and denounce lying men and how to recognize a good man or, in Victoria's case, a good woman.

Mason didn't need a marriage license to treat a woman like

a lady. His father had taught him to always tell the truth in bed and in business, saying, "Son, a dishonest man is a coward. He's scared that if a woman knew the truth about him, she'd kick his ass to the curb. A man who does not protect and put his family first will never prosper. And a man who lies should be ostracized."

The greatest foundation for any man was a smart woman. If a man tore a woman down, he'd torn himself down. If he disrespected women, he first disrespected himself. If a man was so preoccupied with chasing a dollar and his dream that he left his woman behind, he'd fail every time. And if he did achieve material gain, he'd lose his soul in the process. Only when a man cherished women would he prosper.

He'd taught his girls that women had the right to know the truth. Women had the right to know how many partners a man had; whether he was heterosexual, bisexual, trysexual, a sex addict; if he was married, engaged, committed; and how many children he had before kissing him or taking off her clothes. Most of all, Mason realized that given the facts, women had the intelligence to decide if they wanted to become emotionally or sexually involved.

The three gorgeous, independently wealthy women who'd agreed to have his children each wanted a child but no husband. Mason wanted kids. A wife like Déjà's mom would've been nice, but her rejecting his proposal made him realize a wife was not a necessity. His relationship with his daughters' mothers was perfect.

Mason Montgomery loved women and enjoyed his freedom to have as many women as he wanted by his side and in his bed. He was up-front, courteous, and respectful of his women. His ego was reserved for business acquisitions. Mason didn't want a harem or house full of baby mamas catering to his needs. For that he'd hired housekeepers, landscapers, and a personal assistant.

Mason gestured at his server, then asked, "Is everything ready?"

"Yes, Mr. Montgomery," she said. "Everything is ready."

"Tell my girls to get out of the pool. Have them shower and get dressed so I can give them their presents before we leave."

"Will do," she said, heading toward the waterfall.

Mason stood, smiled at his girls, then retreated to his bedroom. Tall white Italian arches graced the entrance. There were no doors separating the walls inside his home. White bed linens, antique furniture, and forest green carpet decorated his room. No woman had the pleasure of entering his bedroom unless she knew her worth. He refused to sex a woman simply because he could, and Mason never sexed a woman he didn't respect.

Entering his bathroom, Mason stepped into the shower, turned the gold knobs, and stood under the dome. Water gushed onto his head as though he was standing under the waterfall over his pool. He stretched his neck side to side, noting to have his assistant schedule him a massage and a facial. Mason never shaved himself or cut his own hair.

Toweling off, he slipped into his boxers, then his white linen pants. Tightening the drawstring, he buttoned up his shirt leaving the top three buttons loose and slipped on his tan leather sandals, then headed downstairs to his family room. Quietly he sat waiting for his daughters to enter.

Déjà entered first, sat to his right as she'd done since they were teenagers. "Morning, Daddy." Her open-toe high heels were crossed at her ankles. Her hair flowed over her shoulders and down her back.

Victoria walked in next wearing a long purple, green, and gold halter-top dress that flattered her figure. She sat to his left, crossed her legs. "I love you, Daddy." Her hair was neatly pent up with soft curls gathered in the back.

Foxy never walked. She strutted into the room, then sat on the pillow at his feet. Not because he'd made her do so. She had to be equally as close to him as his other daughters. "Daddy, you're the best." Her long legs wore a knee-length dress that complemented her curvaceous frame.

"My three favorite ladies," Mason said, adoring his daughters. "Come, I have a surprise for you."

Mason held Foxy's hand, helping her rise from the pillow, then extended his hands to his other daughters. Leading the way, he entered the living room. Three dozen of the best long-stemmed roses sat in real crystal vases on the table before them, one for each of them.

"Foxy, you are my precious daughter. I'm proud of you, baby. You deserve the best," he said, handing her a square black box.

"Thank you, Daddy," Foxy said. She winked at Déjà, then mouthed, "I got mine first."

"Victoria, you are my lovely angel. I'm proud of you, baby. You deserve the best," he said, handing her a square black box.

Victoria smiled soft and wide, winked at DéJà, then hugged her dad. "I'm so glad you're our father. Thanks."

"Déjà, you become more like me each day. You are my beautiful queen. I'm proud of you, baby. You've always been the leader. Thanks for protecting your sisters."

Nodding upward at Foxy and Victoria, Déjà gave him a warm smile and firm hug. "You taught us well, Daddy. Thanks."

Mason smiled as Foxy made the first move toward her bouquet. Victoria and Déjà sniffed their flowers. He watched his girls embrace one another. Mason was pleased. "Open the boxes," he said.

He'd done well with spoiling and educating his girls. There wasn't much their spouses could give them that he hadn't. He'd taught his daughters to value every part of their body. Maybe he'd taught them too well.

Foxy screamed, "Oh, my God! Daddy!"

Victoria and Déjà joined in the excitement when they saw their five-carat black diamond solitaires.

"Let's go. We have to find settings for these diamonds . . . and . . ."

"And?" Victoria said.

Mason replied, "I have one more surprise for my girls. I want you to meet my fiancée. Your father is getting married for the first time."

Book Club Questions

1. How important is sex in a marriage? Could you be married and have an affair with your ex? Do you feel Foxy was justified in having an affair with Dallas when her husband wasn't meeting her needs?
2. Was Victoria cheating on Naomi?
3. Can a person who is a virgin cheat in a relationship? How?
4. Did DéJà betray her husband or her sisters in any way?
5. Do you believe Winton will remain faithful to Foxy?
6. Do you feel an affair can strengthen a marriage? Why?
7. How would you view an officer of the law who raped someone? Should that person go to jail? Do you think the justice system would protect the victim or the officer?
8. Could you be married on Mondays, meaning could you go through the motions of being married, have an affair, and cater to your spouse once a week?
9. Should a woman in the adult industry—strippers, escorts, madams, sex coaches—reveal to her fiancé the truth about what she does to earn her money?

10. Should a woman let her fiancé know how much money she has? Should she have a bank account of her own? If you're married, do you have a separate bank account in your name only?

11. Could you teach women how to masturbate or ejaculate? Could you be a dominatrix or sex slave?

12. Would you have stayed married to Winton if he were your husband?

13. What things do the characters have in common? What do you have in common with the characters?

Would You Marry for Love?

A man worthy of diamonds has paid for the pleasure of pearls. Not the kind embedded in oysters. The precious pearl (clitoris) of a real woman costs men time and money. If a man doesn't provide for a woman and cum bearing gifts that make her smile from the inside out, then no matter how much he loves her, he hasn't earned her hand in marriage. Seriously, if a man doesn't impress a woman, he's not the man for her.

Love and marriage, sad but true, you can have one without the other. Would you prefer love without marriage or marriage without love? Can you have both? Yes, if you give what you'd like to receive. I say this because before and after people marry, their expectations far exceed their willingness to reciprocate.

Life is simple. People are complex.

You don't deserve to receive the things you're unwilling to give. Love. Respect. Honesty. Compliments. Money. Time.

Great sex. It matters tremendously to what degree you please your partner. If you sacrifice selflessly for your mate and family, you deserve the same consideration. If either you or your partner is selfish, your relationship will fail.

Love is the pinnacle of marriage, not the foundation.

It takes a lot of work to reach the highest heights of your goals and your relationships with others, marriage included. Most folk see love in the reverse. "If I love you, you won't cheat on me." That's not true. Instead, before getting married, one should say, "If you cheat on me, I will still love you," and mean it. Infidelity happens. You must determine what's significant to you.

Honesty is the foundation of marriage, but most people aren't truthful with their mates or themselves about everything from losing weight to, you know, that lil' somethin' somethin' you keep on the side so you can hit it, lick it, and stick it every now and then. Or the ex-lover, who you secretly reserve a sacred place for in your heart, wondering if you'll ever see them again. Or those bad spending habits or addictions you try to hide from your mate, fearing they won't love you anymore if they knew . . . if they knew the truth about you. So you go on living lies and having greater expectations of your mate than you have of yourself. Sometimes the things you do would drive you insane if you found out your mate was doing the same, yet you do them anyway. Worst of all you're ill prepared for your consequences and demise, so when your partner discovers your truth, you suddenly have a conscience. You cry, apologize, or even beg for forgiveness only to revert to your deceitful ways.

Realistically, marriage should be viewed as a partnership, an exchange of goods for services. Most marriages are rooted in some form of religion that dictates marriage should be based on love.

The origin of marriage vows is older than any existing marriage, yet most folk recite them anyway. Clueless about their true meaning or what the vows mean to them, they cheerfully oblige when the person presiding over their ceremony says, "Repeat after me." Repeat what? Vows someone you don't even know came up with thousands of years ago? How clever is that?

From religious-based moral safeguards to the biblical duty to procreate to the social definitions of right and wrong to the ultimate belief that family is the fundamental unit of society and the guilt of fornication that states marriage is truly the only legitimate way to indulge in sex, couples stand at the altar craving sex (not necessarily with their partner). That's what marriage comes down to, you know. Partners are reduced to sex objects of desire. They worry more about who their spouse is having or thinking about having sex with than about the overall health of their mate.

I've said it before in another book, and I'll say it now, "We should have a *Worldwide Orgy Day* so we can all fuck and fuck up at the same time." Is initiating sex a husband's duty? A wife's obligation? Would you stop loving your spouse if you caught them cheating? Why? Should you treat your spouse like a child, place them on time-out for bad behavior, make them sit and wait until . . . you're in the mood, not to make love but to have sex? That's cool as long as you don't mind them getting a lap dance in that corner or having their needs met elsewhere in the interim. Let's explore a value that is dormant in today's society . . . morals.

Morals. If most people upheld their own, many more relationships would succeed. But hey, who needs morals when all sins are weighted equally? Shouldn't adults have the right to be happy without feeling guilty for indulging in pleasure? And if being happy means having extra, as in extramarital affairs, then pleasantries are indeed plentiful. Especially since most, if not all, married people merely have a permit. A license that excludes any mention of fidelity, thereby permitting their partner to have sex outside of the marriage. Like it or not, "You can't break what you didn't take."

One can marry for love if they'd like. I wouldn't because most married folk do at some point during their marriage fall out of love with one another and in love or lust with someone else. I swear I didn't make this up. The next time you encounter a married couple that's not on their honeymoon, notice how their marriage has grown into what they should've had from the very beginning, a partnership. Contracts allow individuals to sue for specific performance, breach, monetary recourse, etc. A contract has *enforceable* rights; a license does not. You may disagree with my interpretations, but feel free to email me at (honeyb@marymorrison.com) for the list of *enforceable* rights for a marriage license.

A contract is executed and legally binding by both parties, a license is not. I hear you disagreeing with me on this one, but a contract requires performance. A license grants privileges and permission but doesn't require you to do a damn thing. People stand before one another reciting vows while asking themselves, "What the hell am I doing?" So their "I do" really means, "I think so, but what if this doesn't work out? Am I going to have to start over in five, ten, fifteen, twenty, twenty-five, or thirty years?" If you had a contract, you could've included a "No Penalty, I Quit" opt-out clause. That means you get to keep your shit, I get to keep my shit.

Then why get married in the first place, right? Because people not only want, they need somebody to love. That's natural. Well, in the land of the free and the home of the brave, we do marry for love or lust, but at some point, the two overlap and eventually overwhelm people. Especially when the love or lust is redirected to someone outside the marriage. So how can you control someone's actions? You can't.

The couples who marry for material gain—you know, for richer or richer—become stuck like Krazy Glue to one another because neither can afford the lifestyle they've acquired on their own, or they are just too damn selfish to give up half. Especially if they've contributed more than half of the household income. . . . Aw, damn. Should've gotten a prenuptial. Right?

That's why I believe marriage licenses should be abolished. There are no warranties or guarantees with any license. Married couples allow government to dictate their divorce. You don't need a marriage license to grant power of attorney to your mate, and you hold the right to terminate a power of attorney whenever you want without legal ramifications. If we are free-thinking citizens, then we should have to tell the other person why we want to marry them. I don't mean the things you think the other person wants to hear. Keep it real. Write it down. And draw up contracts that are reviewed by independent attorneys.

Here's my suggestion. If you want to marry someone, don't combine your assets. You'll soon discover how much they really love you. Start off new. Like you didn't have assets before you met them. Consciously grow your relationship. Each party should earn their keep. Being a housewife is cool, but list housewife as your occupation in the contract and make sure you're compensated, whatever that means to you.

Balance the money. Balance the power. If a man wants a trophy wife (you know, the former Miss this or that or the supermodel), then her monetary compensation should be included in the contract. If a woman wants a boy toy, he should be compensated too.

But in reality, if you don't know your self-worth before saying "I do," I can guarantee you one thing, your self-worth will diminish after executing a marriage agreement. "What the hell? Why would HoneyB say something like that? Marriage is a good thing. Right?"

It can be. But it's not good for insecure people who are looking for a reason to be unhappy. I mean checking cell phones, pockets, cars, computers, etc. Go on, marry someone who starts tracking your every move with a damn GPS device. What does that prove at the end of the day? You should've married for money so your answer to the Southwest commercial question "Wanna get away?" wouldn't be, "I can't afford to."

Karma. What goes around comes around. True. But most folk prefer to live by, "Do as I say, not as I do." Oh, hell with that mentality; one might as well draw up the divorce decree before walking down the aisle. Hmm, that's not a bad idea.

Foxy, Déjà, and Victoria Montgomery are the leading characters in *Married on Mondays*. Every woman should be fortunate enough to have Mr. Mason Montgomery as her father, a man who not only tells, but also teaches his daughters how to think like men, saying, "Men are like jobs, accept the job with the best benefits—insurance, working conditions, living environment, severance package, and pension plan."

In a perfect world, women would be free-thinking individuals whose opinions were valued by men. He'd listen to how her day went, and hear her. He'd touch her and feel her. He'd propose to her without being coaxed or given an ultimatum. He'd care about her overall well-being. He'd put her first. Respect her. He wouldn't try to control her. He'd realize caring for the children was not her main responsibility but their mutual obligation. He'd close his eyes while kissing her. He'd open his heart and protect hers. In a perfect world, a man would show and tell his woman how much he loves her.

In return, she'd support her man no matter what. She'd believe in his dreams no matter how far-fetched. Cook his meals. Wash his clothes. Stroke his ego. Warm his heart with her eyes. Rear their kids. She'd make their house his home. In a perfect world, marriage indeed would be satisfaction guaranteed or your love back.

On Saturday, March 14, I was driving home (to Oakland) from Anaheim from the Big West Conference after watching my son, Jesse, play in the men's basketball tournament, listening to a country-and-western radio station. I heard a song that I instantly fell in love with. Toby Keith's lyrics, "I wish somehow I didn't know now what I didn't know then," resonated with me as I hope they will with you.

Some things are better left untold.

Poetry Corner

False Faces
Hide not behind lies
But others' lives
Pointing fingers
Shifting blame
Tarnishing names
Playing games
Going insane
Creating casualties
Escaping their reality
It's all a formality
Of
Self-preservation
Survival of the fittest prevails
All the rest
Can go to hell

Instincts Originate
To protect
Failure to detect
Life or death?
Russian roulette
To ignore
The churn in the gut
Is there
Something more powerful
More aware
Alerts of danger
Ignore
Beware

Daddy's Girls
Mean the world
To a man whose backbone
Is strong
Would give his life
To protect and defend
Real men
Tirelessly fight
Man to man
No sneaking or hiding
Real men
Fight for what's right
Real men
Fight

Real men
Not Daddy's little girls
Neither a woman
Nor his wife

Ticktock

Time waits
For no one
A fraction of a second
Determines fate
Could've told the truth
Hesitation
Should've made a move
Procrastination
A second
An hour
A day
Too late
Devastation
What are you waiting . . .
For
Ticktock

I Don't Suck

Lots of men come my way
Some want a date
Others want to play

Then there are the ones
Who simply want head
Irrespective of the fact
That they haven't paid
For a damn thing

Then there are the men at the club
Who wait until it's late
And they want to take you home to fuck
But refuse to take you on a date
They don't want to leave alone

Two o'clock in the morning
Hard dicks galore
So fucking hard
They could wax the floor

Men stroking erections
With no affection
Spittin' game that's lame
They wanna kiss your lips
Pound your hips
Make you scream their name

Those are the same men
Who walked past you
With a drink in their hand
Acted like they did not see . . . you
And did not speak . . . to you

Those are the same men
Who moved out your way
So you could get to the bar
They didn't offer to pay
Or bother to stay
They checked you out from afar

But right around two
He made his move
That's when you heard him say
Girl, I've been watching you all night
Your body is tight
And the mood is right
Make love to me tonight

Um, um . . .
Excuse me

Are you the same man
Who didn't bother to speak
Or buy a drink
Or ask my name
And now you think
I'm supposed to open my legs
Take you to my place
And give you head

Listen to me
'Cause I'm going to say this once

I don't suck
When my throat is dry
And my stomach is rumbling
And when my rent isn't paid

I got my nails done
My hair is fierce
I paid for this lingerie
That's clinging to my ass
So, no thank you
Keep your dick
I politely pass

Girl you missin' out
On the best sex of your life

Well, I'll take that chance
'Cause
A dick just don't taste right
When I'm walking in broad daylight
'Cause I don't have gas in my car
I don't want to fuck
And I don' already told you
I don't suck

Listen to me
'Cause I'm going to say this once

This good pussy

Can do flips
She can do tricks
My tight pussy
Can make you whipped

Listen to me good
'Cause I'm going to say this once

Your ass ain't slick
And I don't suck
No broke-ass dick

Acknowledgments

I thank God for His creations—birds, bees, flowers, trees, you, and me.

I am grateful for my blessings seen and unforeseen.

I pray the words I write will encourage you to think about your life. I appreciate my readers who love my work; I sincerely thank you. To those who are uncomfortable with erotica, sex, or sexuality, yet you continue to read my books, I appreciate you. When we open our hearts and minds, we find the beauty in our differences is learning to understand one another and not judge our family, friends, and neighbors.

Wholeheartedly, I invite you to either step outside of or slip inside of your comfort zone as you read HoneyB. HoneyB is my pseudonym. Mary Beatrice Morrison is my birth name. My HoneyB novels are erotic. My Mary B. Morrison novels are sexually explicit. All of my books have thought-provoking plots and messages relating to relationship issues, some of which you may have encountered.

Jesse Bernard Byrd, Jr., my loving son, is my perfect child. He brings me joy. Seeing his face lifts my spirit. Son, I'm proud of you and of your accomplishments as a columnist for the University of California, Santa Bárbara *Daily Nexus* newspaper, your determination, dedication, and commitment to the UC Santa Barbara Men's Basketball team, and your being an honorable gentleman. You are a brilliant writer. Keep rising to the top.

There are two more gentlemen I congratulate with pride and joy, my nephews who graduated from Houston High School in Warner Robins, Georgia: Janard Bryant Morrison for his commitment to the United States Marines and Roland Henry Morrison for continuing on to college. I pray for your continued health, safety, success, and happiness.

To my editor, Karen R. Thomas, you're the best. Your endless smile brightens my day. Even when you are overwhelmed with professional and personal obligations, you find time to respond to my concerns. Thanks so much.

To Linda A. Duggins, my fabulous publicist, who gets it all done without breaking a sweat, I thank you. Jamie Raab, you are wonderful. Thanks for having me as one of your authors. And to LaToya Smith, congratulations on becoming an editor, and I appreciate the fact you are never too busy to assist me.

Andrew Stuart, my guardian angel agent. Thanks for understanding my needs as an author, a businesswoman, a single mom, and an individual. There are many words to describe your undying support but *genuine* comes to mind first. I'm grateful for all you do.

Both of my parents have made their transitions into eternity, my mother when I was nine years old and my father when I was twenty-four years old. Now they are my angels in heaven. They've blessed me with the greatest siblings—Wayne Morrison, Andrea Morrison, Derrick Morrison, Regina Morrison, Margie Rickerson, and Debra Noel. I honestly don't know what I'd do without each of you. Thanks for keeping it real.

To my family and friends who support me 24/7, I love you: Treece Johnson-Mallard, James Mallard, Bryan Turner, Valerie Jackson, Angela Lewis-Morrison, John Ferguson, Danette Morrison, Roland Morrison, Desi Rickerson, Edward and LaTasha Allen, Rachelle Davis, Lauren Davis, Angela Davis, Felicia Polk, Vyllorya A. Evans, Carmen Polk, Malissa Tafere, Onie Simpson, Barbara Cooper, Valeta Sutton, Eve Lynne Robinson, Mother Bolton, Shannette Slaughter, Marissa Monteilh, Kimberly Kaye Terry, Noire, Richard C. Montgomery, and my McDonogh 35 Senior High (New Orleans) peeps . . . "Ya heard me."

Mad love and thanks to Michael Baisden, the Bad Boy of radio, for having me as a recurring guest on your show. I appreciate your generosity. And Michael, you know I have to thank George Willborn too. George, you are so hilarious. I love you both.

Real love to my KBLX family, Nikki Thomas, Kevin Brown, Jacques Pryor, and Maria Costen, for heavily supporting me and my "Tell It All" relationship real talk with no limits venues in the Oakland/San Francisco Bay area.

To Bernard Henderson of Alexander Book Company in San Francisco, Vera Warren-Williams, owner of Community Book

Center, Michele Lewis, owner of Afro-American Book Stop (both in New Orleans), to Gwen Richardson of Cuschcity.com in Houston, and to Curtis Bunn of Atlanta, I thank you for always including me at your national book events, in store at Alexander, Essence Music Festival in New Orleans, the National Black Book Festival in Houston, and the National Book Club Conference in Atlanta.

There are many of you who support me by reading, selling, or promoting my novels, and our paths may cross via email, between the pages of my novels, or in spirit, but for everything you do, I say, "Thank you, and I wish you the best of everything."

In loving memory of E. Lynn Harris, a friend and a man with a passion and compassion for life and people. I'm honored to have shared precious moments with him. His spirit and contribution to the literary world will dwell in my heart forever.

Oh, I cannot conclude without giving a shout-out to my FaceBook friends. If you are not my friend yet, please make a request at www.facebook.com/mary.b.morrison.

Feel free to email me at mary@marymorrison.com and sign up for my HoneyBuzz Newsletter at www.marymorrison.com.

DARIUS JONES

by Mary B. Morrison

Darius

CHAPTER 1

For once in my life, I was happy. I mean genuinely happy.

My mother, wife, and son were my world. My mother was my rock. My wife was my rib. My son kept me focused on what was important in life . . . family.

Some thought me to be arrogant, cocky, a shit talker, an asshole. Others thought of me as *the shit*. Fans begged for my autograph, photo ops, or lingered near the arena exit to touch my jersey or shake my hand. Groupies stalked me, followed me from city to city; some even knocked on my hotel door, praying for a chance to suck or ride my dick.

I considered myself the best. I was the best in the professional basketball league. I worked out and practiced every day. Shot around on game day. I lived and breathed basketball. I could easily get into a zone and block out people and the things happening around me.

My wife taught me to make time for her and my son, who by the way wasn't her son. I slipped up and got my stepsister pregnant. At first, that was the worst mistake of my life. But having my son in my life was no mistake. Couldn't have created him with any other woman.

My mother showed me that people are more important than things and that things happen. Not beyond our control, but sometimes because we lost control. Letting ourselves go with the flow, we occasionally chased the people and things we felt were good for us, but not important to us. Mom said, "Sometimes we're right. Sometimes we're wrong. Darius, what's more important than making mistakes is learning from your mistakes."

I was happy my wife hadn't given up on me. Fancy was the only woman who could satisfy me. In my heart, my head, and the bedroom, that woman drove me fucking nuts. My nuts were hers and hers alone. I wasn't tripping off of no groupie chick tryna suck or ride my dick. I'd had enough head to know no woman sucked my dick better than my wife. And Lord, no woman had fucked me senseless until I'd met LadyCat.

MaDear, my grandmother, probably rolled over in her grave whenever she heard me say or even think of using the Lord's name in vain. But I was sure the Lord didn't mind my using his name to express how excited my wife made me.

I didn't ask my wife to sign no prenuptial agreement. I came from a self-made millionaire mom. Made my own millions. Although my wife had earned her own millions selling real estate, my money was my wife's money. Money didn't make Darius Jones. Took me awhile to realize that shit.

I looked at my wife and smiled. "Baby, I love you so much, I want to marry you again."

Her hand was at the top of the steering wheel. She slid her hand down and around, turning onto Wilshire Boulevard, then letting the wheel slide between her fingers as the tires realigned with our SUV. Damn, she had the sexiest mannerisms. Her hair flowed over her bare shoulders. Her titties were perched high under her summer dress.

"I'd marry you again in a heartbeat too," she said, smiling back at me.

"Daddy, I want you to marry my mommy. Can you marry her too?" my son asked.

Kids say the darndest things, but my son was brainwashed by his mother, Ashlee. No telling what would come out of his mouth. Ashlee had planted so many seeds in his head about our being a family one day and how he shouldn't call my wife "mother" or "mommy" but to call her by her first name, Fancy.

Fancy chuckled at DJ. I turned to my son, who was strapped in his car seat, and said, "My man, marrying two women would send your daddy to jail. You don't want me to go to jail, do you?"

"Nope, but Mommy does."

I shook my head, then dialed my mom. She answered, "Hey, baby."

"Ma, what's wrong?" I asked right away. The tone of her voice indicated she was disturbed about something.

Fancy looked at my face. She frowned too. I held up my hand to my wife, letting her know I'd handle whatever was bothering my mom.

"Nothing for you to worry about, sweetheart."

"You still joining us for dinner tonight?" I asked her. "We're almost at Wolfgang's Steakhouse.

"I'll call you back and let you know. I'm not sure," she said somberly.

"Is that Grant Hill guy pressuring you? Is he tripping

again? I told you I can make him disappear from your life permanently."

"He wants me to go to a movie premiere with him tonight. I wouldn't mind if his ex Honey wasn't going to be there. Just not sure I'm feeling up to any drama, that's all."

"I'm sending a car for you, Ma. Come have dinner with us. It's not often we're back in our hometown of LA at the same time."

"I'm okay, sweetheart. I'll call you in a few and let you know what I decide. Give my lil' man a kiss for me."

"That I can do too, Ma. I love you. Thanks for always being there for me. Let me be there for you."

Mom sniffled, then said, "I love you too, sweetheart. Bye."

DJ was too far away for me to kiss his cheek, so I kissed my hand, touched my son's hand, then said, "That's from your grandma."

I had no problem showing my son love and affection. Had no problem keeping him in line either. Didn't want him to become the spoiled brat I was. I'd had so many women, I'd lost count by the time I'd met Fancy. I was glad I hadn't married Maxine, my first fiancée. She'd contracted HIV. Sometimes I wondered if that was my fault. Wasn't sure Maxine would've cheated on me had I not cheated on her. With my promiscuous ways, one would think I would've contracted the disease, not her. Maxine had two lovers: me and the dude that infected her. I was the male whore, so to speak, and not ashamed of my past, mind you. My whoring around before settling down made me a better man.

The women I'd fucked, including my son's mother, Ash-lee, had come to me with their pussies on silver platters.

Well, that wasn't exactly true about Ashlee. I pursued her. There was something pure and innocent about her. Ashlee was beautiful, friendly, and naïve. She believed in me, like my mom. And perhaps, at one time, I was in love with Ashlee. Until she fucked my brother. I would've cut her off, dismissed her, gotten rid of her, all of that, if she'd fucked any other man.

But for her to have fucked my scheming, scandalous, trifling, conniving brother Kevin, the only brother I had alive since my brother Darryl died, was too much. I tried to bring Kevin's ass up, and he tried to bury me by stealing over a million dollars of my money and fucking Ashlee. Talk about ashes to ashes, that dude was dirt. Scum. Blood didn't make him worthy of my respect. Kevin deserved to die in that fire he'd set to my office building. He'd thought I was inside. Instead, Ashlee was the one burned. Her face, like her heart, was permanently scarred.

Fancy's hand slid from the top of the steering wheel to the bottom. "Baby, is your mother okay? We can cancel dinner if you'd like."

That was what I loved about my wife. She always considered my feelings. "Nah, I'll call her from the restaurant."

My wife looked at me and smiled. The steering wheel slid between her fingers.

I pointed at the car speeding in our direction. "Baby! Watch—"

Crash!

"Oh, my God." In seconds, my air bag inflated, jamming my body against my seat. My face was pressed up sideways against the headrest. My wife's air bag hadn't deployed. Her forehead was split from her hairline to her nose.

"Daddy!" my son screamed.

Fighting my way from underneath the air bag, I reached into the backseat and unbuckled my son. I pulled him into my arms and held his body close to mine, shielding his face from Fancy. My wife wasn't moving. All I saw was blood gushing from her head. I don't know how much time passed before a paramedic opened Fancy's door. All I could do was cry, "Please, save my wife."

I got out of the SUV with my son and ran to the ambulance to be close to my wife.

"Sir, we've got to go," the paramedic said, slamming the door in my face.

Anger consumed me. I stormed over to the driver of the other car. "What the fuck have you done!"

His eyes were blood red, but he wasn't bleeding. His face was distorted. His apology—"Look, I'm sorry, man. Hope your wife is okay"—was slurred.

I wanted to punch him in his drunken face. "For your sake, you'd better pray she's all right." Another paramedic and a police officer approached me, so I knew I couldn't leave the scene. So I did the best thing—dialed my mom.

My son locked his arms around my neck. "Daddy, I'm scared," he cried.

"Me too, son. Me too."

Bambi

CHAPTER 2

The way to a man's heart was through his mother.

I had every news article on Darius Jones since he'd played basketball in high school. I also had a video of all his games and his wedding. I was at Madison Square Garden when he was drafted, went to all of his home games in Atlanta, traveled to all the away games. I had photos of his son, his son's mother, his wife, his mother, his step- and biological fathers. Some of the pictures I'd printed from the Internet, others I'd taken. I slept in his jersey each night, made life-size six-nine body-length pillows with images of him. I even picked up a dreadlock that fell from his head when he was sitting on the sidelines during a time-out. I was Darius Jones's number one fan. He just didn't know it . . . yet.

Being a private investigator by trade made me a professional groupie. It was no accident that I'd discovered Darius's mom, Jada, was attending the movie premiere for *Something on the Side*. Savvy groupies befriended celebrities all the time. Velvet Waters, the star of the movie, had become this overnight Hollywood sensation. I added her to my list of people to know because Velvet used to live in Atlanta. She'd stripped as Red Velvet at Stilettos Night Club in Atlanta before landing the lead in *Something on the Side*. She was paid by Trevor to fuck Grant Hill before Grant started dating Darius's mother. Anyone attached to Darius, directly or indirectly, was also attached to me.

I'd been sitting at the bar one day inside LA's most popular five-star hotel, passing time between games, when I met Velvet. While waiting to head to LAX for my flight back to Atlanta to see my Darius play for our home team, I noticed Velvet stroll in. Hair flowing. Makeup immaculate. Money had done her good.

She sat next to me, and I overheard Velvet confirm that Grant Hill would be at her premiere. There was such a thing as luck in the PI world. I was at the right place, right time.

I hadn't been in pursuit of Velvet at that moment. I'd flown from Atlanta to temporarily distance myself from Darius, to avoid having Darius's paparazzi get a snapshot of me in their photos. I was careful because I didn't want to be identified as a maniac stalker like the chick who was pursuing Fisher.

After Velvet ended her call, I said, "Hi, Velvet. Congratulations. You are my she-ro. And you're so beautiful."

She answered with a flat "Thanks."

I leaned closer to her and said, "Girl, you went from stripping at Stilettos to Hollywood." Then I lied, "I used to make it rain on you, but you're big time now. Probably don't remember little ole me."

Velvet had stared at me as if trying to recall my face. How could she remember me? I hadn't sprinkled her with dollar bills. How could anyone remember me even if they'd seen me? I was a chameleon. I changed my makeup, hair, and wardrobe every other day.

As she continued studying my face, I said, "Carl Weber is my favorite author. Is he going to be at the premiere? I'd love to meet him." I smiled at her. Shook my head. "My apology. Who am I to think I could ever go to a premiere? Good luck, girl."

Velvet eased down from her bar stool. Took five steps. I counted each one before she turned around and took five more in my direction.

"Give me your address. I'll mail you a ticket, but I can only give you one."

"Are you serious?" I said, handing her my card with my Atlanta post office box.

She glanced at my card, nodded, then walked away. No "good-bye" or "nice meeting you." A few weeks later I was back in LA to attend the premiere.

Preparing to walk the red carpet, I sat at the vanity in my hotel room. I braided my natural jet black curly hair into eleven cornrows, then covered my hair with a mesh net stocking cap. I applied a small amount of eyebrow glue to the back of my 100 percent human hair eyebrows, then perfectly layered each blonde-colored brow over my jet black brows. Then I glued and attached my light brown eyelashes. I trailed a thin line of glue along the edge of my hairline, then attached my full-lace twenty-two-inch-long strawberry blonde wig. I stood, held my head upside down, brushed, then fluffed my hair. Instantly I went from being a fair-complexioned African American woman to looking like a Caucasian woman with the perfect tan.

I applied my concealer, foundation, and brown eyeliner. I stroked on various hues of sparkling blue eye shadow, toned it down with a hint of magenta, and brushed a soft pink lipstick on my mouth. I inserted my light bluish-gray contacts. After easing into padded butt booster panties that would make Serena Williams jealous, I stuffed silicone breast pads into the sides of my bra to sandwich my D cups into a façade of DDs that gave me amazing cleavage. I stepped into iridescent stilettos, picked up my purse, and double-checked to make sure I had my ticket. I kissed the plastic covering on my photo of Darius, then placed it back in my purse. His picture was my good luck charm. With Darius by my side, all things were possible.

Slipping my room key into my handbag, I left my suite and made my way to the lobby. The bellman smiled at me. "You are one gorgeous woman. Can I, make that, *may* I assist you?"

"Thanks, but no thanks. My driver is outside," I politely said, exiting the hotel.

I eased into the backseat of my white stretch limousine and gazed out the window, lost in thought about how I'd befriend Darius's mother tonight. Was my seat even close to hers? I had the advantage, being that I knew what she looked like and she had no clue who I was.

A long line of limos led to the theater. My driver opened my door, I swooped my hair to one side, thrust my breasts forward, arched my back, and smiled as though I was Mrs. Darius Jones. An usher escorted me to my seat. I sat one row directly behind my future mother-in-law. By the end of the night, I would become Jada's newest best friend or her worst enemy.

A very pregnant woman being escorted by a tall thin man with a long ponytail stepped sideways in front of Grant and

Jada. When the pregnant woman sat down next to Jada, Jada turned to Grant and stared into his eyes. Squinted. Frowned. I noticed Jada's jaw tighten.

Halfway through the movie, the pregnant woman moaned and held her stomach but continued watching the movie. The screening was nice but I was in PI mode. Things moved quickly. After the credits rolled, the director proposed to Velvet, the pregnant lady's water broke, Velvet accepted the marriage proposal, then Grant asked, "Honey, is that my baby?"

My jaw dropped. I thought I was on top of everything, but this was new and valuable information. Jada's cell phone rang, temporarily interrupting the flow of things. Honey answered Grant, "It's not your child, but these babies are your twin boys."

Jada stopped speaking into her phone long enough to call Honey a liar. Jada walked off, then cried, "Fancy was hit by a drunk driver. We've got to go to the hospital."

Bingo! I said to myself.

Jada yelled, "Grant! Did you hear me? Darius's wife was hit by a drunk driver! Let's go!"

I guess people have the right to be consumed with their issues. Jada was worried about Fancy. Grant was worried about Honey. And I was concerned with Darius and finding out what hospital Fancy was in.

My intention to get Darius was no fly-by-night suck-his-dick groupie trick. Oh, no. I was determined to either marry him or massacre him. If I couldn't have Darius Jones, no woman would, especially Fancy. I'd make sure Fancy's hospital stay was permanent.

I stood in the aisle, waiting to follow Jada to the hospital.